A DIS

"Lady Nelson was too much the martyr for my tastes," Alessandra argued, "playing the noble wife while her husband was making her a laughingstock by his public adoration of his mistress. If I had been Lady Nelson, I would have shown his lordship the door and gone on about the business of my own life."

Lucien frowned. "Nonsense," he said sternly. "Nelson was wrong to use her so, of course, but she quite properly acted the supportive wife. She never said a word against him. She made no attempt to interfere with his life or change him in any way."

"And that is your definition of a proper wife, sir?" Alex's voice was filled with quiet laughter. "Pray, is that what you would expect of me?"

Lucien stopped abruptly and stared at her for a long moment, his face unreadable in the shadows. They were quite alone on the walkway, a fact that Alex suddenly found disquieting. He pulled her into one of the alcoves that skirted the path's edge.

"My expectation, Alessandra Ridgely, is that you would never give a man a moment's peace," he said fiercely, his eyes bright with passion. Before she could speak, his mouth descended to hers . . .

Outstanding acclaim for *A Worthy Engagement*:

Jove titles by Eileen Winwood

A Worthy Engagement

Eileen Winwood

JOVE BOOKS, NEW YORK

A WORTHY ENGAGEMENT

A Jove Book / published by arrangement with
the author

PRINTING HISTORY
Jove edition / January 1993

ISBN: 0-515-11017-5

Jove Books are published by The Berkley Publishing Group,
200 Madison Avenue, New York, New York 10016.
The name "JOVE" and the "J" logo
are trademarks belonging to Jove Publications, Inc.

PRINTED IN THE UNITED STATES OF AMERICA

10 9 8 7 6 5 4 3 2 1

A Worthy Engagement

Chapter 1

"I trust you are ready, Alessandra. Guildhall undoubtedly will be a sad crush, especially as Perceval has seen fit to open the ceremony to the public. I only pray we shall not have to rub elbows with all of London. Come, come! I am not averse to being fashionably late, but it would not do to miss the unveiling altogether."

Lady Alessandra Ridgely arched an elegant brow but otherwise allowed silence to speak her opinion of her brother's remark. It would be utterly useless to point out to her sibling that she had been ready this quarter hour and more, while he had dawdled upstairs for an hour, no doubt discarding length after length of crumpled muslin until his long-suffering valet produced a cravat that met with His Grace's approval.

Two more different twigs from the same tree could not have been found than the brother and sister standing in the foyer of Farnsworth House on Berkeley Square.

Lady Alessandra was a study in casual elegance with her moss-colored Spanish pelisse of shot sarcenet trimmed with Egyptian crepe, lemon kid gloves, matching slippers, and a painted velvet reticule. That it was last year's ensemble was not, apparently, a matter of concern, as she wore it with easy confidence. Her clear blue eyes bore no sign of impatience, though she had been awaiting her brother for what seemed an eternity. Her ivory complexion was smooth, with nary a wrinkle or frown to betray her displeasure at this most recent consequence of his thoughtless vanity. Her burnished blond hair was swept into a sleek knot that gave way to a few soft ringlets, a sophisticated version of the popular antique Roman style. Her slender form rose to a considerable height, though no one would think of calling the graceful Lady Alessandra a Long Meg.

She looked, as she was, every inch a duke's daughter. Her demeanor was all that was correct; her bearing bespoke her breeding. On this occasion, as always, she presented a portrait of effortless refinement, as one might expect from the only daughter of one of England's oldest and loftiest families.

Only the irreverent twinkle that so often danced in those lively blue eyes betrayed the lady as something other than she appeared to be. In fact, those who spent much time in her company were wont to think her positively eccentric. For one thing, she had a preference for the rather masculine nickname of Alex, which her father had given her as a child when he despaired (prematurely, as it developed) of ever producing sons. She also had the odd habit of going to operas especially to hear the music rather than merely to be seen. Further, her presence at parties seemed to be determined by her affection for the hosts rather than her status among the *ton*. That she cared not to flaunt herself on the Marriage Mart was viewed as strange, but one only had to be in her presence to see that she was no antidote, even at the advanced age of twenty-five. In short, her beauty was considerable and her fortune even more so. More engaging than those attractions, however, was the lady's utter willingness to eschew social artifice in favor of comporting herself as a real human being.

Not so, however, with her brother, the Duke of Farnsworth.

The delicate, slender nose that gave his sister's face such a refined mien became positively aquiline on His Grace and, along with a pair of beady black eyes, lent him a rather predatory air. His youth, for he was three years younger than his sister, had not yet endowed him with the air of maturity of one entirely comfortable with his own nature. Instead, His Grace carried himself with an exaggerated sense of his own importance, in the manner of one who has not yet discovered that a truly great man need not so openly flaunt such stature but rather wait until it is revealed to the world in the fullness of time.

The lustrous, tawny hair that was responsible for the many admiring gazes cast his sister's way had not, unfortunately, been bestowed upon the duke. His hair was a bit on the thin side and of an insipid yellow that would not tousle properly; it seemed to efface his lofty presence rather than herald it. He had inherited his sister's imposing height, but he was so thin that in no way was he capable of filling out his padded jackets. To make up for his lack of physical presence, the duke attired himself in the manner of one who did not intend his person to be overlooked.

He was dressed this morning in the style of trousers that he favored, as they did not hug the leg so severely as to require padding. They were a golden color reminiscent of mustard. His waistcoat was of aubergine-striped toilinette, and around his neck an intricately tied halter of many-folded muslin buried the extremity of his chin. A long greatcoat with mother-of-pearl buttons as large as a crown piece assured that His Grace would not be disturbed by the brisk breezes stirring this late-April day.

Lady Alex, as she was known, was so used to the ubiquitous assault of her brother's egregious sartorial proclivities that she did not permit her gaze to linger disapprovingly upon his attire or her nose to wrinkle in distaste. As they settled into the comfortable squabs of the town carriage, her mind was otherwise preoccupied.

"I believe I shall leave in a fortnight, Clarence, as the weather should be improving in Dorset soon. I cannot tell you how pleased I am to know that at long last I shall enjoy a Season, simply by removing myself from participation in it."

Her brother's eyes were dark with disapproval. "Must you always embarrass one with your oddities, Alessandra? It will seem most strange if you are not in town for the Season."

"Oddities, Clarence? I am sure I do not know what you mean," his sibling replied in a bland voice.

"Don't play your games with me, Alex. You will one day put yourself beyond the pale with your antics. Last week's episode was a prime example. To think a Ridgely was seen in Cheapside, of all places!"

She looked at him in surprise. "'Twas a benefit for the orphanage, Clarence, as you well know. There is nothing improper in lending my small efforts to such an endeavor."

The duke sat back on the seat, his "humph" offering eloquent testimony to his opinion of that statement.

"Your willingness to allow the use of your name on behalf of charitable causes must be commendable, of course. But I cannot like you gallivanting around the slums of the city. I would choose something more . . . refined for the daughter of a duke."

She glanced out the window, idly adjusting a glove. "How fortunate, then, that I make my own choices in such matters."

The words, delivered in dulcet tones, nevertheless provoked in the duke a fearsome glower. But when he attempted to impose the full force of his gaze upon his sister, she merely continued to look out the window, offering him only her serene profile. An exasperated sigh escaped his lips. With a long-suffering look heavenward, he returned to his original topic.

"Mark my words, Alessandra: One day you will go too far. Everyone already thinks it strange that you have not yet snagged a husband. It is more than time that you did."

"And more than time you and Mama stopped singing that particular tune," Alex replied cheerfully. "I am quite on the shelf, you know, and happily so. I have no wish to continue parading myself before all those unfortunate gentlemen who think that my esteemed family name, passable looks, and eventual fortune present a pleasant way to spend their remaining coddled years. And I do not believe Mama has the heart for another round of it, if you want to know the truth."

"Nonsense! Mother only wants what is best for you," Clarence replied dismissively.

"Because we have never allowed her to think of herself," Alex retorted. "There is no use arguing about it again. I have decided that what is best for me is to rusticate by the sea rather than to endure the frenzy of another Season and become burned to the socket. At all events, George wishes me to look in on Vivian."

"Huntsley? Surely he can look after his own wife. Our neighbor's goings-on are not our concern."

Alex frowned. "It is more than 'goings-on,' Clarence. Vivian is due to give birth next month. And George is not even in the country, as you would remember if you kept up with anything as important as the war. I received a letter from him just yesterday, in fact. He is in a fit of dismals at not being home with her now. I have known George all my life. You cannot think I would refuse his request."

His Grace, observing his sister's set features, bore that statement silently. He had learned over the years that her ultimatums were capable of withstanding any challenge he could mount. There were two matters upon which he intended to be firm, however. He cleared his throat with the air of one about to issue an important decree.

"I am certain that *I* will do my duty when the time comes to set up my nursery, although thankfully I have a few years yet to think about that responsibility," he said ponderously. "But you are, by your own admission, already on the shelf. To compound the situation, you insist on wearing last year's fashions—"

"There is nothing wrong with my attire," came the brisk interruption. "This pelisse has been barely worn. I see no reason to consign it to the rag heap."

His Grace frowned, his nose elevating itself into a position indicating extreme distaste.

"If you want to ruin your chances of catching a husband," he continued, "I suppose that is your business, but you must not bring disgrace upon this house by gadding about without a companion. If you intend to become an ape-leader, at least observe the proprieties." He stopped at her disdainful look, but as she said nothing, he continued, relieved that she had borne this pronouncement in silence. "There is no use in arguing about it again. Mother and I are agreed on this. You may be of age, but you are not beyond scandal. I must insist that you take a com-

panion upon the occasion of your birthday. In fact, I was thinking of Cousin Agatha for the post."

Alex shuddered at the vision of her father's humorless second cousin, a sour woman of no particular intellect or humor.
Sharing her days with a woman like that would be sheer torture.
Her birthday was a little more than two months away. Idly she
fingered her reticule. She would have to think of something.

Taking heart from his sister's silence, Clarence proceeded to
issue his second decree. "And I must insist that you present
yourself in town for Prinny's fete," he said in his most forbidding voice.

Alex's elegant nose wrinkled disdainfully. "You mean, of
course, the dreadfully obscene party he intends to throw to celebrate the king's insanity."

"To celebrate his Regency, as well you know," Clarence declared in an awful voice, jerking his head around angrily, to
unfortunate effect for his perilously high neckcloth. "I will not
have such disrespectful talk in my carriage, Alessandra."

To His Grace's chagrin, his sister showed no sign of retract-
ing or regretting her remarks. Indeed, she was staring at him
with an amused elevation of those exquisite brows. To cover his
discomfiture, the duke hastened to add: "To be precise, of
course, it is a celebration to promote the use of national manu-
factures."

Alex laughed, a rich, deep-throated sound that had captivated
many a gentleman and provoked them—unwisely, since Alex
did not like fulsome compliments—into comparing the musical
sound to a sweetly running brook or perhaps a Mozart sonata.

"You cannot believe that drivel, Clarence! Everyone in town
knows the real reason. Anyone who has any sensibility feels the
inappropriateness of such excessive gaiety in the midst of the
king's increasing decline, about which there is little, surely, to
celebrate."

But Clarence had turned his attention to his cravat and was
fumbling with its folds.

"Nevertheless," he stated firmly, "I expect you to return in
time to attend. Our position carries certain responsibilities, after

all. You cannot forget that you are the daughter and sister of a duke."

"No," Alex said evenly, watching her brother's ineffectual efforts, "unfortunately I cannot."

The unveiling was well advanced by the time they were able to maneuver a position in front of the new monument to the distinguished Lord Nelson, such task being accomplished with the aid of minions who had been deployed for just such purpose as assuring that no members of the *ton* were prevented from viewing the naval hero by the presence of an enthusiastic public. One fortunate benefit of being late, Alex decided, was that they were spared having to listen to most of the speeches, although the last speaker, Lord Grantham, insisted on reading aloud the entirety of Mr. Sheridan's inscription on the tablet. First there was a recital of Lord Nelson's virtues and his rapid rise through the ranks. Then followed a listing of his most famous battles, the unfortunate circumstances of his death, and the sadness into which it had plunged the nation. Then came tribute to those public officials who devised the idea of the present accolade.

"The lord mayor, aldermen, the Common Council . . ." Lord Grantham intoned as Alex's eyes wandered over the crowd. Like her brother, most of those present stared admiringly at the gray marble obelisk and listened in apparent rapt attention to the reading of the inscription.

" . . . of the City of London have caused this monument to be erected . . ." Lord Grantham was saying. Alex stifled a yawn.

"Better they were gagged to the rigging than produce such a monstrosity," muttered a deep voice close by her elbow.

" . . . Not in the presumptuous hope of sustaining the departed hero's memory," Lord Grantham droned on, "but to manifest their estimation of the man . . ."

"Drivel!" came the same raspy whisper.

" . . . And their admiration of his deeds . . ."

"Exceeded only by their admiration for themselves," the voice grumbled.

Alex quickly put her gloved hand to her mouth and tried desperately to restrain the tiny bubble of laughter that threatened to erupt uncontrollably. She forced her eyes to remain riveted on Lord Grantham and her face to sustain its mask of polite respect. But she was filled with curiosity about the mysterious critic at her elbow. She clutched her reticule tightly as Lord Grantham continued:

" . . . This testimony of their gratitude they trust will remain as long as their own renowned city shall exist . . ."

"And their own esteemed personages shall reap the benefit," the voice muttered in disgust.

Blithely unaware of the condemnation his remarks had occasioned, Lord Grantham puffed out his chest to deliver Mr. Sheridan's final triumphant words: " . . . The period to Nelson's fame can only be the end of time!" he declared as the throng erupted in wild cheers and applause.

"Bloody hell!" came the low, caustic response.

Alex could no longer suppress her laughter and turned to discover the critic's identity. Her eyes, accustomed to finding those of the masculine gender at the same level, encountered only the plain gold buttons on a dark green kerseymere coat that covered a rather broad chest. As she gazed upward in search of the face that accompanied this attire, she found herself looking into a most extraordinary pair of amber eyes. They had apparently wanted to be brown, but flecks of gold had intruded. They glinted rather fiercely, like the gleam of steel in a newly sharpened blade. She quickly decided that the speaker's eyes were his most singular feature. His shock of deep auburn hair was likewise most extraordinary, however. The thick, luxuriant mass tumbled around his head like flames leaping from the devil's own halo, and that fallen angel was uppermost in her mind as her mesmerized eyes drifted down to a pair of unruly auburn eyebrows. They were raised in imperious inquiry, and suddenly Alex realized not only that he had spoken to her, but also that she had treated him to a shocking lapse of manners. Her recovery was instantaneous.

"I beg your pardon, sir. Did you address me?" she said politely, staring at his unsmiling face, its complexion darkened as if by the sun.

"I merely asked whether I passed your inspection," he said in his deep baritone, not pretending to hide his contempt. "That was your purpose, was it not? To see what manner of beast dare defame such a noble monument?" His eyes gleamed even more brightly, fueled by his scorn.

Alex refused to rise to the bait. "Certainly not," she denied calmly as one of her perfectly formed eyebrows arched in mute reproof of his boldness.

He crossed his arms on his chest and studied her with an arrogance that would have discomposed a less collected woman. Alex, however, pointedly ignored the insolent eyes that raked her person. It took considerable effort, though, to retain her customary detachment, for she felt her pulse quicken alarmingly. She surveyed the crowd, searching for the quickest path away from his unsettling presence. Unfortunately the milling throng had closed about them. Suddenly someone jostled her into him.

His arms reached out instinctively to catch her about the waist and prevent what would otherwise have been her ungraceful tumble onto the floor. The movement brought her against his body, and Alex drew a sharp breath as she found his face mere inches from her own. Surely she only imagined that his hands tightened warmly about her for an instant before falling away. Yes, that must be the case, for now she saw that his uncompromising visage displayed no inclination toward warmth. If anything, the scorn on his face was even more patent. She felt utterly disconcerted as she stared into his face, unable to force her eyes away from the compelling features. Suddenly she was severely irritated at her uncharacteristic discomposure.

"Oh, botheration!" Alex snapped, brushing her sleeve off and transferring her reticule to the other hand. "Pray, excuse me, sir. I must find my brother and depart this madness."

He barely touched her arm with the tip of his finger, but it was enough to halt her movement.

"If you are referring to that self-important fop who was standing next to you earlier, I regret to inform you that he is now holding forth to that cloying group of exquisites over there, no doubt on the wonders of Lord Nelson's monument. I would imagine, alas, that it will be some time before he tires of the sound of his voice and is able to escort you."

At those words, Alex turned on him with icy anger. "You, sir, have no manners," she said in her chilliest voice.

"Oh, I'll admit that readily enough," he replied easily. "But manners are merely a veneer of civility, are they not? They do not in themselves serve to civilize, nor are they any indication of a man's—or woman's—worth. In the end, of course, they are as superficial as that monument."

Alex greeted this comment with silence, completely unprepared to find her attempted setdown met by such a lecture. Her interest was now thoroughly piqued by this strange man and his harsh pronouncements. Her curiosity overcame her anger.

"And what do you have against Lord Nelson's monument, pray?" she asked finally.

"Only that it pays hollow tribute to the sacrosanct public image of the hero without so much as acknowledging the real man, with all of his flaws. You have only to look at the thing to find it utterly ridiculous."

His jaw was clenched, and his full, domineering mouth was drawn into a rigid line, so that he looked quite forbidding. Alex, having decided that she had had quite enough of his posturing, refused to be intimidated.

"You have been wishing that monument to the devil these long minutes, sir," she said challengingly. "Do you care to explain precisely *what* it is you find so offensive?"

Abruptly he grabbed her hand and, parting the crowd with amazing ease, rapidly walked her to the front of the monument. He pulled her along so quickly, she was forced to stifle a gasp.

"There," he commanded. "Tell me what you see."

Trying to regain her breath, Alex glanced at the large object. "Well, there is a group of three figures on a pedestal," she said uncertainly.

"What figures?"

She moved closer to the monument and studied it. "On the

right is Neptune, looking rather horrified—I suppose at the battle that is raging—and there is Britannia on her lion, evidently mourning Lord Nelson's fate," she said.

"And?" he demanded impatiently.

She shot him an annoyed frown. "Well, the central figure is that of a female, emblematic of London, I suppose. She looks to be completing the process of inscribing the names of the three great victories—Nile, Copenhagen, and Trafalgar." Alex turned to him, perplexed. "I repeat, sir, what do you find so offensive?"

His derisive laugh caused several heads to turn in their direction. "Does it not occur to you, madam, that you have left something out?" His thick brows arched in thinly veiled contempt.

Alex waved her hand impatiently. "I am tired of this guessing game, sir. I must ask you to be done or be gone."

The words had come out rather more bluntly than she had meant them, but perhaps it was just as well. Surely he would leave her alone now. But the amber eyes kindled anew with what might have been surprise or amusement or something else altogether. Alex wondered less at their meaning than she did the little hop-skip they triggered in her pulse. Her heart beat even more furiously when he leaned over her quite deliberately and whispered softly in her ear.

"What of *Nelson*, madam? What of our fallen hero?"

Taken aback, Alex looked again at the monument. "Well," she said hesitantly, "I believe that little medallion Britannia holds bears his profile."

"Ah, yes, a tiny little thing, isn't it?" he said with heavy sarcasm. "And did you expect to see the great warrior, whose memory this monument is intended to commemorate, no more than a mere profile on a very small medallion?"

"Well . . ."

"Do you not think that at the least there might have been a statue of the hero himself? Or any kind of exhibition of the man on his own public monument? Can you tell aught of his appearance from such a tiny profile so poorly chiseled that it might as well be Perceval himself? Is niggardliness thus superior to extravagance?"

She squinted at the medallion, a reluctant twinkle beginning to form in her eye. "I begin to see your objection, sir," she murmured.

"You also have overlooked another striking aspect of this shrine," he said, and Alex nearly caught her breath when a dimple appeared suddenly in his cheek.

She waited expectantly, no longer bothering to hide her amusement.

"I cannot think why we have been given the posterior view of the figure of London who is inscribing the marble," he said, staring disparagingly at the crouched female figure. "See how strangely she turns her back on the spectators as she records Nelson's triumphs. Are we to admire this aspect of her demeanor? What, pray, is she trying to tell us by posing in such a position?"

"Indeed," Alex agreed, her blue eyes dancing. She turned to him with a playful air. "Since you seem so determined to thoroughly humble this poor tribute, sir, perhaps you would care to say what you would deem appropriate to stand in its stead."

He crossed his arms and rocked back on his heels, as if giving the matter much thought. He stroked his jaw consideringly, and Alex noticed with pleasure how his own amusement had softened those hard features.

"Oh, I do think we must have Lord Nelson himself, in full dress regalia, a patch over one eye and an empty sleeve where his arm once hung."

He stopped, and Alex caught a mischievous glint in those amber eyes as he cast her a sidelong look before continuing.

"The inestimable Lady Nelson, of course, standing behind him to his right—she was ever supportive, you know. Then we must cast the ample Emma Hamilton at his feet, looking up at him adoringly. Horatio will have a slightly silly expression upon his face, uncertain whether to go to his dear mistress or out to sea again. In no case, of course, will he turn to the woman who shares his name. His captains will look on disapprovingly.

Perhaps we ought to have Britannia blindfolded to protect her sensibilities in the face of such scandal." He smiled in satisfaction. "There. I believe that begins to approach the man himself."

The roguish lights in his eyes grew brighter, and Alex thought they quite transformed him into a breathtakingly attractive man. He was obviously expecting her to voice ladylike outrage at the indelicacy of his remarks. Alex was determined to refuse him that pleasure; indeed, she knew his portrait of the hero was no more than honest. And so she merely turned to him with a placid air, her pleasant countenance seemingly unperturbed.

"You speak as if you knew the man," she said, a teasing note in her voice. "Are you also a naval hero, sir?"

Abruptly the humorous expression vanished, and his face darkened, as if a pair of shutters had closed upon his countenance. He was once again the forbidding critic.

"In my youth, I had the pleasure of serving with the admiral," he said brusquely. "Good day, madam."

Suddenly he was gone, melting into the crowd with a speed and ease that she would not have thought possible in one of his size. After staring blankly at the spot where he had disappeared, she turned to study Nelson's monument with new eyes. A tiny frown settled upon her generous mouth. He was right, she decided. It was woefully inadequate.

"There you are! I have been looking for you this age! Let us be gone from this dreadful place," Clarence said, taking her elbow and propelling her through the crowd.

In her preoccupied state, Alex allowed him to steer her, but her mind's eye was seeing a pair of amber lights and that unruly auburn hair. Had she embarrassed him with that inane remark about being a naval hero? It might have been tactless, but why had he taken it so severely? Clarence noted her silence and frowned.

"Who was that tall chap you were talking to?" he demanded. "Not of the first circles, surely. I could not even place his tailor."

Alex shook her head. "I believe he was at sea with Lord Nelson," she said thoughtfully.

Clarence stopped abruptly and fixed her with a disbelieving gaze. "You were conversing with a common *seaman*?" he asked in utter horror.

"Oh, no, Clarence, you mistake the matter," Alex replied sweetly. "Indeed, he was most *un*common."

Chapter 2

Lucien ripped open the packet from the Admiralty. The coded letter inside told him precisely what he wanted to know. The *Pandora* was rumored to be ready to set sail again for France, perhaps finally bringing to England the mysterious spy long-rumored to be plotting to infiltrate London diplomatic circles by posing as a Royalist. How many times had Lucien made that journey, only to have it end in futility! This indeed was good news. He took the note and burned it carefully at his desk, tossing it at the last minute into the hearth. He rubbed his hands together in satisfaction. If he rode through the night, he could be in Dorset by dawn, preparing to trim the *Pandora*'s sails. After the crossing, it would be a simple matter to mark the spy and trail the group inland to London.

About time, too, for this racketing about at Admiralty headquarters was trying stuff. If he wasn't careful, he would find himself sent off to represent the office at ribbon cuttings or ceremonies like that stultifying ordeal at Guildhall today. He had only gone there on a lark, thinking somehow that he had owed Nelson that. But he was wrong. Nelson would rather have been dumped into a tub of burgoo than find himself commemorated for all time by that silly monument.

He frowned. There was another letter in the packet. It was from Sir George Huntsley, captain of the *Vanguard* and part of a British flotilla that commanded the Tagus River north of Lisbon. Last month, Massena had given up his lengthy siege of Wellington's entrenched positions there, but it was too soon to celebrate. George knew it, and he implored Lucien to see to the care of his wife, whose confinement was imminent. He had en-

closed a letter to be delivered to Vivian in Dorset. The missive
to Lucien concluded:

> *I know this comes at an inconvenient time, old friend,
> but I had expected to be home long before now. It is hard
> as hell to be away, but I would feel better if I knew you
> were seeing to Vivian. She can be shatter-brained at times,
> and it would be just like her to get herself in a tizzy when
> she learns I won't be home in time for the baby's birth.
> Perhaps if your mother would go to stay with her? Nothing
> like family at a time like this.*

George was correct about one thing. His request couldn't
have come at a worse moment. Lucien folded the paper and put
it into his desk. It was just like George to throw an obstacle or
two into his path. He sighed. Of course he would do it. George
was not only a good friend, but a relative of sorts, since Vivian
was Lucien's distant cousin. His mother would be horrified, in
fact, to learn that Vivian was down in Dorset about to give birth
alone. Everyone had assumed that Vivian's sister had gone to
her.

Lucien rose impatiently. He could never keep straight the
comings and goings of the ladies of his acquaintance. The only
thing that mattered now was that he was going to have to make
yet another trip to Dorset after this business with the *Pandora*
was done. He wandered out of his study to break the news to his
mother.

As her dark green traveling carriage rumbled out of London,
Alex gave a sigh of relief. She was delighted to bid farewell, at
least for now, to the crowded routs, silly masquerades, Venetian
breakfasts, come-out balls, and tedious Wednesday nights at
Almack's. Her spirit soared as the city noise and traffic faded
into the verdant Surrey countryside.

Not that she despised the *ton*'s rituals, for she knew she was
indisputably part of that world. But sometimes it was tiresome
always to be about the matter of appearances. That was some-

thing she and Clarence could never agree upon. Like so many men, he viewed a woman's proper role as that which showed a gentleman to best advantage. Ladies, whether astute hostesses or beautiful mistresses, were essentially ornaments.

What grated most of all was this notion that one had to find a husband or wither into that dreaded state of spinsterhood, which, in society's eyes, was tantamount to removing oneself completely from any prospects of happiness. Alex could not see what all the fuss was about. She herself was perfectly happy in the single state. Moreover, although the men in her circle were generally pleasant company, more often than not she simply preferred her own.

She could not imagine why, fortune and family aside, she had any suitors at all, especially since there were many gentlemen whose insecurities required that their height exceed a female's in order to converse with her. Alex's essentially modest nature prevented her from seeing just how winning were the twinkle in those blue eyes and the easy confidence with which she bore her willowy stature. Nor did she realize the delight with which persevering gentlemen discovered that beneath her elegant poise was a woman of lively humor and spirit, with little concern for whether her dance card was filled or whether she was taken into supper by the *ton*'s most eligible bachelor.

As to why none of her admirers had been able to persuade her to offer them anything but her friendship, Alex had no ready explanation. If asked, she might have said that they were not precisely what she was looking for in a man. Not that she was looking, of course.

Unbidden, the image of a pair of extraordinary amber eyes interrupted her meanderings. They belonged to a man quite out of the ordinary mold, of that she was certain. She did not even know his name. Most likely he was entirely unsuitable, even for polite company. But a common seaman? No, he was not that.

She was equally certain that respectability was not what he would offer a lady. He would be thoroughly unrespectable and outrageous, for she could see that he was too much ruled by passion, unlike the men she knew, whose manners were cool and impeccable. What had he said about manners, anyway? The corners of her mouth tugged into a tiny smile.

It was no use thinking in that vein, Alex realized, and suddenly frowned so deeply that her maid privately wondered whether it was not time to mention the new wrinkle cream she had discovered. But no, she could see when her mistress's face cleared with a sudden idea that this was a passing aberration; Lady Alex's complexion was as unlined and smooth as ever.

"I think I shall ask you to ride with the baggage coach when we change horses beyond Bagshot," Alex said. "It's nothing against your company, Mary, but I simply need to be with myself for a bit."

"But, my lady, you cannot mean to travel alone—" Mary broke off when she saw her mistress's resolute face.

"I shall not be alone. There are Tom and William, as you well know. No harm can come to me in such stalwart company. I have a mind to push on to Salisbury tonight, by the by, although I do not expect the baggage coach to make such good time. If only we had gotten an earlier start, we might have made it farther."

The maid remained silent. It would do no good to point out that ladies of quality did not barrel along country roads with only a coachman and groom in tow. Lady Alex would ever go her own way.

Alex relaxed into the cushions and allowed a contented smile to cross her face. She would put London and all of its pesky irritations behind. Now that she could look forward to a journey in comfortable solitude, with nothing more stressful to do than watch the villages of Hampshire and Wiltshire pass by her window, she began to relax.

Her family would have been horrified had they known of her solitary mode of travel. She did not know why she always found herself at odds with their notions of propriety. It was not as though she were truly a rebel, although she knew she had acquired some rather unconventional notions in the flower of her womanhood.

Alex sighed and closed her eyes. The only rebellion she

could muster for now was a small one, eschewing the Season for the serenity of the country. Later, perhaps, she would dutifully hire back to London for the Regent's fete. For now, Dorset awaited.

A few hours later, Alex was smiling in amusement as she imagined the horrified look Clarence would bestow on the Ducks and Drakes Inn. To be sure, her estimable brother was not stranded in a driving rainstorm with no better possibilities in sight. Even he could not have foreseen the disastrous change in weather or that her carriage would plunge into a muddied rut and break a wheel.

The inn was a mean sort of establishment that only a charitable eye could judge respectable. Alex knew she herself was barely so at the moment, attired as she was in the costume of a serving girl, her tawny and still-damp hair falling about her shoulders like some Covent Garden strumpet. Her blue eyes twinkled. At least she could be thankful there was no looking glass to give her back the image.

It required no great feat of fancy to imagine her brother's stinging rebuke: "A Ridgely comporting herself as a member of the *lower* orders? Father would perish of mortification!" It would be useless to point out that their revered parent had already gone to his reward, but then Alex had ever stood accused of having a singularly inappropriate sense of humor.

Still, she was somewhat uneasy as she paused in the dim, dingy corridor to survey the taproom ahead. She had no wish to call untoward attention to her situation, which she knew was entirely owed to her stubborn and independent nature. If she hadn't been so set on enjoying her solitude, she would not have sent Mary back with the baggage coach or pushed her coachman on toward Salisbury. They had not gotten even that far in this weather. She supposed the baggage coach had put up for the night miles back. In this weather, that lumbering vehicle would be lucky to make Dorset by week's end.

Her sigh was inaudible amid the relentless pounding of rain outside and the raucous laughter ahead. She felt her spirits sag a bit as her stomach again reminded her that it had been an unconscionable time since she had eaten.

She hesitated. Her immediate intent had been to discover her host's whereabouts and order dinner. The wheel could not be repaired until the morrow, her coachman, Tom, had dourly reported, and in any event the weather prevented further travel tonight. They had done well to walk the quarter mile to this place. The innkeeper had been unable to suppress his shock at the appearance of a lady in such a bedraggled state; however, he had managed to rustle up a dry frock for her from his tavern maid.

As she peeked into the taproom she could see no sign of her host now amid the large and ill-assorted throng. Alex supposed he was busy attending to matters in the kitchen. That would also explain why no one had come to offer her so much as a cold collation. Her eyes flitted over the assemblage. The group appeared to be composed of local farmers and laborers, although a darkened table in the corner held three decently attired men. There was not a female, respectable or otherwise, in sight. To proceed further, she knew, would be most unwise.

By now, her smile had vanished. As doing without dinner was evidently to be her fate, the adventure was losing its appeal. She would have to return to her room and pray for easy sleep. As she turned back toward the stairs a rough voice came from the nearby shadows.

"I was beginning to think you were going to occupy that post all night."

Alex had barely registered the exasperation in the man's tone and opened her mouth to protest such rudeness, when a large hand covered it to stifle what he evidently feared would be a shriek. His other hand grabbed her shoulders from behind with a force that made her wince.

"If I had wished to call attention to my presence, girl," a voice rasped, "I would have hoisted my colors."

She had begun to struggle instinctively, but now his words immobilized her. She could not see her assailant, but she easily recognized that voice.

The callused hand that silenced her was large, nearly covering her nose as well as her mouth. It smelled rather pleasantly of rope and seawater. As its owner turned her slowly around she encountered a familiar pair of amber eyes.

"You!" he said in surprise, the eyes radiating flashes of what might have been irritation.

Alex wondered idly what infraction she had committed to give rise to such a look, but he soon jerked her wandering thoughts back to the present.

"None of your female screeching, please. Hold your tongue, or else I will gag you to the rigging." His voice was low and urgent.

This man was as incomprehensible as ever, Alex thought, stifling her irritation to nod cautiously at his order. She remained mute as the hand slowly withdrew, leaving only its mate still wrapped most improperly about her person. She shook her head to collect her senses, but found herself distracted as he moved to stand before her. The face was the same as she had remembered from the London unveiling, but its hard planes were lined with what appeared to be fatigue. Several days' growth of stubble covered that well-defined jaw. His clothes were no better than the servant's rags she wore and a good deal worse; his rough-woven shirt was stained and torn and had about it the odor of fish. His height was as imposing as she remembered, quite eclipsing her own. She felt the intensity of those eyes as they bored into her.

A thoroughly unsavory fellow, she thought in disgust, bringing her wayward brain back under control. She drew a large, calming breath and rejected as unwise the urge to demand an immediate apology. Best simply to make her escape from this dangerous man.

"If you will excuse me . . ." she began with a coolly dignified politeness that would have been quite fitting in the drawing room, but that sounded laughable, even to her own ears, in this setting.

He did not immediately answer, and she saw that his attention was claimed by a movement in the taproom. Holding her breath, she began to ease past him to the relative safety of the stairs. Clearly he had other business in this corridor besides her.

"Not so fast," came a low growl as a great arm snaked out to take hers and a speculative look appeared in his eyes. "You just might be able to help me plug a few shot holes."

I am the prisoner of a madman, Alex thought wildly as she tried to suppress a surge of panic.

She saw his glance move quickly back to the taproom, appearing to focus on the respectably attired trio who had been sitting in the corner. One of them was coming toward them. Perhaps rescue was in sight!

Her hopes were dashed as his grip on her arm tightened. His fierce eyes held hers with a new sense of urgency.

"I mean to have your help," he whispered, impervious to her wince of pain, "and I don't have time to do the pretty. Do what I say, and you'll come to no harm."

Alex stared dumbly at the fierce mouth that was suddenly descending to hers. She tried to draw back, but just before she thought her heart would beat itself into oblivion, she caught sight of a shiny glint of metal neatly hidden in his hand. The blade traced its way along her slender neck, and she gasped aloud.

"Remember," he said in his low and threatening rasp, "follow my lead. And say nothing."

The full lips came down upon hers with brutal force. His body pressed its full length and weight against hers as one large arm held her immobile. She was vaguely conscious of the other arm at his side, and she knew it held the dagger in readiness. She forced herself not to struggle. In truth, she could barely breathe, but did not know whether that condition arose from fright or from the altogether strange sensations being produced by this envelopment.

The kiss was purposeful in its passion, and Alex surmised that it was entirely for the benefit of the man coming toward them. Still, while she had not attained five and twenty without having experienced an occasional kiss, she had certainly never endured one quite like this. His bruising mouth bore no resemblance to the polite lips of the gentlemen of her set. Indeed, she was quite sure that if she survived this night, her mouth would long bear swollen testimony to her ordeal. If she weren't so frightened, she might find other interesting aspects of the kiss, but her attention was increasingly claimed by the rude manner in which her body was being pressed into intimate acquaintance with his.

"Luke!"

The startled male voice that spoke from the doorway had the effect of causing her assailant to raise his head slowly and gaze at the intruder with a languid eye.

As Alex watched her captor shake his head and attempt to rouse himself from what appeared to be passion's depth, she marveled at his acting skills. There was no sign of the desperate man who had compelled her into this strange performance. There was only the fervid lover reluctantly responding to a voice that summoned his attention from the object of his lust.

"Captain Harnsby," he said finally, no longer whispering, and Alex heard in the rough accents a baritone that was low and melodic.

"I did not think to find you here. I thought our business was done," the other said, and now Alex thought she detected a note of displeasure, perhaps even menace in the intruder's voice. She must have imagined it because the man was very nearly dwarfed by her captor and clearly no match for him. Still, there was an undercurrent in this conversation she could not quite make out. She waited, her body tense with fear, for the next move.

Luke, for that was apparently her assailant's name, gave her shoulders an affectionate squeeze with one arm. The other remained carefully out of sight, and Alex was sure she was not imagining the threatening prick from the blade at her side.

"Aye, sir, 'tis well and done." The words were slurred just a bit. "Didn't know you were here, to be sure. I've only got eyes for my Sally. Warm comfort on a night like this, eh?" He winked crudely and brushed his unshaven face against hers, leaving a roughened area that Alex was certain would require hours of soothing with her maid's special skin cream. She almost giggled at the inanity of such a thought at a moment like this. Instead, she managed a silly smile under Luke's deceptively lazy eye.

The captain stared at them until his two companions joined him. One of them—a short, slight man with a mustache—said something in an incomprehensible French that did not begin to approach the polite language Alex had learned from her proper governess. The third man remained silent. Alex's discerning eye noted the unmistakable signs of London tailoring in his garb, although he was by no means attired in the manner of a gentleman of consequence. She would have said that he resembled nothing so much as a clerk, as he wore a ditto suit of dingy brown fustian. This individual was frowning nervously, and Alex formed the distinct impression that he wished to be about his business.

Clearly none of them would do so tonight, however, the storm outside having only increased in intensity. A loud rumble of thunder sounded overhead as if to underscore the fact.

The awkward stillness in the corridor continued for an agonizing, prolonged moment. Suddenly Luke scooped her up and headed for the stairs. Alex could not stifle a gasp, and he gave a rough laugh.

"Like to stand around jawing with you, Cap'n, but I've got other fish in my net tonight," he said with a slurred voice and a meaningful wink. Holding her close to his chest in what appeared to be an ardent embrace, Luke began an apparently drunken stumble up the stairs as the three men watched silently.

The Frenchman's eyes narrowed to slits. "That man was on the boat, *n'est-ce-pas*?" he said quietly to the captain.

"Aye," Harnsby replied. "A fine seaman, Luke. Reads the currents like the back of his hand. Saved our bacon during that squall on the crossing last night."

"What do you know of him?" the Frenchman asked.

Harnsby shrugged. "Much as I know of any of them. Showed up several months ago looking for work. Seemed done up. I hired him in a thrice after I saw how he handled my *Pandora*.

He's been with me ever since. Comes and goes, though, like all of 'em."

The man in the brown suit watched distastefully as Luke paused on the landing to bestow a lascivious kiss on the wench he was carrying.

"Can he be trusted?" The man's voice held a nervous note.

Harnsby laughed. "The ladies seem to trust him well enough," he replied with a smirk. At the other's frown, Harnsby cleared his throat and added: "I wouldn't worry. His head is so fogged that by morning I daresay he'll have forgotten that he saw us."

The man shifted uncomfortably as he stared silently at the retreating couple.

"Where is your room?" he whispered fiercely as they reached the landing, still in sight of the trio below.

"I beg your pardon—" Alex began indignantly, but he swiftly silenced her with a vigorous kiss that looked for all the world like a besotted suitor unable to control his ardor.

"You may beg all you like, my girl," he rasped into her ear, "but if you do not play your part through, we may both be dead before this night is done!"

At his words, a chill fear shot through her. She looked up questioningly into the amber eyes, hard with a desperation that seemed to be willing her to cooperate.

"Down the hall, there, on the left," she whispered, and saw his eyes close briefly with what might have been relief.

Swiftly he carried her to the door. With one powerful movement, he opened it roughly, set her down on her feet, and bolted it shut. Finally he leaned his large frame against the door and closed his eyes in fatigue. His face looked suddenly pale, and Alex wondered if he were in pain. He moved his head quickly, as if to shake off whatever plagued him. She heard his labored breathing. After a moment, he opened his eyes.

"I believe I am growing too old for this," he muttered, and sighed deeply.

Alex blinked in astonishment at his words and fought an unexpected urge to laugh. This man was full of surprises.

He had another one, it seemed, because he reached into a pocket and pulled out a purse, tossing it to the floor at her feet.

"Take that as your compensation for that little bit of acting back there," he said, "although I must say, your performance was less than . . . inspired."

The fragile restraint that had held her tongue suddenly snapped. She drew her lithe frame into rigid erectness, her tone exuding the cold anger of a lady offended beyond all endurance.

"You dare to offer me money? I'll not take one farthing from such an ill-mannered oaf! All the gold in the realm would be poor compensation for this night's work and the indignities to which you have submitted my person." Her words came more rapidly as her anger gathered steam. "If you were a gentleman, I might appeal to your sensibilities. As there is ample evidence that the term holds little meaning for such a poor specimen of humanity as yourself, I fear that my breath would be entirely wasted."

With that, she perched gingerly upon a spindly chair that was the only stick of furniture in the room besides the narrow bed and a small chest. The fire in her blue eyes cooled to ice as she sat, head tall, surveying him with utter disapproval.

His broad mouth suddenly pulled upward in an appealing, almost boyish grin, and his eyes twinkled. There was that devastating dimple she remembered from London. It erased the lines of fatigue and made him look almost boyish. He couldn't be much above thirty, she thought, shifting uncomfortably under his impertinent stare.

"So speaks the grand London lady beneath the servant's rags," he said, walking around her rigid form and flourishing his hand to an imaginary audience. "Not at all in the usual manner of tavern wench." His thick brows arched speculatively. Her servant's rags did not dispel the impression he had formed in London that she was definitely of superior birth.

His eyes took in her finely sculpted bones, delicate ivory

complexion, and lush tawny hair that fell about her shoulders like dark spun gold. The long fingers that she clasped elegantly in her lap bore no sign of any labor more taxing than moving a needle across fine linen. Underneath that unattractive frock appeared to be a slender body that he knew would move with grace on the dance floor. Even in servant's garb, she exuded the kind of elegance that could only come from superior breeding. She belonged in a London drawing room, surrounded by mahogany, rosewood, and silk. Only her height, far greater than fashionable, and her mouth, almost nakedly sensuous in its fullness, were at odds with her ladylike image. He offered a silent prayer that he would never lay eyes upon her after this night.

Alex watched his changing expressions with a detached curiosity that had begun to supplant her anger. What manner of man was this? He held himself with an erectness that bespoke poise and pride, making no effort to efface his height or to cover the sharp and challenging light that radiated from his eyes. A keen intelligence lay behind those amber lights, she was certain. She already had seen his superb acting skills. And those stained and torn clothes certainly did not hide his attractiveness.

She nearly laughed out loud at the lunacy of her thoughts. This was no time for woolgathering. She was in the hands of a madman, or at least a supremely dangerous man. She must not forget that!

He saw the irreverent look come into her eyes, followed by a wary one. With an effort, he recalled his own wandering thoughts. Perhaps a different tack was needed.

"Look," he began, almost contritely, although there was no penitence in his eyes. "I apologize if my actions have given offense. I would never have willingly involved you in this, but your presence in that corridor gave me no time to do otherwise."

Alex shot him a doubtful look, thinking that his contrition was just the latest in his repertoire of acting skills. If he saw her skepticism, he ignored it.

"I would like to explain, but I cannot," he continued, his rough tone almost pleading. "All I can tell you is that those three are up to grave crimes against our country. They will stop at nothing. I do not know who you are; nor, indeed, do I wish to. Neither do I know whether I can trust you. But if money will not buy your silence, can I at least count on your patriotism?"

Alex pondered his words, trying to divine the truth in them. The three men she had seen looked relatively normal, whereas he looked like a man at the end of his rope. He had dressed well enough in London, but here he wore the rough garb of a seaman. Was he in possession of his senses?

He saw her frown. "What is it?"

Alex cleared her throat. "You ask much, sir. I do not know you, after all. And there is much about your story to give one pause. In London you implied that the sea was the occupation of your youth. But you are still engaged in that pursuit, are you not? Your conversation tonight with that captain and the slight air of . . . ah, fish about your presence seem to indicate that."

His eyes narrowed, and Alex fought to suppress a shudder at the sudden look of menace they held.

"As I said, I am not at liberty to explain," he growled. "At all events, it would not do for either of us to be forthcoming about our identities now that we find ourselves in this compromising situation."

Alex's back stiffened. She had not thought of *that* aspect of their predicament.

"Indeed, it behooves us both to make certain no one learns of this adventure," he continued, surveying the room. "For now, there are more pertinent matters before us, such as how we intend to spend this night."

Alex started, and her eyes grew wide in alarm. "*We*, sir?" she repeated dubiously.

"Surely you do not think I can simply saunter down the stairs now and seek my own bed?" he said incredulously. "Our very lives may depend on the success of our charade. I have no doubt that those three would try to kill us if they thought we were onto their game. They must believe us to be harmless lovers—drunk on lust and with no thought of leaving each other's presence until dawn's light."

A slow blush spread over her face. But as horrified as she was at his remarks, her irreverent mind suddenly conjured up an image of her brother's reaction to this latest turn. She laughed out loud and then abruptly halted at her captor's look of consternation.

"Well?" he demanded. "What's it to be? That is, if you are quite finished with your enjoyment of this little nightmare, for I assure you it is that."

She colored guiltily but still could not bring herself to respond. Impatiently he moved closer, bending down so that his face was level with hers. As she looked into those burning amber eyes, inches from her own, Alex felt an involuntary shiver sweep through her body. She hoped he had not noticed, and she forced her expression to remain impassive.

"I promise I have no designs on your virtue," he said quietly. Then his voice took on a more urgent tone: "I *must* stay here tonight. Will you trust me?"

His words hung in the air for a long, portentous moment. Alex could not suppress the eerie feeling that she would remember them long after this night had ended. She gave a sigh, feeling as if her orderly world's sanity had entirely slipped away in the scant time she had known this man.

"I cannot see that I have any choice in the matter, sir," Alex replied with dignity, and prayed fervently that dawn would come quickly.

Chapter 3

"What the devil are you doing?"

Alex jumped at the rough voice that pierced the silence of the darkened room. In a moment, he was at the window, where she was fumbling with the sash. His hands seized her wrists.

"If you think to escape, you must have windmills for brains!" growled the familiar voice, low and menacing. "Even assuming I could sleep through your clumsy efforts, how do you expect to manage such a considerable leap to the ground in those skirts?"

She turned toward him, mustering all the dignity she could in the rumpled frock in which she had been trying to sleep upon the hard, narrow bed.

"You are mistaken in your impression of my activities, sir," she said coolly. "I sought only a little air."

He gave a rough bark of laughter and shot her a look of incredulity. As she quietly stood her ground he sought to study her face, but her features were cast into shadows by the fire's dying embers. Still, he was certain she played him for a fool.

"You expect me to believe such a bouncer? Why, it's storming like a man-o'-war outside! Opening the window would drench us both!"

"Nevertheless," Alex insisted crisply, "I find the prospects of a drenching preferable to the constant and stifling odor of dead fish that pervades this room."

Taken aback, he was silent for a moment, and she took the opportunity to shake off his impolite hands, glancing ruefully at the red marks on her wrists. He began to laugh, a full and hearty sound. Finally he brought himself under control.

"You refer, I take it, to my . . . ah, person," he said, his sensuous mouth breaking into a grin.

Alex looked at him with cool imperturbability. "Oh, I would never be so rude as to do so, for that would be quite improper," she said matter-of-factly. "But perhaps it would not be amiss to suggest that there is a distinct . . . air about you that only seems to grow more noticeable in the stifling stillness of this room."

His thick brows arched in amusement. "I have no wish to offend your sensibilities, madam, but I am at a loss as to how to best reduce your inconvenience," he said, his deep voice carrying a hint of laughter. "I have only the one shirt, and though it is nearly in tatters, I did not think you would much care for my removing it. As for the rest of my clothes—" He broke off, obviously waiting with interest for her next words.

It was fortunate that the darkness hid her face, as Alex was quite certain that it was a shade of deep red. She stared at a dancing shadow cast on the wall by the fire's faint flickering. There was no evidence of her discomfort in her next words.

"I am sure you have acted most considerately, sir," she said with perfect poise. "Quite obviously there can be no discussion of doing otherwise with your apparel than that which you have already done. I believe my original suggestion still holds merit, however. If the window might be opened just a crack, I daresay the only drenching will occur to the floor and immediate area. I confess myself quite willing to inconvenience our host to that extent."

He studied the calm figure before him. To her credit, she was not one for hysterics. She was really quite beautiful, with that golden hair and classic profile that he could easily envision as the figurehead on one of those fast new brigantines the Dutch were producing. He frowned at the direction his thoughts were taking. Abruptly he grabbed the sash and, with one silent effort, raised it. The wind immediately swept a small torrent of rain onto his breeches and her frock, and he cursed as he quickly lowered the window to only a few inches above the sill.

"My fault," he snapped, although his tone clearly indicated that he blamed her. "Should have had you step back out of the way. I only hope there is enough heat left in the fire to dry out these rags."

Alex gratefully inhaled a breath of the fresh air, not at all minding the wetting that his precipitous act had wrought. After a moment, she followed him to the hearth, waiting patiently as he stirred the fire and added the punk from a box at the edge of the fireplace. For several minutes, they stood silently before the rejuvenated flames and the dry, comforting heat. It was not an awkward silence, hostility having somehow evaporated in the obvious necessity for warmth.

She glanced over at the thin blanket on the floor, which he had made his bed after they had resigned themselves to each other's company for the night.

"I wonder that you have been able to sleep on such a poor pallet," she said, and then immediately felt the impropriety of such a remark. Still, she *was* curious.

He shrugged. "I am long used to such discomforts."

"But too old for them, by your own admission."

He looked at her in surprise, wondering whether she was jesting. Surely not. Most females would be quite terrified in her situation. Nevertheless there seemed to be a distinct twitching about her mouth.

"I am not so old as all that," he growled indignantly. "I merely suffer from time to time from an old injury. By the bye, you are by no means an insignificant burden to haul up two flights of stairs."

A disdainful arch of her brows told him what she thought of this comment. "It is not as though I do this sort of thing regularly," he added brusquely. "I—oh, damnation!" He broke off with a dark look and lapsed into silence.

She was filled with curiosity as to what precisely he *did* do regularly; however, she supposed that any request on her part for elaboration would be met with evasion. His earlier suggestion that they remain circumspect about their backgrounds was probably for the best. After all, both of them must fervently wish never to meet again after this horrible evening!

Well, it was not so horrible, she amended. Rather more in the nature of an adventure, now that she knew he meant her no harm. It was unfortunate she would never be able to tell anyone about this night, but a least it would provide her with a secret source of distraction whenever Clarence's prosing became unbearable.

A sudden chilly breeze from the window interrupted her thoughts and caused the flames to flicker violently. She shivered. Without warning, a strong arm reached out and drew her close.

"Is this better?" he asked.

"Certainly not," she said primly, and stared resolutely ahead at the fire, not a little alarmed by this turn of events. The effort to maintain her poise in such proximity to his body was considerable. She felt an odd sense of lethargy steal over her and found that she was strangely unable to move away from the tantalizing warmth that had suddenly enveloped her.

Once again he watched the conflicting expressions flit across her face and felt himself captivated by those limpid blue eyes and generous mouth. Her deep golden hair, which had dried to a delightfully undisciplined mass, had taken on the fire's radiant glow. Even in the face of his impertinence, her profile was serene. She was every bit a lady, even in those rags. He smiled to himself. He would wager that the lady was having some unladylike thoughts about now. He turned her toward him.

Alex knew a moment of panic when she saw flames leap to his eyes, no reflection of the fire but something else of his own making.

"I have said you have no need to fear for your virtue," he murmured softly, and she trembled as she felt his warm breath on her cheek. Then his rough face was brushing hers.

Alex wanted to step away, but she found herself mesmerized by the glowing lights in those eyes. Standing at the hearth's edge, she was conscious only of his presence and the steady drumbeat of rain on the window. She felt surrounded by the sound, surrounded by his touch, enveloped in some warm and comforting cocoon.

"Of course," he added lazily as he brought his lips toward

hers, "there are methods other than force. I believe I am not without some small powers of persuasion."

Even as Alex's brain absorbed that outlandish statement he kissed her, and it was a very different sort of kiss than the one he'd inflicted upon her earlier in that painfully public and unabashedly crude display.

This began as a sweet caress, a gentle grazing of her mouth that set off a torrent of delightful sensations. His were exceedingly soft lips for such a rough man, she thought wonderingly as they brushed hers again and again. Gradually his mouth became more insistent, and Alex marveled that her own lips seemed to be responding in kind. In fact, she now seemed to be the one pressing her body rather rudely to his, which had the effect of sparking in her companion the most unsettling response. His arms suddenly crushed her along his length with a fierceness that robbed her of breath, and his hands began an unrelenting exploration of her person. They moved up toward her breasts and hesitated not a moment at the obstacle of her clothing, quickly burrowing under the offending and obviously unnecessary cloth.

Alex never doubted that it was urgently necessary to put an end to this exercise; the difficulty seemed to be in the doing of it. She seemed to have become utterly helpless in that regard, and indeed, could not but admit that she was shamelessly enjoying this activity in full measure. The roughened face moved lower, assaulting her slender neck as his mouth progressed to the roundness of her breasts, and Alex gave herself over to the enjoyment of the sensations that were engulfing her. She knew she was being quite wanton but, oddly, could not rouse herself to excessive concern.

There was a burning in the pit of her stomach that drove her hands to run wildly through his thick hair, a burning in her brain that left her feverish in anticipation of what awaited, and a burning at the tip of her toes that, in fact, had suddenly become quite uncomfortable.

"Oh my!" she exclaimed, jumping away from him with an

abruptness that nearly propelled him into the fire before he caught himself.

"What the—" He broke off as she jerked off her smoldering slipper and began beating it upon the hearth.

"The fire . . ." she began, gesturing helplessly at the slipper, into which an errant spark had burned a neat, round hole. Then her senses caught up with her brain, and she grimaced in pain at the large red blister that was rapidly forming on her foot.

Quickly he scooped her up and deposited her on the hard narrow bed. As she watched with wide eyes, he unceremoniously tore a strip of cloth from her skirt, holding it at the open window until it was saturated. Gently he began to bathe the reddened skin. She closed her eyes as the cool water began to lessen the pain.

"'Tis not so bad," he said finally, and wrapped the burn with the wet remnant. "We'll let that be for a few minutes."

Alex opened her eyes and, suddenly conscious that he was holding her bare foot, flushed deeply. "I thank you for your assistance," she said, gingerly withdrawing her foot from his hand, "but I confess to excessive embarrassment at the necessity of such an intimacy, which I am persuaded must be as mortifying for you as it is for me."

He sat back, and those disconcerting amber eyes danced with amusement. "I would have thought that the somewhat greater intimacies of a moment ago would cast the matter of my attentions to your foot quite in the shade, madam."

In acute mortification, Alex turned her head away from those mischievous eyes. She had indeed gone beyond the pale, as Clarence always warned her she would. What had she been about? She could not believe her own conduct. She had been on the verge of total ruination with an unprincipled stranger and had objected not at all. She was thoroughly horrified. But after a moment, her mouth began to twitch, and she could not suppress a tiny bubble of laughter at the ridiculousness of it all. She looked over at him, a small smile on her lips.

"I fear you are correct, sir, but how infuriating of you to point it out! I am not in the habit of comporting myself so, and I must believe that I have quite lost my sanity this evening to allow myself to forget myself with such—"

She stopped and looked at him uncertainly. She had been about to say "abandon" but could not bring herself to confess how complete had been her weakness.

"With such 'an ill-mannered oaf' and 'poor specimen of humanity'?" he finished. "I believe that was your earlier description of me, was it not?"

"That was not what I was—" she began, but was stopped by the look on his face, devoid now of all humor.

She squared her shoulders. "If I spoke precipitately, sir, it was no more than you deserved. What do you expect a lady to say at such abominable treatment as you have served me with this evening?"

His eyes glinted dangerously as he leaned closer, only to stand with an abruptness that prompted a creaky protest from the bed. He walked over to the fire, and when he turned to her, the flickering light gave his silhouette a strange, glowing aura.

"You raised no objection to my 'abominable treatment' a moment ago, I recall. Indeed, I would say that you seemed very close to enjoying it immensely."

Alex flushed with humiliation but held her head high. He was correct, of course, to her lasting embarrassment, but she did not intend to discuss it further.

He evidently intended to, however. He crossed his arms and fixed her with a hard stare as a flash of lightning illuminated the room. A clap of thunder followed almost instantly, signifying that the storm was directly overhead. Alex jumped, but whether from the sudden noise or the suddenly forbidding figure before her, she did not know.

"Tell me, madam, are all the ladies of your set such consummate teases? And do you enjoy pretending to mingle with the lower classes, as you are tonight? Or does your clever costume simply allow you the convenience of meeting a lover undetected?" His mouth was curled into a harsh sneer. "Is that the usual way of a lady?"

Alex flushed. She had not explained her attire to him, nor

would she. He clearly knew from their London encounter that she was wellborn, although she prayed he would never learn that she was a duke's daughter. Suddenly a terrible thought occurred to her. Was blackmail his intention? She shuddered at the thought of Clarence having to pay off such a rogue to prevent this episode from becoming the scandal of the Season. She might as well stay in Dorset, for she would never be able to show her face in town again. Not that it would be such a dreadful fate, but she would never hear the end of it from Clarence.

"Ah, I see I am correct in my assumptions," he said, his voice carrying a nasty edge. "That cool poise, even now, bespeaks a higher breeding. 'To the manner born,' of course. So what are you, then? A gentleman's wife? A baroness, perhaps? Shall I look even higher?" He gave a bitter laugh.

"It does not matter, for I can see by the look in those chilly blue eyes that you think you divine my purpose. You are quite wrong, however. I do not intend to blackmail you. Indeed, you may go your way after this sorry night with my blessing."

At her look of surprise, he laughed again, but it was not a pleasant sound.

"I intend only to point out the folly of your game. What do you know of a serving girl's life? Like all of your class, you conveniently overlook the vast majority of humanity you consider beneath yourselves. Your life no doubt revolves around parties and routs and balls and the burning question of what to wear to the opera. You expect England's rabble to fight your wars for you. I have no doubt that your greatest tragedy has been the inability to find a ribbon in the correct shade of blue to match your charming eyes."

Alex flashed him a look of cold anger.

"Your indictment of an entire class is unfair, sir, although your accusations may well find some easy targets," she said with composure, trying not to think just how closely Clarence resembled the portrait he had drawn. "But I do not care to discuss the matter with someone whose views are so obviously prejudiced as yours."

He studied the figure on the bed and suddenly wanted to

shake her out of that cool aplomb. He crossed the room in a stride and jerked her to her feet. "You dare to talk to me of prejudice when you are a prime example of the most rigidly hypocritical people this country has produced?" he said fiercely.

Her icy rage triumphed over the fear that surged at this rough treatment. "Hypocritical? And what about you, sir? You pretend to be a common seaman for those men downstairs, and yet it is quite clear to me that the only thing common about you is your boorish demeanor. 'To the manner born' indeed! What manner of seaman goes about quoting Shakespeare? For that matter, what knowledge have you of routs and the opera? I do not know what deep game you are playing, but I do know that you are not who you seem. Do not preach to *me*, sir, about hypocrisy. Now if you will excuse me, I intend to retire. I hope when I awaken you will have proven to be merely a *most* unpleasant dream."

A clap of thunder filled the silence generated by this statement, but it did not faze her as she grabbed the thin coverlet and wrapped it around her. Then, without another look in his direction, she lowered herself onto the narrow little bed with dignity, gingerly extending her injured foot. Finally she lay down, the coverlet clutched tightly to her chest. Her eyelashes fluttered closed.

He stood in the darkness staring at the motionless figure, illuminated only by the faint firelight and occasional flash of lightning. He saw by her stillness that she was determined to ignore his presence, and felt a reluctant admiration for her stubborn composure. That thought renewed his anger, oddly now directed at himself.

After a long moment, he walked over to his thin blanket and lay down on the hard floor. He tried to listen for the sounds of even breathing that would indicate her sleep, but they did not come. After a while, he was lost in the rhythm of his own slumber.

Chapter 4

"Alessandra Ridgely would make you a perfect wife, Lucien."

The Marquess of Canfield, for it was to him the remarks were addressed, opened one sleepy eye and beheld the petite figure opposite him in the carriage.

"Thank you, Mother, but I prefer to choose my own wife." He closed his eyes and prepared to sink again into the comfortable somnolence induced by the gentle rocking of the coach and the *clip-clop* of his team. The last week had been exhausting, and he was grateful to relax at last.

An affectionate smile danced about the lady's mouth, which was as tiny as the rest of her. In fact, she was so dwarfed by her son's size that a casual observer would be forgiven for disbelieving the connection between the two. What the dowager marchioness lacked in stature, however, she more than possessed in determination. In that, mother and son were much alike.

"It is not at all necessary for you to do so, my dear, since Marisa and I have already chosen her for you. I know you hate to be reminded, dear, but you have only two months in which to wed. Marisa and I thought to save you the time of looking."

Her words found him somewhere on the edge of slumber, and the tiny alarm they sounded in his brain drew him reluctantly back to the present. "Marisa?"

"Alessandra's mother—the dowager Duchess of Farnsworth. Surely you have not forgotten Her Grace, Lucien! She was so kind to us during my . . . *difficultès*."

He frowned at the bitter memories that suddenly traveled across a decade gone by. "One of the few of your *tonnish* 'friends' who were, if I recall."

The marchioness sighed. "I wish you would put that behind you, Lucien. I have."

He sat upright in the coach and studied the beloved figure who sat across from him, her chin held high. His face softened as he met the piercing gray eyes. "You are too forgiving, *maman*," he said softly.

"And you not forgiving enough," she retorted sharply, though her smile robbed the words of their sting.

"With good reason," he persisted. "Those tabbies treated you abysmally." Even now he did not like to recall the sight of his mother repeatedly receiving the cut direct from those "ladies."

"Why must you persist in this needless condemnation of society, Lucien? You must admit, we gave them *raison* to wonder about my loyalty."

"Because Uncle Guy turned out to be a Bonapartist spy? That was no reason for them to paint you—and all their French emigrés—with the same brush. Anyone could see you were no threat to England."

The marchioness chuckled. "How flattering, Lucien. Do you refer to my size or my intellect?"

The marquess threw up his hands in a playful gesture of mock futility. "You always have the last word, don't you, Mother?"

"Yes, as it happens. That is one of the privileges of being a marchioness in this country of yours. Had your father come into the title before the *scandale*, I daresay we would have weathered it in better style. And now the entire episode is long forgotten."

"Not by me."

"Come, come, Lucien! It is time to get on with enjoying the happy things in life. You cannot be the embittered young man forever. *En vérité*, you are no longer so young—thirty is time to begin thinking about the future. Your father knew you would wait an eternity unless you were pushed. Which brings me to my *premier sujet*—Lady Alessandra Ridgely."

Now the sigh came from the other side of the carriage.

"Father understood me only too well. He never would have imposed such conditions on Derek."

Lady Canfield laughed. "And I know you think it unfair that he imposed them on you. But you see, while he had no fear that Derek would not do his duty in *that* area, he knew that your first love was the sea. That was perfectly *agréable* to him, *tu comprends*, unless it happened that you became marquess. *Alors*, he gave you eighteen months to wed or lose the unentailed properties to that despicable cousin in the colonies. You have only two months remaining. So here we are." She shrugged. *"Il n'y a rien de mieux à faire que de s'amuser.* It is not so dreadful."

"Despite your words of wisdom, I find it impossible to 'enjoy' the barbarity of the Marriage Mart, Mother," the marquess replied evenly. "Nevertheless I believe I am perfectly capable of finding my own bride. I daresay you have no notion of the type of woman I would like."

Something flared briefly in his amber eyes and was gone, but his mother had not missed it. Lady Canfield studied her son thoughtfully.

"Alessandra Ridgely is considered quite an Original, Lucien. She is intelligent, beautiful, and not at all in the usual mold of fashionable young ladies. She states her own mind. And, she is accepted in the best circles."

He groaned. "I am not interested in an Original, Mother, or a flower of the *ton*. I must marry to fill my nursery and save my estates. I don't need a woman who will be dashing about doing all manner of outlandish things. No, since my father's will decrees that I must marry, I'll wed an entirely biddable lass, one of those pale, insipid misses who won't upset my way of doing things. I am too old to change now."

With that, Lucien settled back in the cushions, his features set in the way of one who has said his piece and expects that to be the end of it. He was not entirely surprised, however, that it was not.

"I think it is you, *mon fils*, who has no notion of the type of wife you would like," the marchioness persisted, not at all daunted that her son's face had darkened ominously.

"Mother . . ." he began in a stern voice.

"And anyway, no doubt we shall meet the Lady Alessandra at Vivian's, and you shall have ample opportunity to see for yourself," she continued placidly. "I believe she is at Farnsworth just now."

"The only thing I intend to do at Cousin Vivian's is to deliver this missive from George. I shall be leaving you both as soon as is seemly. A woman's confinement is no place for me."

Lady Canfield smiled in amusement. "I think we have a little time before Sir George's *héritier* is born," she said. "And Dorset is so beautiful this time of year. It is Alessandra's home, you know. *Peut-être* she will show you the sights."

Lucien frowned. He did not care for the way this trip was shaping up. Thankfully he had compelling business in London that would provide a ready excuse for his departure.

"What is an unmarried duke's daughter doing in Dorset while the Season rages in London?" he asked suspiciously.

"As I told you, Alessandra knows her own mind. She has refused another Season, Marisa says, to rusticate this spring. At twenty-five, I suppose she has earned that right."

"Ah," he said, smiling. "It becomes clearer now. This paragon you and Her Grace have picked for me is completely on the shelf."

"By her own choice, I think."

"Then what, Mother dear, makes you think such a particular young lady would condescend to accept someone like me?" His mouth shaped itself into a bitter line. "Despite what you say, there is about our family the lingering hint of treachery. My society manners have been rubbed away by years at sea and activities other than dancing attendance on debutantes. I already have a reputation as a cad, having jilted one rosy-cheeked young innocent, in the process driving my father into an early grave—"

"*Zut!* That was *not* what happened!" his mother broke in angrily.

The marquess's shrug was much like his mother's. "That is the way the *ton* sees it, so what difference does it make? You have interrupted my list, Mother. Let me continue: I am persuaded that your Lady Alessandra will not be the slightest bit interested in a disreputable marquess. My fortune will not tempt her, for she obviously has her own. As for a title, well, she is a duke's daughter."

He crossed his arms and studied the carriage ceiling before continuing. "All of that, *maman*, pales before the reasons *I* have for finding such a match detestable. Marriage to a paragon of the *ton* would be intolerable. I cannot abide women whose most strenuous task is deciding what gown to wear each evening. Nor do I have the slightest interest in a woman who cares only for parties where she can be seen surrounded by her court. No, if I wed, as I must, it shall be to some milk-and-water miss who will obey my wishes and leave me alone."

Lady Canfield drew a deep breath and fought to control her temper. "Ah, Lucien, *que tu es cynique*, this does not become you. You were such a loving child, so eager to please, so *joyeux*. What happened?"

The marquess closed his eyes. "I think you have confused me with Derek, Mother. He was the perfect child. He was the perfect marquess, and I assure you he would have found the perfect wife. He even would have married Alessandra Ridgely, if you had wished it. By all rights and odds, I should have been the one taken, not him."

A sharp gasp came from the other side of the carriage. Lucien opened his eyes quickly and winced at the expression of pain on his mother's face. Cursing his wayward tongue, he reached over and took her small hand in his.

"I should not have said that, *maman*. Please forgive me," he said, giving her a gentle squeeze.

The marchioness withdrew her hand to fumble with her handkerchief, dabbing it quickly at her eyes, bright with unshed tears. She looked into her son's face and saw amber eyes shimmering with compassion and regret. She cleared her throat and spoke with quiet dignity.

"I have been fortunate to have two loving sons, Lucien, in whom I have been exceedingly proud. It is our deep loss that

Derek is gone, and I know it has been *difficile* to give up your beloved sea for a title and position you did not want. But I have never been more proud of you."

She smiled, and he shook his head ruefully.

"You see, *maman*?" he said lightly. "It is so easy for me to hurt the person I love. You surely cannot wish such a fate on the daughter of your old friend."

A tiny dimple appeared in her cheek, not unlike the dimple that occasionally transformed her son's stern countenance.

"*Peut-être*, Lucien, Alessandra Ridgely will not be so faint of heart as you think. Perhaps she can even discover what to do with my son."

The marquess scoffed disparagingly, leaned back into the cushions, and closed his eyes.

"I suppose it's no use hoping that George will get here before the birth, only I *do* wish it. Thank goodness he has only this last assignment. I simply do not understand the appeal of being on a musty ship with dozens of other men who have not bathed in months!"

"Although I do not know about these things myself, Vivian, and would not be so bold as to venture an opinion, could it be possible that he views his service as a duty to his country?"

The first lady eased her swollen body into a more comfortable position on the chaise longue and took a sip of tea. The expression on her face as she glanced at the second speaker could only be described as one of pique, although she quickly replaced it with a smile as she addressed the third lady in the room.

"My sister is right to remind me that George has other concerns besides my small worries," she said, shooting that young lady a look that was not entirely charitable. "No doubt," she continued after a measured moment, "my condition makes me impatient. At all events, it is most unfair of me to burden you with my ill temper."

"Nonsense," Alex responded congenially, although she was tiring of the subtle drawing-room warfare that seemed to be ongoing between the vivacious Vivian and her somewhat mousy sister Emma. "I am certain that the waiting must be very difficult. When do you expect to hear from George?"

Vivian threw her visitor a grateful look. "My cousin Lucien is bringing my aunt to me, and I expect he will have word from George. He is with the Admiralty, you see, and he and George are old friends, having served together under Lord Nelson. I have always admired Lucien excessively. Had I not met George, I own I might have been tempted to set my cap for him, for he is not such a close relation as all *that*."

Vivian giggled, but Alex could see that this confession was met with frowning disapproval by Emma who appeared to lack the ability to recognize a lighthearted remark when she heard it. Indeed, although Emma was younger than Vivian, she already seemed to have the humorless disposition of the most dour spinster. Which she would fast become, Alex thought, if she kept on in this vein. Her insipid brown hair and dull countenance were in stark contrast to Vivian's rosy cheeks and brightly glowing green eyes, which were crowned by a glossy chestnut halo.

As George was Alex's longtime neighbor and childhood playmate, she had been delighted to look in on Vivian, whose company she vastly enjoyed. Since her arrival in Dorset last week, Alex had become almost a daily caller at George's comfortable old manor house. Alex thought that George need have no cause for worry about Vivian's health, but she did wonder about his wife's spirits. For Vivian, whose activities now were quite limited, had welcomed her with such enthusiasm that Alex wondered whether Vivian was finding Emma's companionship trying in the extreme.

Although Alex usually was most interested in Vivian's loquacious chatter, today she found her thoughts wandering, as they had quite often since her arrival, to her strange adventure on the journey down.

There had been no sign of her fierce companion when she had awakened that morning at the inn, and Alex guessed he must have taken his leave at dawn. She did not know whether any of the three men had been awake to see him step from her room in the final act of their bizarre charade. The storm had long since spent its fury, and by the time her carriage was repaired and her host commissioned to find more suitable attire for her from the village, it was midday. It seemed odd to be on her way again, as if nothing out of the ordinary had happened, as if she had never encountered the man named Luke. The sense of unreality continued until Shaftsbury, when the sight of the chalky downlands and the familiar undulating countryside reassured her that she was indeed home. Southward to the coast she drank in the sight of the downs as they disappeared into rounded covers and sharp cliffs. When finally the carriage pulled up at Farnsworth, the gentle rustle of the fresh sea air was a balm for her troubled thoughts. Now, surely, she would relax.

Except that it had not gone quite that way. The solitude of Farnsworth had not banished the image of the contemptuous man who had injected himself so memorably into her life. Why was he so angry? And why, given his obvious disgust of her, did she continue to think of him? Perhaps it was because his aversion had not prevented him from those rude assaults on her person. She still flushed with embarrassment, remembering the scene before the fire. Who would have thought she could be such a wanton? Thank goodness none of her acquaintances had witnessed the exemplary Alessandra Ridgely led astray by a pair of mischievous amber eyes!

Alex forced her attention back to Vivian's prattle. She had launched into a glowing description of her cousin, who seemed to be a marquess of some dubious reputation.

"Mind you, I don't say that it was proper to leave the young lady at the altar—well, actually he cried off before the wedding date, but only *just*," Vivian was saying. "And although he allowed her family to put out the notice, everyone knew it was his doing. But if truth be told, the chit was playing him false. She was enamored only of his medals—Lucien was highly decorated after Trafalgar, you know—and when he was invalided home shortly thereafter, her eyes wandered. We were most out-raged to find that she was dangling after a toplofty earl."

"I see," Alex replied politely, although she didn't. "But surely, a marquess . . ."

"Oh, Lucien didn't have the title then, you understand. That's why he went to sea. He was the younger son." Vivian broke off, a frown marring her brow. "There was a scandal of enormous proportions when Lucien hobbled on his crutches into a party at Lady Greenville's and planted the toplofty earl a facer. Then he told the chit's horrified parents that he was certain their daughter would wish to end her engagement to such an ill-mannered boor as himself and that he had no doubt of soon seeing a notice to that effect in the *Gazette*. Then he left!"

"But that is famous!" Alex said, laughing. "Why have I not heard of it previously?"

Vivian smiled. "Oh, that was several years ago. It was a nine days' wonder, at all events, and no one would remember it at all if Lucien's father had not died a few weeks later. He had been in ill health for some time. The scandal had nothing to do with that, of course, although the chit's parents were unkind enough to suggest that Lucien's behavior put the marquess's other foot in the grave."

Alex sobered. "How unfortunate!"

"Yes, well, it was not the first time that the Tremaines had weathered scandal, but that's neither here nor there. Lucien went back to sea after his injuries healed—against his doctor's advice, I might add. I do not know how he did it. We did not see him again until his brother Derek died over a year ago. Now he is the marquess, although I am sure he does not wish to be."

"You seem to know him well. I suppose that is because he is your cousin," Alex said.

"No, Lucien keeps his own counsel. It is George who pro-vides me with such information, for he wishes me to help find Lucien a wife. Now that my husband is settled—or will be, once his duty to the Admiralty is finished—he thinks all of his unmarried friends should be introduced to the pleasures of mar-ried life." Vivian smiled. "I think he even fancies it his obligation to get Lucien leg-shackled. Although in that, I confess, my dear husband may have taken on a Herculean task."

Alex's eyebrows arched skeptically.

"I don't doubt, Vivian dear, that there will be plenty of young ladies willing to take on such an enticing challenge, despite your cousin's tarnished reputation. Unless of course there is some other reason. He lacks conversation, perhaps? Something amiss with his looks? Too fond of spirits?" She frowned in mock horror. "Don't tell me he has put himself beyond the pale at Carlton House, for I simply won't believe it. The Regent offended by a shady marquess? Never!"

Vivian gurgled with laughter. "For shame, Alex! Your wicked wit will get you in trouble one day."

Emma, who had been listening silently to this exchange, spoke up in colorless tones. "Still, Vivian, you must admit that Cousin Lucien lacks a certain . . . sensibility."

Her sister frowned. "I do not know what you mean, Emma!" she said sharply. "There is nothing whatsoever wrong with Lucien." Vivian turned to address Alex. "In truth, most ladies find Lucien excessively attractive. His demeanor is perhaps a trifle . . . fierce, but that is off-putting only to those females who have unrealistic notions of male behavior."

Alex was certain that this last remark was intended for Emma, and she was forced to hide her smile.

Vivian leaned forward with a confidential air. "As for his looks, well, they are rather unusual, but I am persuaded that you would find nothing displeasing *there*. In fact—"

There was a sound at the doorway, and Vivian abruptly broke off with a delighted smile. "But you shall soon see for yourself, Alex dear," she whispered. In a more audible tone, she gave a cry of welcome: "Aunt Celeste! Lucien!"

Alex turned with a friendly smile that greeted the petite lady in the doorway and traveled up to the tall man standing behind her. As the older lady advanced briskly into the room Alex's eyes suddenly widened in shock. The man remained riveted to the spot, his amber eyes locked with hers in appalled disbelief.

"Good God!" he said.

Chapter 5

Vivian's delighted chatter covered the awkwardness of Lucien's exclamation. Indeed, as the effervescent hostess performed the introductions, thus removing for Lucien and Alex every hope that their worst fears had not been realized, she did not seem to notice the stunned stares each of those two parties fixed upon the other. Nor did Alex and Lucien appear to hear the conversation about them; Lucien was taken aback when Vivian finally pulled on his sleeve, demanding for the third time that he produce the promised letter from George.

"What? Oh, of course, Vivian. My apologies," he muttered, and noticing the ladies had seated themselves, did likewise. He settled on a camel sofa, realizing only belatedly that it was but a few feet from the chair on which Alex had tensely perched. His thick brows drew together ominously.

Vivian quickly became engrossed in her husband's missive. Discourse in the room halted, as no one wished to intrude upon their hostess's absorption in her long-awaited letter. Lady Canfield, comfortably installed in a peacock-blue wing chair, was content to avail herself of the opportunity for observation. Her son was behaving most strangely, she thought as she watched his inexplicably glum expression deepen. As for the worthy Alessandra Ridgely, Marisa's beautiful daughter seemed to have no conversation at all, which Lady Canfield would swear was not in the young lady's nature. There seemed to be a tension in the room, originating in the vicinity of Lucien and Lady Alessandra. Then again, perhaps she was only imagining it.

At that moment, Emma chose to speak, perhaps thinking it

her place in the face of her sister's temporary abdication of her hostess duties to fill the silence.

"I hope your journey was most unexceptional, Aunt," she said politely.

"*Naturellement.* We would have come sooner, but Lucien had business in Wiltshire that prevented him from returning to London to escort me until this week. But we are here in plenty of time, it seems. Perhaps Sir George will even have time to get home for the blessed event."

At this, Vivian looked up from the letter, her eyes shimmering with tears. "He will not be here for the birth, although he expects to be home in June. Of course, he cannot be certain. Oh, it is so hard, this waiting!" She refolded the papers and looked at the group apologetically. "I am sorry. It is just that at times I think the sea is more competition for my husband's affections than any mistress he might take it into his head to acquire."

Her sister colored at that comment, but Lady Canfield reached over and patted Vivian's hand.

"My dear, all women feel thus. But do not worry, your George will be home soon enough. And when he does, you will have the satisfaction of knowing that it is *finis*. For this is his last voyage, is it not?"

"Yes—at least if all goes well on the Peninsula," Vivian replied mistily. "You are kind to sympathize, Aunt. I know it was difficult for you when Lucien was at sea all those years."

Alex had been following the discussion with a dazed air, still attempting to absorb the news that this distasteful man was Vivian's marquess. And he had dared to lecture her about hypocrisy! She fixed him with a narrowed gaze.

"You were formerly at sea, my lord?" she asked in a polite voice that did not obscure the daggers in her cool blue eyes.

"In my youth," Lucien replied curtly.

"Ah, yes. Well, I am certain that it seems like only last week," Alex responded innocuously.

He glowered at her, and Alex was thankful that they were not alone; she had no doubt that in his current mood he wished to do her violence. Was he that kind of man? He was dangerous, of that much she was certain. The memory of that powerful body pressed against hers suddenly made her shiver. His sudden presence here was an unfortunate turn of events; nevertheless she refused to be intimidated. He would know that she was a woman to be reckoned with. As Lady Canfield and Vivian continued their conversation she renewed her polite offensive.

"Your mother said you had business in Wiltshire, my lord. Coincidentally I myself was traveling near Salisbury last week on the way down from London. A lovely place, is it not? I trust your business was not too fatiguing to prevent you from enjoying the area." She smiled charmingly.

Lucien leaned forward, the full force of his amber eyes upon her for the first time since that moment when he had stood at the threshold. His blazing look made Alex catch her breath. There was contempt there, along with a lazy speculation that she found both insulting and provocative. Alex felt her pulse flutter.

"My business must be utterly insignificant to a *lady* such as yourself, Lady Alessandra."

His voice did not carry to the others, but she heard the implied insult in his emphasis of the word and flushed. He seemed not to notice, but his eyes and contemptuous mouth spoke volumes about what was left unsaid as he continued what must have seemed to everyone else a perfectly unexceptional conversation.

"My work for the Admiralty is rather dull, mostly involving the shuffling of papers. Occasionally a more challenging task comes my way. I have been working on such a project during the last few months, and an important development took me to Wiltshire. I do not believe you would care to know the details. It involved associating with company one does not usually find in the drawing room. Though of course," he drawled, "some *ladies* do take an inordinate interest in the affairs of the lower orders."

Alex bit her lip in anger, though one corner of her brain could not help but watch the scene with a sort of detached amusement. Very well, then. She would not give him this round without delivering a parting shot.

"I would be wary, my lord, of making hasty judgments about

what ladies consider acceptable drawing-room company," she said pleasantly, and pointedly turned her attention away from him to the others.

It was his turn to flush as he stared hard at the seemingly serene profile before him. While he had no doubt that she felt the heat of his gaze, her controlled demeanor was evidence of the same gritty determination she had displayed in the inn. Here, as there, her self-possession drew his grudging admiration. He wanted to shake that complacency out of her, to crush that lady-like facade that he was certain masked an abundance of hypocrisy. But he also wanted to do other things, he realized quite unexpectedly. His eyes followed the sleekly coiled blond hair, the ivory complexion, the lithe form encased in an enticingly thin sprigged muslin. He could not help but remember how that tawny hair had flowed loose around her shoulders and the feel of her soft flesh under his probing hands. Inadvertently a grin stole over his face, lightening his hard features.

As if she was aware of the change in his mood, Alex suddenly glanced in his direction. The smile that spread across his features transformed his face into something altogether breathtaking, and she found herself unable to look away.

"I am happy you see the humor in our situation, sir," she whispered in irritation, her eyes regarding that elusive dimple dancing near his mouth.

"Oh, no, madam. It is not that," he said in a low, caressing voice. "I was merely thinking about the more pleasurable aspects of our last encounter. I am reminded that we have not always been at daggers drawn."

Alex felt her face redden. What an impudent man! But she would not let him see her discomfiture. She merely elevated her exquisite eyebrows and returned with patent unconcern to the ladies' conversation. Somehow, she joined in the discussion for a full half hour before taking her leave; later she realized she had no notion of what she—or the others—had said.

The morning air always lifted Alex's spirits, and this day was no different. It was almost possible, she thought as she felt the brisk breeze on her cheek, to forget she had ever encountered Lucien Tremaine.

She stopped at the crest of a hill, from which she could see the main house at Farnsworth and the sea beyond. Why Clarence never chose to come here was a mystery. It was such a beautiful spot. She knew she should be grateful that he preferred town life, as it meant that she had Farnsworth all to herself. On days like this, it was a privilege. Here she was free of the trappings of society. She could even ride astride in a pair of old breeches. There was no one to question her behavior.

The question of a companion nagged at her brain. If Cousin Agatha came to live with her, she might as well be tossed into a prison, for all that she was of age. And yet Alex knew that Clarence and her mother had a point. Ladies, even ape-leaders such as herself, simply did not go about by themselves. Moreover, Alex knew it was not fair to expect her mother, who had played her dutiful chaperon for so many Seasons, to give up her own pursuits to continue to keep her company. But Cousin Agatha! It did not bear thinking about. She would have to come up with some alternative. Perhaps this time of freedom and relaxation at Farnsworth would provide fertile ground for an idea or two. She would savor all of Farnsworth's delights, perhaps for the last time, without anyone around to point out her various improprieties at every turn.

A gurgle of laughter rose within her chest and burst out unexpectedly as she thought about the events of the past week. To call them improprieties was rather to understate the matter, and now the very same man with whom she had engaged in them had turned up yesterday at Vivian's—nearly at her own doorstep!

Quite literally so, Alex amended with sinking spirits as she spied the rider even now handing the reins to a groom on the gravel drive that swept past the front of Farnsworth. He had not caught sight of her position on the hill above him. No doubt he did not think she was the type of person to rise at dawn and ride for hours before breakfast. She could turn her mount around, and he would never be the wiser.

Abruptly she stiffened her spine. Alessandra Ridgely was no coward. With a sigh she bid her mare forward.

She found him pacing in the morning room, oblivious to the glass of sherry that had been placed on a tray near a comfortable leather chair.

"Good morning, my lord," she said, and he turned quickly.

She nearly gasped in shock, unprepared for the elegant sight before her. He was dressed rather formally for one paying a morning call on horseback in the country, wearing sage-green kerseymere breeches and a corbeau-colored double-breasted coat with French riding sleeves. His white neckcloth was tied in a formal style, usually seen at the best occasions in town. His only concession to his mode of travel was a pair of deep brown top boots; however, they were so exquisitely polished as to have been acceptable in the most elegant London salon.

His unsmiling eyes traveled over her form, and suddenly Alex was conscious that she stood before him in a groom's faded breeches and shirt. She realized with a blush that her attire far from disguised her figure. Once again, she thought, she had proven herself a veritable hoyden. He must think she did nothing all day but run around in strange disguises. Alex's demeanor betrayed none of those concerns, however, and her tone was coolly formal.

"Pardon me, sir. I did not expect morning callers," she said smoothly. "If you will excuse me, I shall change. It will not take a moment."

"It is not necessary," he said politely, although his tone seemed strangely unsure. "That is, I did not mean to disturb your morning and would not want to inconvenience you, though perhaps—" He broke off, seemingly at a loss for words.

Alex hesitated at the threshold, puzzled at the uncharacteristic display of uncertainty from this man.

"Yes?" she prompted.

"I have come to speak to you about a grave matter, that is, one of some importance. Perhaps you will feel more composed in some other attire." His closed countenance revealed nothing more about this cryptic statement, and Alex could not quiet a tiny surge of alarm.

"Vivian . . .?" she began.

"She is well. This does not concern her," he growled tersely, and Alex thought the room fairly reverberated with the tension in his voice. Indeed, his imposing form seemed poised for battle, or for flight.

"I shall be no more than ten minutes, sir," Alex responded, and quickly disappeared through the doorway.

When she returned, good as her word, no more than the promised time had elapsed. She saw that the glass of sherry was now empty, and the marquess was standing rigidly at the mantelpiece. When she entered, he walked over to the decanter and poured another glass. She shook her head when he silently offered to pour her some.

He drank deeply and set the glass down sharply on the table, fixing her with an enigmatic expression. For one moment, Alex thought he looked like a little boy about to confess a misdeed. The look was gone almost the second she discerned it, however, to be replaced by a mask of rigid control. He expelled a deep breath.

"I have come to ask you to do me the honor of becoming my wife," he said, and Alex thought it was the merest luck that he did not choke on the words.

She stood quietly with her hands at her sides, waiting in stunned silence for some explanation. When it became clear he had nothing else to say, she spoke.

"I cannot think why, sir," she responded placidly. "Or do you mean to tell me that you hold me in great regard?"

The thick auburn brows came together like a thundercloud, and the amber eyes glared, but her cool blue gaze did not flinch. After a moment's silence, he spoke in clipped tones.

"I should think it would be fairly obvious. I have compromised you beyond repair."

If he had expected a response to this announcement, one was not immediately forthcoming.

Alex wandered to a lemon brocade divan and sat down upon

its comfortable cushions. Her perfectly smooth hair gave no evidence of its former wind-torn state; her green cambric gown was so far from the disreputable garb she had just removed as to cause anyone to wonder if it had been the same female in those tight-fitting breeches. Indeed, she was every inch the lady, and at the moment, a lady curiously contemplating the glowering man across the room.

She regarded him for a long moment.

"That may well be, my lord," she said politely, as if discussing the merits of a new play at the Royal. "But as I think it is unlikely anyone will ever know of our . . . evening together, it is hardly necessary to go to such extremes."

He threw out his arms impatiently. "That is irrelevant, as you well know," he retorted, his deep baritone carrying a decided edge. "I was not at sea so long that I lost all sense of honor or manners. No matter how unintentionally, I have wronged you. I mean to correct that."

"If you think that forcing us both into an unwanted marriage is righting a wrong, then I take leave to quarrel with your reasoning," Alex responded calmly. "As for your vaunted sense of honor, my lord, may I remind you that you yourself have in the recent past voiced no great respect for the manners of my class. Or, I should say, *our* class."

His jaw tightened, and those thick brows drew together as anger glinted in his golden eyes. But he remained silent for some moments. A look of indecision crossed his face, but it was quickly replaced by one of sternness. Finally he spoke.

"I am certain you think I deserved that, and perhaps I did. My code of honor is my own, however, and I can only repeat that it requires me to demand your hand in marriage."

"Ah, now we are getting nearer the nub of it," Alex said, and swept gracefully to her feet. "When you did not know who I was, it did not matter to you that I was 'compromised.' Now that you know my identity, your conscience awakens. A strange sort of honor, my lord, that allows transgression when the victim is unknown but protests when a name is put to the face."

He advanced to her side, his expression fierce. "You go too

far, madam," he said through clenched teeth, his face so close to hers that she could feel his warm breath. She forced herself to ignore the disturbing sensation.

"Nay, I have not yet finished," Alex insisted. Her voice was firm, belying the turmoil she felt. "Let me conclude, sir, by easing your mind: what happened in that inn does not matter one whit to me. My reputation is intact, unless you plan to spread scurrilous rumors all over the country, and somehow I do not think your curious code of honor will allow that. Your contempt for me is only too plain, sir. I wish I had the time to tell you why it is also wrongheaded, but that is neither here nor there. I do not intend to accept your proposal, so you may be on your way."

He stared at her in disbelief, and for one wild moment, Alex thought he was contemplating simply carrying her away with him. Finally his startled features dissolved into that mask of control.

"I hope you do not regret your answer, madam," he said in a constricted voice. "I remain at your disposal, should you reconsider." With that terse statement, he bowed and left the room.

Chapter 6

"I must return to London tomorrow, Mother," Lucien said as he escorted Lady Canfield down the wide oak stairway leading from the second floor of the Huntsley Manor.

"I do not see why you cannot stay longer with us. You cannot have had time to further your acquaintance with Alessandra," the marchioness replied, wrinkling her nose.

Lucien cleared his throat. "I know the lady as well as I care to," he said stiffly. "At all events, I have important business in London." He did not look at his mother but focused his attention on a spot on the floor at the end of the stairs.

Lady Canfield studied her son's profile. She had not missed the speaking glances Lucien and Alex had exchanged that first day or the tension that had continued between them since. It was clear to her that they were neither easy in each other's presence nor on the best of terms. She was not, however, ready to give up her hopes of a match in that quarter.

"*Il se recule pour mieux sauter.* He draws back to make a better leap forward."

Lucien's brows drew together ominously. "Where do you get these sayings of yours, Mother? I assure you, my quitting Dorset has nothing to do with any clever strategy to win the Lady Alessandra."

Lady Canfield shrugged. "You must do as you will, my dear, as always, but I would urge you to make the best use of your time here. Two months is not so very long to find a bride." At her son's frown, she added cheerfully, "Come, come! Perhaps you will enjoy the expedition today to the old abbey. Vivian will be resting, of course, but the rest of us ladies will be in need of your escort."

Lucien looked at her with narrowed eyes. "By that I assume Lady Alessandra is included in this little outing?"

His mother laughed. "*Mais oui*, Lucien. *Mais oui*."

The marquess gave a shake of his head and shot his mother a pained smile. "You always could shorten my sails, *maman*."

The group set off at midday, the weather having cooperated in presenting them with a fine, clear Dorset day. Lucien rode alongside the landau that carried the ladies. A picnic lunch was in the keeping of two footmen who followed in a gig.

The abbey itself was only a few miles from Farnsworth. It was a delightful old ruin, parts of which dated from the fourth century. Alex and Clarence had often played there as children, and Alex loved to wander through the ruins and the sky-ceilinged chapels that had been built and rebuilt over the centuries until the abbey fell into ruins after the monasteries were dissolved during the reign of Henry VIII.

Today, however, Alex was conscious of an uneasiness that quite spoiled the accustomed pleasure of this favorite haunt. It was due entirely to the presence of the Marquess of Canfield, who, to her dismay and horror, suddenly seemed to be everywhere she was.

When she scrambled over the stones, he was at her elbow, so that when she tripped slightly, a large hand reached out quickly to steady her. That only served to leave her more unsettled and to provide him with a further reason to remain at her side. He said nothing beyond the merest commonplace about the weather, and his continued silence only served to make her more conscious of his troubling presence. She was constantly aware of his large form, his hand ready in a thrice to touch her elbow helpfully or assist her over a pile of rocks. Was this some new game of torture? At one point she turned to him in exasperation.

"Oh, do allow me space to breathe, sir!" she exclaimed when she accidentally bumped into him as they were exploring the remains of the old smoke room. As this contact was entirely due to her own clumsiness, she could not help but blush in chagrin at having upbraided him so unfairly. But he gave no sign of feeling ill-used, merely grinned in that irritating way he had that transformed his face into true magnificence.

By nuncheon, Alex was exhausted and exasperated with the effort of maintaining her equanimity. As she watched the marquess help his mother and Emma settle onto a quilt under a shady tree, Alex knew she could not bring herself to join the picnic. Instead she walked quietly toward the old apple orchard and began to wander aimlessly, enjoying the smell of apple blossoms and the breeze that rustled through the trees. The lush carpeting of grass and moss felt soft under her feet, and at last she felt herself begin to relax. She could almost feel the old childhood magic of this special place.

A spot under a magnificent old tree looked suddenly inviting, and Alex did not hesitate to pull off her walking boots and plop down under its canopy. As she leaned back against the old trunk her eyes gazed upward in mute appreciation of the leafy patterns the branches made against the sun. For a moment, she was transported to another world, one in which there was no infuriating marquess. She closed her eyes in peaceful contemplation.

But a pair of disconcerting amber eyes intruded into her mind's eye, and Alex found her thoughts much occupied by their owner. How odd that he should offer for her. It was patently clear that he had no wish to shackle himself to a woman who represented everything he despised, yet he did seem to have a desire—that was not quite right—a need, perhaps, to marry her. Most perplexing.

Alex curled her legs up under her, giving herself up to the lazy warmth that stole over her as she thought of Lucien Tremaine. Such a strange man! He hesitated not a moment in giving one a piece of his mind, and his speeches were filled with the passion of one who truly believed in what he said. Now that Vivian had acquainted her with a bit of his history, Alex could begin to understand why he was so bitter toward society and her sex. Moreover, she supposed the sea had added some rough edges. But surely such a life as he had led would also have told him that not all of humanity was shallow and superficial. There was evil everywhere, if one looked hard enough. But there was also good, and more that could be done if one stopped complaining about life's injustices and began to do something about them. It angered her that he was so biased against her and her world.

She envisioned that hard-planed face, those molten amber eyes, and unruly auburn hair. Arrogant man! Why must he always be about the business of cutting up her peace? She would dearly like to teach him a lesson or two. With that thought, Alex rested her head on her arm and closed her eyes, determined to enjoy a brief respite from the marquess's disturbing presence.

Alex's absence had not gone unnoticed, although Lucien allowed a decent interval to pass before casually excusing himself from the others and sauntering off in the direction of the orchard, relentlessly ignoring his mother's interested eyes.

Part of him had been relieved when Alex refused his offer. Despite his title, he knew he could never be part of her superficial world. Moreover, he was certain she would lead any husband a merry dance and that he should count himself fortunate to have escaped such a fate. Still, there was no getting around it: He must marry, and soon. He had not been able to confess that fact to her. While he did not need the money from the estates that would be forfeit if he refused to marry, he knew it was his obligation to preserve them for his heirs. Lucien understood too well his father's reasons for putting such a pistol to his head; they both had known he never would marry otherwise.

He smiled grimly. His father had been proud of him, never caviling about his chosen career as some members of the nobility might have done when faced with a seafaring son. He had given his wholehearted support until the last, when his health failed him and he could barely rise from his bed. Lucien knew his own scandalous behavior at Lady Grenville's had not helped matters. By the time he had calmed down enough to think about someone other than himself, his father was dead. Then Derek, carried off by consumption not so many years later. He owed his father much, and he would pay his due.

He would begin by trying again with Alessandra Ridgely.
She wasn't the biddable woman he preferred to wed, but no
other females of his acquaintance were even remotely suitable.
That she could be his salvation was galling in the extreme. He
had been surprised that she cared as little as he for the fact that
he had compromised her; some women might have accepted
him with alacrity. It grated to bow to society's strictures by offering such a shabby rationale for his proposal. Yet he could not
confess the truth to her. It was too complex, too tied up with a
package of guilt, shame, and some other emotions he did not
care to examine too closely. Moreover, since the unpleasantness
of his previous engagement, Lucien Tremaine had never
wanted or needed a woman for anything other than satisfaction
of physical desires. He could not so easily dismiss the habits of
a lifetime now and ask a woman's help in resolving his di-
lemma.

Lucien kicked at a small stone that lay in the path as he me-
andered through the woods. He could well imagine that the lady
in question would, if she knew the whole, take great delight in
pointing out the irony of his marrying simply to save his estates.
He remembered how brutally he had accused her of hypocrisy
at the inn; he was loath to show her just how justified she was in
throwing the accusation back in his face.

Strangely, though, he was drawn to her. It was not just her appearance, although that was enough to dazzle any man. There
was something about her spirit that was intriguingly at odds
with that elegant facade. It fascinated him and conjured images
of that stormy night before a flickering fire. Her passion then
had been an aberration, he felt certain, for she was steeped in a
station in life that would never condone such behavior. If she
really had been a serving girl, or even a mousy chit like Vivian's
sister, they would have gotten along far better. It was only this
type of female, this polished, cool-as-ice lady, that he did not
know what to do with.

Time was running out. He must leave on the morrow; the
men he had tracked from the inn had left a cold trail behind
them. The Frenchman would no doubt surface in London diplo-

matic circles, but the other man—likely one of those nonde-
script, underpaid government clerks who knew how to efface
himself—was another matter. He could continue his treacherous masquerade for months, if not years, with no one the wiser.
The Admiralty was most eager to ferret out the traitor.

As for his immediate quarry, Alessandra Ridgely, Lucien had
been unable to corner her today despite dogging her heels for
most of the morning. Someone was always too near for private
conversation. Suddenly he stopped in the path. She was lying
not a dozen yards before him, fast asleep under a shady apple
tree. There would never be a better opportunity. Resolutely he
moved toward her.

She presented such a lovely picture that he paused a few feet
from her to drink in the sight. Her stockinged feet were curled
up close to her body, her boots lying a few yards away. In sleep,
she appeared painfully vulnerable, her long fringed lashes cast-
ing delicate shadows on her cheeks and a few errant tendrils of
golden hair carelessly caressing her smooth skin. Her full
mouth parted ever so slightly, as if waiting for a kiss. He tried to
put that thought aside.

"Lady Alessandra . . . Alex," he said tentatively, using the
nickname he had heard Vivian call her.

She stirred at the sound but did not waken. He called to her
again and bent down, gently placing his hand on her shoulder.
He shook her slightly as he spoke her name again.

Alex's eyes fluttered open, and she gave a start. Abruptly she
sat bolt upright.

"Must you positively *haunt* one, sir?" She rubbed her eyes
and frowned. "Is there no escape, even in sleep?"

"I see your disposition does not improve with rest," he said
with a half smile. "Pity."

To her surprise, he sat down under the tree, his shoulders
nearly touching hers.

Alex looked quickly around, not a little alarmed at being so
alone with this baffling man, who had positioned himself uncomfortably close. She squared her shoulders. When she spoke,
her tone was brisk.

"I collect that you wish to explain the reason you have followed me about all day. Pray do not keep me in suspense any longer, sir. I do not think I could stand another minute of this treatment."

He played with a long tuft of grass. "I merely wanted speech with you," he said with a sigh, "but I suppose it is only to be expected that my manner of seeking it would not meet with your approval."

Alex bristled. "If by that you mean that I do not care for being tracked constantly like some prime bit of game, you are quite correct, sir. Could you not have simply *asked* for a moment of my time?"

Unexpectedly he grinned. He brushed a hand through his thick auburn hair and reached out almost as an afterthought to push a wisp of her own hair back from her face. Alex buried her hands in her skirt so he would not discover that they were cold and damp. Drat the man!

Seemingly oblivious to his effect on her, Lucien continued. "Actually I shan't trouble you after today. I am leaving for London in the morning."

Alex felt a sudden constriction in her throat and was irritated at her reaction. Why should she care whether he took himself off to the devil?

"I wish you a pleasant journey, my lord," she said politely, her voice frosty.

His brows arched in amusement. "I am certain that you do," he said and there was a suspicious note of laughter in his voice.

Alex frowned in vexation. "Be done with this cat-and-mouse game, sir. What is it that you want?"

He threw back his head and laughed out loud. "Now *that* is the woman I remember. Not one to mince words, are you?"

"Nor are you, sir, I had thought."

At her retort, his face became suddenly serious. A soft light shone in his eyes. "I simply wish to apologize for bungling my offer of marriage. My temper sometimes gets the best of me and—well, somehow you seem to bring out the worst of it." He paused, but she said nothing, only continued to stare at him with those clear blue eyes.

He cleared his throat. "I could not leave allowing you to think that my offer was not sincerely given. I confess I even have the temerity to hope you might reconsider your refusal." Still she remained silent. He rushed on gruffly: "I would be honored if you would become my wife. I know it is not precisely what we expected—oh, blast it all! We do not even like each other, do we?"

He shrugged and offered her a crooked smile that made Alex's heart turn somersaults. "But perhaps," he continued, his voice low and caressing, "we could learn to speak civilly before too many years pass." The amber eyes flared suddenly with lazy speculation.

Alex found herself drawn into their depths, captivated by his unexpected warmth, humor, and something that might have approached humility. She could almost believe that this man had a human side. Nevertheless she knew that his offer arose out of a reluctant and misguided obligation to rescue her reputation. He had no more wish for her hand than he had for the moon. She gave him a tentative smile.

"I believe you overestimate the damage you have done me, sir," she said frankly. "It is not required that you do penance for the remainder of your natural days for the small act of sleeping on the floor in my bedchamber while endeavoring to avoid being killed."

He grinned, that tantalizing dimple suddenly appearing in his cheek. "Ah, but there was a bit more than that, wasn't there, dear lady?" He nodded as a blush stole over her. "Just so. I do not believe your friends in the *ton* would exhibit much sympathy or understanding of our behavior. You may be a duke's daughter—" Alex heard in the phrase just a touch of scorn— "but you are not immune to scandal."

A slow burn crept over Alex's features, replacing the first flush of embarrassment. That statement sounded precisely like something Clarence would say. In fact, he had said something very like it in his prosy lecture on the way to the unveiling. She was suddenly very angry with the men in her life who presumed to preach to her about her behavior.

"I have no use for your sermonizing, sir. And once again, your indictment of my set is unfair," she said coldly. "But then, I should expect as much. Oh, I know you were betrayed long ago by some silly chit with an eye for titles." She ignored the sudden angry blaze in his eyes. "But not all of society is composed of such superficial ninnies."

"So the duke's daughter"—this time the words were unmistakably suffused with cold scorn—"dares to lecture me on the superficialities of the *ton*?" His eyes were chilling.

Alex swallowed hard at his look, but she plunged ahead: "I dare and I do, sir. It is too bad you lack the courage to take up your position in society with style and conviction. You might actually do something about the evils you rail against. But then, it is so easy to criticize from afar, is it not?" She fixed him with a look of cool disdain. "You may be a fine seaman, sir, but I think you must be a coward at heart."

The amber eyes were nearly black with rage, and Alex wondered whether she had gone too far. He looked as though he wanted to strike her. But he merely rose after a moment, dusted off his breeches, and gave her a mocking bow before turning away.

His refusal to defend himself sent a bolt of fury through her. Before he could walk a dozen feet, Alex scrambled up, her outrage pushing a reckless idea to the forefront of her brain.

"Just a minute, sir. I have not given my answer to your kind offer," she said in a firm voice laden with sarcasm.

He turned, one eyebrow arched in pure contempt. "Haven't you?"

Angrily she shook her head. Her pulse throbbed, and her head suddenly ached. She clutched her hands tightly, willing them not to tremble.

"The answer, my lord, is yes."

An apple fell to the ground between them, punctuating her reply with a resounding thud. Then there was silence, absolute silence; her words seemed to linger in the air like a dead leaf that, swept along by the wind, refuses to fall to its fate.

He stared at her for a long moment. But if she expected any further reaction, she was disappointed. There might have been the slightest clenching of his jaw, but it was impossible to tell. Silently he offered her his arm.

"Allow me to escort you to the others," he said in a flat voice. "I believe we are missing the picnic."

What was it about that infuriating man that caused her reason to all but disappear? She had rarely lost her carefully constructed equanimity, even in the face of Clarence's most insufferable remarks. Riding alone back to Farnsworth later, Alex felt foolish and ashamed. Goaded by his contempt, she had been unable to resist shocking him by accepting an offer she knew he had no real wish to make. For that one reckless moment, she had even seen Lord Canfield as the solution—albeit a temporary one—to her problems. Yes, a betrothal would still Clarence's nagging tongue and allow her time to find a more acceptable companion than Cousin Agatha. It was not as though they would really wed, she thought, barely suppressing a shudder at the notion. She would cry off at the Season's end, and that would be that. But could she pull it off? Could she spend the rest of the Season—nearly two months—with this man as his betrothed?

Her pulse fluttered alarmingly at the thought. But again she envisioned his arrogant features and remembered how scornfully he had uttered the words "duke's daughter." She would not mind taking this lord down a peg. How better to do it than to force him to squire his betrothed around in those very London circles he despised? Perhaps he would even see that society was not so bad. She frowned. Well, perhaps that was going too far.

Thank goodness she did not really have to marry him. Despite all his talk about her being compromised, Alex knew that her reputation had not been in jeopardy; no one could possibly know of that night. No, she and Lord Canfield could part in June with no one the wiser except the marquess, who would have learned a thing or two about Alessandra Ridgely. Alex smiled grimly.

The group at Vivian's that night heard Lucien's announcement in stunned silence. Lady Canfield shot her son a puzzled look before moving delightedly to embrace her daughter-in-law-to-be. Emma murmured some words of congratulation, and Vivian, once she had recovered from her speechlessness, began to chatter like a magpie.

"But this is famous!" she exulted. "How sly you two are! Why, no one would even guess that you were on such friendly terms. You fooled us all! George will be thrilled!"

Lucien and Alex exchanged awkward smiles at this remark, but their smiles froze at Vivian's next statement.

"When is the wedding to be? Oh, I do hope you will wait until after my lying-in. I would dearly love to attend. Will it be in town?"

Alex looked quickly at Lucien. She had not anticipated this question.

"I have never believed in long engagements," he stated smoothly. "We will wed in a month or two. The location of the ceremony, of course, is up to my betrothed."

A month or two! Alex fought her rising panic. He had never said a word about haste. She gave Vivian a too-bright smile.

"I daresay it shall not be so soon as all *that*," she said lightly, carefully oblivious to the frown forming on her fiancé's features. "Luke—that is, Lucien—is returning to London, and I have decided to return also and enjoy the remainder of the Season. We shall be too busy enjoying all the parties to think about such details."

She observed with some satisfaction that Lucien nearly choked on the champagne that had been brought out to celebrate the news.

"Parties?" he asked quietly.

"Oh, yes," she trilled gaily, taking his arm. "The Season has suddenly become so much more interesting, don't you think?"

He muttered something incomprehensible and finished off the contents of his glass.

Chapter 7

The Duke of Farnsworth stared down his elongated nose at the cream-colored pages on which familiar bold flourishes comported themselves with utter disregard for the more refined aspects of penmanship. With a scowl, he crumpled this missive and tossed it onto the table at which he was taking breakfast with his mother, the dowager Duchess of Farnsworth.

"How like Alex to send word of her betrothal two days *after* her prospective bridegroom has presented himself upon my doorstep to arrange the settlements!" He picked up a teacup and sipped the contents before setting it down again with a resounding rattle. Then, warming to his subject, he cast his mother a baleful look.

"I am sure she is welcome to Canfield. Indeed, I rather think they deserve each other. Although I suppose one *could* wish that the only sister of a duke was not throwing herself away on a disreputable cad." He sniffed disdainfully. "A less amicable man I have yet to meet. No conversation. And he cares not a bit about his appearance."

The dowager, who had been immersed in a newspaper during this monologue, looked across the table at her son.

"Lucien Tremaine is perfectly respectable, Clarence. He is accepted by everyone nowadays," she said in her soft, genteel voice.

That remark drew a distinct "humph" as her son tackled his plate of kidneys. "Father never would have tolerated a son-in-law who publicly insulted Baron Chenilworth's daughter and whose uncle was a traitor to boot!"

The duchess sighed. "I suppose the marquess was doing the

69

honorable thing by informing you of those foibles in his past, but you mustn't credit them overmuch, Clarence. The Chenilworth chit was entirely to blame, a fact Lucien is too honorable to mention." Her blue-gray eyes regarded him gravely. "As for his uncle, well, one can hardly choose one's relatives, you know."

Clarence eyed her suspiciously at that last remark. But his mother merely smiled blandly and resumed her perusal of the paper. Lately his normally meek parent had not been herself at all. Since Alex's departure, in fact, she had been positively free-spirited, even defiant. He had been certain she would be plunged into the doldrums at not having the opportunity to shepherd her daughter through another Season. But his mother had seemed almost happy to be relieved of those responsibilities. He frowned. He would never understand women.

"I intend to question my sister thoroughly about this matter when she arrives tomorrow. There is something havey-cavey about this business. It is too precipitous."

"Precipitous? Clarence, Alex is five and twenty. There is nothing precipitous about a betrothal at this date."

He looked up questioningly. Her normally placid pewter eyes bore a decidedly militant glint. No, his mother was definitely not herself these days.

"That is not what I mean, as you very well know, Mother. A fortnight ago, Alex was laughing at the very notion of a husband, professing herself perfectly content to rusticate in the country. Now she hears wedding bells and scurries back to town." He paused, struck by a sudden thought. "I wonder if he has forced her into it. You don't think . . .?"

The duchess frowned repressively. She folded her delicate ivory hands on the table in front of her and fixed her son with a decided glare.

"Lucien Tremaine is the son of my dearest and oldest friend, and he is a gentleman, no matter what you may think of his tailor," she said firmly. "I cannot imagine that he would have forced himself on Alex. If you think she would place herself in such a situation, I fear you do not know your sister at all."

Momentarily abashed, Clarence coughed into his napkin. "Nevertheless, Mother, I am sure you are as eager as I to discover what has transpired. I cannot credit it to Canfield's mysterious appeal. If you could have seen him in my study—he had the disposition of a crocodile."

"Clarence." The dowager's gaze narrowed, and her eyes took on a flinty gleam. "Alex has made her decision. I daresay it will turn out to be the correct one. Your concern is admirable, but there are times when one simply has to cease interfering in other people's lives. Why do we not just wait and see how this engagement goes along?"

The duke's eyebrows arched in mute reproach. "I have a position to maintain, Mother, and I am responsible for this family. I would not want Alex to take a misstep that could sully our name."

The duchess tossed her napkin onto the table and rose. She was by no means as tall as Alex—that had been the former duke's legacy to his daughter—but she carried herself with an elegance that befit a woman long used to her unassailable position in society. Her silvering hair crowned a face that was used to reposing in a state of benign and sometimes resigned agreement with the forceful personalities that surrounded her. Today, however, the duchess had the appearance of one who would not be gainsaid.

"Alex is of age, Clarence," she said sharply. "Even your father would have been smart enough to realize that." With that, she left the room.

Now what, Clarence thought with a frown, did she mean by that remark?

Her maid was putting the finishing touches on a new hairstyle devised especially for this occasion, although Alex privately wished everyone would not make such a to-do about the dinner celebrating her betrothal. It was but a simple family gathering, after all, although she knew there would be nothing simple about this evening. Clarence, regardless of his views on the Marquess of Canfield—and he had made those plain to her after her arrival yesterday—would spare no effort or expense in gifting Lucien with the most lavish display of Farnsworth splendor.

"My dear Alex," he had said, "your betrothed is a marquess so you are not *precisely* marrying beneath you, but I do intend that he shall be fully aware of the singular honor he has won in engaging himself to the daughter and sister of a duke."

As if Lucien—or any of them—could forget it, Alex thought glumly as she regarded the effect of her tunic of apricot silk, her newest dinner gown, although it was several months' old.

"There!" Mary said, stepping back to admire her handiwork. "You'll draw all eyes tonight, my lady! Fitting it is, too, for such a happy occasion."

There was no denying that she was in looks tonight, Alex thought resignedly, that is if one could ignore the rather feverish appearance of her eyes. She wished she could somehow escape this feeling that her engagement was a disaster waiting to happen. Every time she looked into those stormy amber eyes, she saw the warning signs. What had made her think she and Lord Canfield could manage even a brief betrothal? She ought to cry off this moment and tell him the truth—that she never intended anything but a temporary engagement. Surely he would understand. A shiver raced down her spine as she envisioned his thunderous reaction to her explanation. No, he most definitely would not understand. The eyes of the woman in the mirror expressed an uncertainty Alex had never before noticed.

He was waiting with her brother at the foot of the stairs to greet the ladies. He bowed nicely over her hand and brushed it lightly with his lips, as if it were the most natural occurrence in the world. But Alex saw as he raised his head the combative gleam in his eyes. No, he would never understand why she had done this. Her only choice was to continue with her plan and at Season's end inform him politely that they did not suit. In the meantime, they would likely remain at daggers drawn, and the charming rogue she had occasionally glimpsed would remain hidden behind this cold, contemptuous facade.

"My lord," Alex said politely, and then turned to allow him

to greet her mother and Emma, the latter having traveled with Alex to London after Vivian prevailed upon Alex to accept Emma's company. "For I shall never have a moment's peace if you do *not*, dear Alex," Vivian had pleaded.

Lucien bowed deeply, offering his arm to the dowager. The evening had begun.

At least it was not a disaster at first, Alex thought later. Lucien and her mother had rubbed along especially well; her fiancé seemed to hold the duchess in exceptional regard and was surprisingly friendly in her presence. Her mother, moreover, showed every sign of monopolizing Lucien's company until a look at Clarence's stony face recalled her to her obligations.

"Clarence reminds me that I must not keep you all to myself," the duchess said with a smile, and moved off to chat with Emma, a task she found singularly unrewarding as Miss Manwaring seemed to have little to offer beyond commonplaces.

At dinner, Clarence presided over the magnificent Hepplewhite mahogany dining table and a sumptuous feast he had been pleased to command for the occasion. Indeed, he had given precise instructions for every detail of the meal, being one who enjoyed giving his personal attention to such matters but who lacked the finesse that would assure his guests' comfort. Consequently they had been positioned quite formally around the enormous table at some distance from each other. Lucien and Alex had been placed together on one of the table's long sides, an arrangement that left Emma alone on the opposite side, since the duchess and Clarence sat at either end. After a few minutes, the duchess frowned.

"This will not do at all, Clarence!" she said. The duke looked up in surprise from the head of his carefully ordered table. To his mortification, his mother removed herself from the hostess's position, promptly took a seat beside Emma, and signaled a footman to move the table settings closer.

"Mother!" Clarence exclaimed in embarrassment, but the duchess took no notice and had soon engaged Emma in conversation as the parties arranged themselves more intimately. Alex was startled and puzzled by her mother's gesture. In her father's day, the duchess would never have challenged the duke's right to order the table as he wished, nor would she have objected to a formality that served only to prevent the guests from conversing easily with each other.

"Bravo!" Alex whispered under her breath, unable to suppress a smile. Without thinking, she looked at Lucien and was surprised to see an answering smile upon his face. The amber eyes looked at her assessingly, and she felt her face flush as she met his lazy gaze. Their looks held until they were abruptly recalled by Clarence's petulant words.

"I daresay all this moving about has left the food cold. I never could abide a chilled turtle soup! Fallows, you may take it away." The butler bowed and promptly removed the offending bowl from in front of His Grace. The servant looked questioningly at Her Grace, but the duchess merely smiled and shook her head.

"I shall keep mine, Fallows. It is just now becoming cool enough to taste." With that, she took up her spoon, a lively twinkle in her blue-gray eyes.

Lucien calmly did likewise. Alex was hard-pressed to stifle a laugh at the outraged look on her brother's face when she, too, took up her spoon and sipped her soup. Only Emma, her eyes downcast and her hands in her lap, made no move to her bowl.

"I hope you do not think it improper of me, Your Grace, to ask that my bowl be removed also," she said quietly. "I, too, have a reluctance for soup that has lost its heat." She looked up at him with timid eyes. "I hope your chef will not be offended."

Clarence looked over at the diffident young lady and beamed an approving smile.

"On the contrary, Miss Manwaring. My chef desires only to please me, and therefore my guests. He would be offended only if you did not send back a dish that displeases you. You have acted quite properly."

Emma blushed and looked down again. "You are most kind, Your Grace," she murmured.

It was not long after the ladies adjourned to the drawing room that they were joined by Clarence and Lucien, the gentlemen not having overmuch to say to each other or any particular desire for the other's company. Clarence immediately took up a pose at the marble fireplace and idly began polishing his quizzing glass.

Lucien hesitated for a moment and then surprised Alex by coming to sit beside her on a gold brocade divan.

The duchess favored him with a warm smile. "When may we expect to see your mother, Lucien? I know she remains with your cousin, but I declare myself most eager to closet myself with her and discuss all the plans for the wedding!"

Lucien grinned. "My mother awaits the pleasure of Sir George's heir, Your Grace. Moreover, she may not feel free to leave Dorset for some weeks after the birth. If George returns in good time, she will, of course, come to you posthaste. I assure you that she is as eager as you to plunge into the wedding plans. But I should warn you, ma'am, Alex and I do not plan a long engagement."

Alex frowned and opened her mouth to take issue with his imperious statement, but she closed it abruptly when he reached out and patted her hand. Knowing that such a show of affection was purely for her mother's benefit, Alex tried subtly to pull her hand away, only to find that his grip had tightened. She knew she could do little else that would not draw attention to them and cause unwanted speculation as to the way matters really stood. She sat motionless and was relieved when her mother began to question Lucien about his naval experiences.

"I know your mother is happy to have you back with her, Lucien, although I am certain you miss your former post. I remember she was especially proud of your last position, but the details escape me now—you had a ship, I believe?"

Lucien hesitated and then cleared his throat. "At the time of my retirement, ma'am, I was privileged to command a ship of the line. The *Intrepid*, sister ship of the *Victory*, was given to me after Trafalgar."

From across the room, Clarence raised his eyebrows, and even Emma looked suitably impressed.

"What an honor to have your service to Lord Nelson rewarded in such a manner," the duchess said with a warm smile. Lucien shifted uncomfortably on the divan.

"It was indeed an honor, ma'am, but I would not have you think I was always held in esteem. Indeed, I started at sea at a very early age and at the lowliest of positions. The fact that I was from a good family held for little amid the rigors of sea life. The pay was low, the food wretched, and discipline harsh. Much of the crew, you know, was raised by press gangs. Others came to avoid prison, or worse. We had criminals, vagrants, debtors, men impressed against their wills, and a few foreigners who had deserted from their own ships."

Alex found herself fascinated and eagerly leaned forward to hear more. But Emma gave a little shiver, and Clarence's nose wrinkled in distaste.

"No, it is not a pretty picture," Lucien said, a thin smile on his face as he caught their expressions. "Conditions of service have not changed so very much over the years, I'm afraid, but I have not yet persuaded anyone that there is an urgent need to change them. Shore leave is still practically nonexistent. The food remains an abomination—a seaman's staple is weevil-infested biscuits made of pea flour and bone dust. The meat is gristly and encrusted with salt. It is so tough that men even carve figures out of it. Burgoo—an unpalatable mixture of oatmeal and water—is quite inedible and the butter rancid."

Alex was quite moved by Lucien's recitation, but she saw that Emma was beginning to look sickly. Her mother, meanwhile, was fanning herself weakly. Clarence looked as if he had just come upon a large, repulsive insect swimming in his soup. Alex turned to suggest to Lucien that perhaps this was not an appropriate subject to discuss after dinner, but he had already begun to speak again.

"Not surprisingly there is disease aplenty aboard ship— typhus, scurvy, and horrible ulcers that refuse to heal. Excessive economies by the Navy Board left us little in the way of dressings. Sponges are used instead, and there are not enough of them to go around, so the spread of infection is inevitable. Amputations are not uncommon."

Emma had begun to slump in her chair, and even Lucien noticed when her head fell forward toward her lap. Clarence rushed to Emma's side and picked up her hand, slapping it about somewhat ineffectually.

"Miss Manwaring? Mother! I do believe she has fainted!"

The dowager rose hastily and pulled the bell rope.

"Some hartshorn, Fallows! And send Miss Manwaring's maid to her immediately!"

There was much running to and fro, and suddenly the room was filled with people. As the dowager, Clarence, and a bevy of servants quickly clustered around Emma, Lucien looked over at Alex.

"Perhaps you feel yourself similarly afflicted, my dear?" he asked sardonically, his voice low amid the din.

"Not at all, my lord." She arched her brows in reproof. "The only affliction I have at this moment is a surfeit of your presence, sir. If you will excuse me, I find I am in need of some fresh air."

Alex swept to her feet, intending to take the air in the courtyard and garden that opened off the drawing room. She strode briskly through a set of French doors, inhaling the night air and embracing the silence in relief.

Trying to calm her wildly throbbing pulse, she realized that what had shaken her was not his recital of the rigors of life at sea but that contempt, that damnable contempt he exhibited at every turn. She wanted to shake him, to throttle him out of that arrogant scorn. She took a deep breath, aghast that she had flown up into the bows like the haughty society miss he believed her to be.

"Odd," came a low, raspy voice behind her. "I had thought for a moment that you were interested in the plight of our poor men. Alas, it seems I was wrong. Like your brother, you seem to prefer pretty chitchat to unpleasant matters of substance."

Alex whirled to face Lucien. Her face was calm, but her

words seethed with cold anger. "Your arrogance once again misleads you, my lord, but I suppose it is useless to waste my breath. Any gentleman of breeding knows that such conversation is highly inappropriate for such a setting." Alex bit her lip. She had not meant to sound so pompous. Hastily she continued. "It is not because no one cares for such things but that some sensibilities do not tolerate such revelations delivered so bluntly and vividly. If you sincerely wish to change these harsh conditions, my lord, you surely can present them in such a way as not to render my family and guest senseless!"

"I do apologize, madam," he said sardonically. "I had not thought your sensibilities so delicate."

She stared in outrage as a slow grin spread across his face. A suspicious thought shot into her brain. Her eyes flashed dangerously.

"Why, I almost could believe you staged that little scene for our benefit," she said, her voice low and even as she studied his face.

He said nothing, but she saw in his bland gaze all the confirmation she needed. Her voice was very quiet when she spoke.

"You think to mock us, my lord, do you not? You think we are all shallow nodcocks with not a care for humanity, only for our balls and gowns and precious parties. It gives you a perverse sort of pleasure to be confirmed in your view, does it not? Well, I tell you, your *lordship*"—and she pronounced the word with sarcasm—"you are one of us, whether you like it or not." Her voice began to rise. "If you really cared about those unfortunate seamen, you would find the people in town who can help you improve their lives. You would not waste your time trying to shock my family and proving yourself much the better specimen of humanity."

Suddenly Alex broke off in frustration. "Oh!" she said angrily. "Now you have *me* preaching!"

She sat down abruptly upon a garden bench, her hands clutched tightly in her lap. She felt utterly spent.

"Please go away, sir," she said quietly and with as much dignity as she could muster.

Lucien stared at her for a long moment. His eyes took in her heaving breast, her pale hands nervously kneading wrinkles into her beautiful apricot gown, and her golden hair, which had begun to work itself out of the sophisticated style her maid had no doubt spent considerable time creating. She was no longer looking at him, but he detected the shimmering of unshed tears in those blue eyes.

This engagement was all wrong, he thought suddenly. The realization lurking in the recesses of his brain since she had stunned him by accepting his proposal came to the fore with crystal clarity. If nothing else, tonight had given him ample evidence that she would never be the biddable, complacent bride he wished. Oh, he knew he had behaved abominably by regaling the company with subjects unfit for the drawing room. The pompousness of idiots like Alex's brother brought out the worst in him. But he had not meant to go this far—giving Emma a case of the vapors and upsetting the dowager. Alex's righteous indignation had pricked his conscience.

He sighed. This woman would always stir things up. Her world was not his, and he would never be at peace in his own house. She would always wish to change him, never allowing him simply to lead his own life. He could never endure it. He should have known that from the first turmoil of their earlier meetings.

But he must find another bride, and soon. At least he was in London, where such things could be accomplished in short order. Could he persuade her to cry off? Lucien did not doubt that she was angry enough, but he suspected that if he suggested it, she would refuse just to spite him. There must be another way, he thought as he studied the beautiful woman before him. And she *was* beautiful. He would regret not having the opportunity to explore with her the delights of the marriage bed. Then again, perhaps she preferred to confine her passion to words. He remembered how mortified she had been at the inn by the liberties she had allowed him. Yes, a woman of her class would be. One of those cool ladies of the *ton* who enjoyed displaying herself

like a flower ripe for the picking but who remained horrified
and disgusted by the feverish, untidy delights of passion itself.

Slowly an idea began to form in his brain. His pulse quickened in anticipation, and his lips curved in a slow, sensuous
smile.

Chapter 8

Alex held out her long, slender arms so that Mary could button her new limerick gloves, which were of such thin and supple leather that they clung like a second skin. She gave her reflection a pleased smile. There was nothing about her appearance to fault tonight, nothing to suggest she felt anything other than the confidence and poise she exuded. Her celestial-blue ball gown looked bang up to the mark, she decided, even though it was last Season's. Sky-blue satin shown through a nearly transparent silver overnetting slashed dramatically at the hem to allow a fuller view of the underskirting. The color flattered her ivory complexion and emphasized her eyes. The neckline plunged deeply to offer a tantalizing glimpse of her creamy breasts, saved from making promise a reality by a snippet of netting at just the right moment.

Yes, Alex thought, she was quite satisfied. All in all, the gown had a buoyant insouciance that was just right for her mood tonight.

It was not vanity that had made her give such care to her appearance. It was pure fear, she acknowledged as she contemplated the woman in the mirror. What was it, precisely, that she dreaded? Perhaps it was the possibility of losing control, as she had with confounding regularity since her acquaintance with the Marquess of Canfield.

Most recently, of course, there had been that horrible dinner party two days ago. She had completely lost her composure, delivered a righteous lecture worthy of a Methodist reformer, and, all in all, sounded like the supercilious snob Lord Canfield believed her to be. He had said nothing after her sermon, merely bowing with exaggerated politeness and bestowing an enigmatic smile upon her before taking French leave. She had not seen him since. Oh, why was it that she was never at her best with him? And why should it bother her so?

Alex studied the figure in the mirror, willing the uncertainty to vanish. Finally she was satisfied that the woman who looked back was the epitome of poise and elegance, a woman who would never allow herself to be swept into such a state. No, they would play the game on her terms now. The Melville ball was a perfect place to start. All of the *ton* would be there.

She gave a rueful laugh. Certainly much of her world was concerned with mere appearance and in that respect deserving of his censure. But at least it was a world she had mastered, one in which she was certain of her position. And if there was anything she needed right now, it was to rediscover that calm and confident woman she had been a few short weeks ago. She squared her shoulders and drew her silver pekin shawl around her shoulders.

Lady Melville greeted the Farnsworth party with the effusiveness of one in a state of breathless anticipation of at last confirming a juicy piece of gossip. "Alex!" she exclaimed, tittering delightedly when introduced to the Marquess of Canfield. "And the marquess, of course! Alex, you sly minx! Am I given to understand that we may expect an interesting announcement from you and Lord Canfield? One hears things, you know, but is never quite sure how much store to set by them."

The look with which Lady Melville fixed them was reminiscent of a dog contemplating a new bone that had just arrived from the butcher's, Alex thought. They had made no formal announcement of the betrothal, but she had not thought word would get around so soon. Since Lucien seemed to enjoy informing everyone of his penchant for short engagements, however, she would allow him the joy of confirming Lady Melville's suspicions. Alex waited expectantly.

But Lucien merely bowed politely.

"I am certain, my dear madam, that if there are any announcements to be made, you will be among the first to hear them. No one would dream of keeping such a charming hostess in suspense."

With that, he put a hand at Alex's waist and steered her toward the ballroom. Lady Melville stared after them in some confusion. She turned to Clarence, who stood with Emma, Lady Farnsworth having refused to accompany them on grounds that they could all adequately chaperon each other. Lady Melville considered asking the Duke of Farnsworth about his sister's plans, but abandoned that thought the moment she beheld Clarence's stern face contemplating Lucien's departing figure.

Oblivious to the speculating looks that followed them, Lucien promptly deposited Alex in a corner near some greenery and offered to fetch her some punch. He seemed so eager to be off that Alex reached out to stay him before she could stop herself.

"I am puzzled, sir, by your response to Lady Melville's question. Is there any reason to withhold the announcement of our betrothal? Clearly word is out, so why cavil at formalities?"

A startled look came into his eyes but vanished in an instant. The thick brows arched innocuously. "Of course I shall announce it from the treetops if you wish it, my dear," he said smoothly. "You will pardon me for thinking that you were perhaps having second thoughts."

Lucien waited, his breath held. Perhaps the matter of ending this engagement would be easier than he thought.

Alex colored. Of course! After that abysmal dinner party, he would think that she was angry enough to cry off. And now he had gallantly offered her the perfect opportunity to put paid to the whole miserable plan. She took a deep breath.

"Alex! What a surprise. I had thought the Season was to be robbed of its brightest light when I heard you were rusticating in Dorset. How happy I am to see that it was only a ridiculous rumor."

Alex turned in confusion to greet the newcomer, and Lucien muttered a curse under his breath.

"Gerald!" she said with a quick smile as the dark-haired lord bowed charmingly over her hand. "Such flummery! May I present Lord Trayhnam, Lucien? Gerald, Lord Canfield."

The two men exchanged pleasantries, but it seemed to Alex that Lucien was preoccupied. Soon he excused himself, saying he would return with the promised punch. Alex watched him disappear into the crowd, her eyes not quite able to drag themselves away from his imposing figure and that shock of thick auburn hair. Lord Trayhnam studied her face thoughtfully.

"So it is true, then? I thought it but a mad rumor. Alex Ridgely betrothed to 'Lucifer' Tremaine. Imagine that," he said with an exaggerated sigh. "I suppose it explains why you have turned the rest of us down!"

Alex turned to him with a frown. " 'Lucifer'?"

"Never say you have not heard of Captain 'Lucifer' Tremaine? Why, he was decorated for valor several times over after Trafalgar. Took a bullet with Nelson on the deck of the *Victory*. One of Nelson's lieutenants, you know. Grabbed a musket and returned fire into the *Redoubtable*'s rigging. Got a couple of frogs, I believe, and managed to help carry the wounded below deck as well. Why do you think he has all those medals?"

"Medals?" Alex asked faintly, attempting to reconcile the heroic image with the irritating, infuriating man she knew.

Lord Trayhnam fixed her with an incredulous look. "Alex, do I understand that you honestly have no idea that you have betrothed yourself to a war hero?"

She shook her head. "No, of course I am aware of Lord Canfield's war record. That was the problem with his first engage—" She broke off abruptly. "Never mind. I suppose you think me a nodcock, Gerald. Truly, I had not heard of the precise nature of the deeds that earned him his decorations."

"And here I have been consoling myself with the thought that that was why you chose him over the pink of London manhood."

He stared at her mournfully, a fact that finally brought a smile to her face.

"Oh, pooh, Gerald!" she said, tapping his arm lightly with her fan. "You have not offered for me this *age*. Besides, you know we should not suit. We are friends, after all."

He broke into a smile, but it bore a trace of wistfulness.

"Yes, and perhaps that was my mistake. I was too much the friend and not enough the ardent suitor," he said, his expression grave. "Somehow I do not think the marquess would make such a mistake with the woman he loved."

Alex blushed and found herself at a loss for words. There was no way to explain to Gerald that he was entirely mistaken in his presumption about her relationship with Lucien.

Lord Trayhnam led her out for the first set, Lucien having not returned, and soon Alex was feeling more like her old self. Her dance card was quickly filled, and she was surrounded by her usual admirers. Had an hour passed since Lucien had left her side? More? She barely had time to wonder before she was led out for another dance. She supposed the others had also heard the rumors about her betrothal, but in the absence of her supposed fiancé, they were only too happy to step into the breach.

That suited her mood perfectly, she thought as she whirled about the dance floor and briefly caught sight of the reflection in a gilt mirror. She was pleased to see that the woman reflected there was the epitome of confidence and elegance, her hair swept back into a cool chignon from which wispy tendrils had been allowed to escape. Her blue eyes were glittering with flirtatious laughter, although Alex realized with a start that she could not even remember who was partnering her.

This was what she had intended, Alex thought, pleased at how thoroughly she was enjoying herself. She would carry it off. There would be no misstep tonight, no awkwardness, no opportunity to display to the world how Lord Canfield could unsettle her with a look from those devastating eyes. Let him think her the worst sort of social butterfly. That was what she wished, was it not? To force him to endure her world, to make him dance to her tune, here where she was indisputable mistress. What was he doing at this moment? Probably propping himself sourly in a corner, glaring at the gaiety, condemning them all with those disapproving amber eyes. No doubt he was utterly miserable. Perhaps she ought to rescue him from his misery, she thought magnanimously.

"You may be alone among the ladies tonight in ignorance of Captain Tremaine's achievements," said Lord Trayhnam, resuming the thread of their earlier conversation as he arrived to partner her for the cotillion. "Or perhaps it is merely his lordship's other considerable attributes. Whatever it is, I would dearly like to know the secret."

Perplexed, Alex followed Lord Trayhnam's gaze and spied Lucien a dozen or so feet away, surrounded by several adoring young ladies. That several other gentlemen seemed to be in the group appeared to be irrelevant, for the ladies had eyes only for Lucien. The men, too, were watching him in admiration. Lucien, she realized with a shock, actually seemed to be enjoying himself. The amber eyes were bright, and his mouth was smiling at some remark addressed to him by a dark-haired young miss. Alex stared in stunned disbelief.

"Oh! I beg your pardon," she said as she stepped on Lord Trayhnam's foot.

"My fault entirely," he said nobly, and she responded with a rueful smile.

"It is not, as you know," Alex said in chagrin.

She did not need to elaborate, she realized as she felt Lord Trayhnam's eyes on her. They danced in silence for a few moments. Finally he spoke.

"I do not know what is afoot, Alex, but I do know that something is quite wrong. You have not spent five minutes in the company of the man to whom all of London believes you betrothed. Meanwhile he draws the rapt attention of all the ladies in this ballroom while you have set up your own court here. Does that not strike you as a bit odd?"

Alex favored him with a cool look. "I am quite happy to enjoy my old friends, Gerald. I do not think it is required that Lucien and I sit in each other's pocket. If Lucien wishes to dance with every young lady in the room, I am sure it is nothing to me."

" 'The lady doth protest too much, methinks,' " he said gently and was rewarded for this observation by the sight of her charming mouth pursed in irritation and her exquisite eyebrows arched in mute reproof.

He repaid her with a haughty look of his own and picked up his quizzing glass to look at her ostentatiously.

"Ah, the lady is on her high ropes now. Any more of that, and I will think you are truly your brother's sister, all previous contrary evidence notwithstanding."

Alex eyed him in indignation and finally, unable to contain herself, burst into laughter. She gave his arm an affectionate pat.

"You have caught me out, Gerald," she said merrily, and then added soberly, "but I don't think I will thank you for it."

There was a question in his eye. She took a deep breath.

"Yes, I have been putting on airs tonight. Indeed, I have recently discovered in myself a disturbing tendency to seek refuge in such familiar displays when faced with unfamiliar territory. It seems the only way to preserve my sanity and dignity." She gave him an embarrassed, apologetic smile. "I am afraid I am the last person to know what is the state of affairs between Lord Canfield and me. As you have pointed out, I seem to be woefully ignorant about anything pertaining to him."

She hesitated. He touched her arm gently. One of the things he most loved about Alex was her frankness. Did she know how touchingly vulnerable she appeared at this moment?

"Please do not feel you owe me any explanations. You need not tell me anything you do not wish to," Lord Trayhnam said. "My friendship need not intrude into your private affairs."

Alex sighed. "It is such a long story. The short of it, however, is that Lord Canfield is a most infuriating man." She looked at him helplessly. "I do not think I can explain it, Gerald, perhaps because I have not yet worked it out myself."

He smiled, but a mischievous look flitted over his features. "Then perhaps you had best try a bit harder."

"What—" she began, only to break off in confusion as Lord Trayhnam, one hand in the small of her back and the other firmly on her arm, half dragged her across to the spot where Lucien was just escorting his latest partner off the dance floor.

"What are you doing, Gerald?" she whispered fiercely.

He smiled blandly. "It should be clear, my dear," he said in a low voice. "You see, I have never thought Alessandra Ridgely was a coward."

With that, he deposited her in front of Lucien, bowed politely to the surrounding ensemble, and left.

The others looked at her uncertainly and then at Lucien. So Gerald was correct. All of London knew of their betrothal. Lucien did not precisely look delighted to see her. His thick brows knit together, and his mouth drew into a something approaching a scowl before he replaced the expression with a polite social mask. Well, Gerald was correct about something else: She was no coward.

Alex gave a broad smile that took in the company in general before sliding into a deliberately intimate look directed at Lucien alone. The orchestra was striking up the music again. A waltz.

"My lord," she said sweetly, giving him a graceful curtsy, "I believe this is our dance."

Alex heard a collective gasp, whether at her boldness or the dance itself—which was not generally accepted by the high sticklers—she did not know and cared not one whit.

Lucien merely bowed politely and led her out onto the floor.

"My dear Miss Manwaring, you are an excellent dancer," Clarence was saying as Emma colored with pleasure.

"You are too kind, Your Grace," she murmured. "I fear I have not had much practice."

He frowned. "But surely your parents gave you a Season?"

She bowed her head. "Only the briefest one, Your Grace. I was too young when my sister made her come-out to accompany her to any of the parties. The next year, Mama brought me to town for the Little Season, thinking to prepare me for the following spring. But she and Papa were carried off by consumption that winter."

Clarence regarded the top of the brown head before him with compassion. "But how dreadful, Miss Manwaring! I knew, of course, that your esteemed parents were . . . no longer with us, but I did not know that you had been deprived of the joys of a Season. Notwithstanding the opportunity of contracting an acceptable marriage, many of us do enjoy the comforts of town—myself included, even though I have no pressing obligation to wed as yet. It must have been terrible being forced to endure the deprivations of the country for so long."

She raised her head and smiled in gratitude at his understanding.

"Indeed it was, Your Grace. Vivian had married, you see, and although she was often alone—Sir George being at sea—we really do not enjoy each other's company enough to seek it out. It is odd, is it not, how siblings can have such close blood ties but so little in common?"

A jostling movement interrupted them, and Clarence happened to catch sight of Alex standing in a group with the Marquess of Canfield.

"Indeed," he agreed glumly, and involuntarily clenched his hand, which, since it was holding Miss Manwaring's, had the effect of making his partner wince in pain.

He started as he realized what he had done. "I do beg your pardon, Miss Manwaring!" he said. "I hope I have not injured you?"

Emma's doe-brown eyes widened as she looked past his aquiline nose into black eyes filled with concern. "No, Your Grace," she said quietly. "I realize that you must have concerns much more important than partnering me in this little dance."

Taken aback, Clarence regarded her with horrified remorse.

"Indeed, Miss Manwaring, I hold myself in the deepest reproach if I have allowed you to believe I have anything more important to consider at the moment than enjoying this dance with you. I do apologize most sincerely. It was the height of bad manners."

He pressed her hand gently and seemed to be anxiously awaiting her reply.

Emma lowered her eyes. "There is no need for an apology, Your Grace. You have behaved most properly. Indeed"—and here she began to flush deeply—"I am persuaded that all of society could look to your excellent manners as the standard of good breeding and behavior."

Clarence beamed, and this time the firm grip on her hand was no accident. He whirled her exuberantly through a complicated turn, which he was pleased to see that she followed precisely.

"Perhaps, Miss Manwaring," he began when the figures of the dance brought them together at the end, "you might tell me a bit of your family's history. Your father was a baronet, I believe?"

Emma smiled shyly, giving him a deep curtsy. "The title is a modest one, Your Grace. We can make no pretensions to your level of society. My mother, however, was the niece of an earl. His title goes back to the Normans, I believe."

Clarence regarded her with delight as he escorted her off the dance floor. A few daring couples—among them Lucien and Alex—had begun to assemble for the waltz. He frowned at them but then returned his attention to Emma.

"Perhaps, Miss Manwaring, you might call me Clarence."

As Lucien moved to the strains of the waltz he realized he was thoroughly enjoying the feel of his partner, a surprising fact when he considered that he was not at the moment in a state of harmony with her. What had Alex intended by presenting herself before him and claiming the dance so outlandishly? He had been doing his feverish best to get to know as many young ladies as possible, and hard duty it was, too, to stand around gabbing about such inconsequential matters as who was to be invited to that silly Carlton House fete. Then there were those who wished to talk about his naval record. It was embarrassing in the extreme. Didn't anyone care about the machine riots or anything consequential?

Lucien wondered fleetingly whether the woman in his arms might give such matters a second thought. But no, she was like the rest of them, was she not? Look how she cut up with him over his speechifying after dinner the other night. That he had set out deliberately to be provocative was, of course, beside the point. Now his challenge was how best to induce her to cry off as soon as possible. A smug smile crossed his features. He planned to have that well in hand before this evening ended.

They danced in silence, and Alex was not surprised that he made no effort at polite conversation. Her high-handed behavior could not have earned his charity, after all. It was all Gerald's fault, she decided, then almost laughed out loud at the ridiculousness of that notion. No, it was no one's fault but hers. She had gotten herself into this, rashly accepting his ill-considered offer of marriage, and she would make a show of going ahead with it. But, oh, when June arrived, when she had found an acceptable companion, then she would enjoy showing this arrogant lord the door.

If only he were not holding her quite so closely. If only they did not move together quite so well in this scandalous dance, her body encompassed so nicely by his strong, solid arms. He was almost a head taller than she, and she found that experience as thrilling as it was novel. When he pressed her to him during one heart-stopping turn, she felt her breath leave her. She supposed she should not be surprised that he excelled at a dance few in London had even dared to learn. He must have learned the waltz in Europe on his travels. Despite his years at sea, Lucien Tremaine clearly had considerable experience with the fairer sex.

As if to underscore that point, he brought her closer to him, so close, in fact, that this action verged on impropriety. Her satin gown was a scant buffer against his long, sinewy body. She looked up at him in protest, but her words died as she encountered those molten eyes. His lips were slightly open, and as she watched in horror, he brought them closer, depositing the lightest of kisses on her temple.

"Sir!" she said in protest. "Surely everyone can see us! We are nigh to courting social disaster as it is."

He moved away slightly, and his eyes narrowed provocatively. "And that is so important, is it not? Very well." His tone was harsh as he drew her off the dance floor. "We will remove ourselves from any offended eyes."

Before she knew what he was about, Alex found herself propelled into a small room off the hallway that led from the ballroom. It was apparently a butler's pantry, although its chief use tonight seemed to be as a place for the musicians to store their equipment. An open violin case gaped at her feet, but otherwise there was no sign that anyone had entered the room recently.

"What is this about, sir?" she demanded.

Lucien's thick brows elevated slightly at her imperious tone.

"Why, I merely wished a few moments alone with my fiancée," he said lightly. "There is nothing amiss in that, I imagine."

"Since you have not sought even a minute of my time this entire evening, sir, you will pardon me if I do not give your words a shred of credibility." Her voice dripped with scorn.

A tantalizing smile slowly crept over his mouth, and he deftly caught one of her hands, bringing it toward his lips. Instead of the expected kiss, however, he idly brushed away a speck from one of her gloves. Alex gave an involuntary start at his touch.

"And did you miss me so very much then, my dear?" His voice was silky smooth.

Alex colored but willed her face into a mask of cool imperturbability as she carefully withdrew her hand, her body rigid. His smile broadened.

"Are you always so obstinate, Alex?" he asked softly, and then moved closer to whisper in her ear: "Or is it merely that I bring out such behavior?"

She felt her skin tingle at the feather-soft brush of his breath against her skin, but she tried to ignore the sensation.

"Since you know me not at all, sir," she said stiffly, "you cannot be in a position to judge my behavior one way or the other."

He caught both of her hands then and pulled her gently to him. She averted her face and tried to pull away, but he merely strengthened his grip.

"That is true, of course, a fact I would like to remedy in short order. You see, Alex," he said, his hands warm on her soft, bare skin, "I am most eager to get to know my charming fiancée."

The hands moved up her arms, the palms lightly—perhaps only accidentally—brushing the sides of her breasts before continuing over her shoulders and down her back with increasing pressure. Her pulse raced alarmingly as she gazed into his face, now a heartbeat from her own. She wanted to pull back, but his relentless hands were playing havoc with her resolve.

"What are you about, my lord?" she managed weakly, her trembling voice not sounding anything like her own. He directed a heated gaze at her lips as his own parted slightly.

"Nothing improper, I assure you, my dear," he murmured soothingly, his voice low and seductive. "It is fitting that a betrothed couple gain some understanding of what awaits them in married life. Indeed I would not want you to be unpleasantly surprised at my demands. For I assure you, Alex," he added with a half smile, "I am a very demanding man."

With that, he pulled her hard against him and brought his lips down fiercely upon hers, his tongue probing, seeking entry. Her resistance seemed to evaporate as his hands moved lower down her spine to cup her backside and crush her crudely along his length. She felt the evidence of his arousal, and somehow—inexplicably and incredibly—her hands were clinging tightly to his shoulders, seeking even closer contact. A sense of desperate need suddenly overwhelmed her, and she heard herself make a strange sound like a whimper.

Now his lips were everywhere, moving down over the deep neckline of her gown, finding underneath her sheer chemise the curve of her breast that his hand had already begun to caress. She heard his labored breathing and was startled to find that it matched her own. Helpless to do otherwise, she gave herself over to the strange and delightful sensations racing through her, silencing the tiny corner of her brain that told her she was headed toward disaster.

She gasped as his mouth found a nipple, and she knew now that she was powerless to call a halt to his insistent exploration. Her reason had evaporated in the face of his demanding passion.

Suddenly, dizzily, she was no longer on her feet. He had whisked her to a nearby divan and tossed her upon it with careless abandon. The breath was nearly knocked out of her as Alex landed on her back, arms and legs flailing. But Lucien seemed not to notice her plight. He positioned his own body over hers, his thighs holding her pinioned. Alex felt as if a bucket of cold water had been thrown upon her.

"Sir!" she cried as she struggled with all her might to thrust him aside. In her distress, she did not notice that her efforts met with no resistance whatsoever. In a split second, she had brought herself up to a sitting position.

Lucien stared at her, his own expression unreadable. As if from a great distance, he spoke in a rough voice with some effort.

"If you are worried about someone interrupting us, I took the precaution of locking the door."

Alex stared at him incredulously. "You, sir, are intolerable!"

His face remained blank. "I have been told that."

With an outraged cry, she rose shakily to her feet and began to smooth her skirts. Her hands moved mechanically over the fabric and continued on to her hair, which was, she realized, in great disarray.

"Oh, no!" she said, sounding perilously close to tears.

"There is a mirror on the other side of the cabinet there," he said quietly, not unkindly, and Alex looked up to see him regarding her gravely. She squared her shoulders and lifted her chin.

"You need not trouble yourself further, sir," she said curtly. "I shall come about in a thrice."

With that, she walked over to the mirror and shakily began to repin her errant tresses. By the time she had succeeded in this task, she had also regained some measure of her composure, although she felt as if she were in the midst of a strange dream. Nightmare, she amended. But she intended to think about that later. For the moment, the challenge was to return to the party with no one the wiser. She whirled to face him.

"Perhaps you might wish to leave the room alone," he said before she could speak. "I will wait here for a suitable interval." So he could read her thoughts, in addition to everything else.

"Yes," she said shortly. "I think that is best."

Alex moved to the door. She put her hand on the knob, but it did not turn.

"Allow me," he said quietly, and moved to her side to unlock the door. His hand brushed hers, and she shivered inadvertently.

"Thank you," she said, and found that for the first time in her life, she was unable to look at a man directly. Her eyes remained riveted on the tips of the blue satin slippers that so nicely matched her gown.

No, she thought suddenly. She would not let him see her humbling devastation. She lifted her head, willing all of her self-control into the cool blue gaze that swept him from head to toe.

"You are a brute, Lord Canfield," she said evenly. "May you and your medals rot in bloody hell."

With that, she swept through the doorway.

He watched her leave, her lithe figure a study in elegance as she made her way down the hall with all the determination and poise he had come to expect. Her bravery made him feel all the more despicable. What had he done? He had expected her to repulse his advances with the first kiss, if not sooner. He had not expected that it would be necessary to go so far to unsettle her. Too far. He had almost lost control. Not that he would have ravished her, of course. He had put on a show at the last just to scare her when he realized that he was fast losing himself in her. Thank God she had come to her senses, for he was on the verge of losing his. In order to save them both, he would have had to stop and confess everything. He could well imagine her reaction to his explanation that he had merely thought to give her a disgust of the marriage bed to induce her to break their engagement.

What had his mother said? That Alessandra Ridgely was not so faint of heart. He smiled ruefully. Yes, the joke was on him, was it not? If he was going to proceed with this plan, it would take every ounce of control he had to remember that his show of passion was a charade, that he cared nothing for that elegant firebrand.

He shook his head. Despite their differences, Alessandra Ridgely had the power to leave him foundering in deep seas. With that disturbing knowledge, he softly closed the door.

Chapter 9

"We are examining the background and movements of every employee with access to sensitive information, Tremaine, but we need more than that, I'm afraid. You are the only one who has seen this weasel. Ought to round them all up and let you have a look at them, by Jove! Of course that would give the game away. Pity."

Lucien smiled at the older man in whose office he stood. Admiral Donley was known for his impatience and reluctance to waste time with niceties.

"And would accomplish nothing, as you know very well, sir. The fact that I could identify a man who was seen at a seedy inn one night in the company of a Frenchman is not, I believe, grounds for hanging."

Admiral Donley grimaced and for a moment stopped his relentless pacing across the length of his office. "You always did cut to the heart of things, Tremaine. But this method of doing things is taking a damnable lot of time when we can ill afford it. Edgeworthy has long suspected that someone inside the government has been funneling information to the French. The stakes are extremely high just now. We may have reached a turning point on the Peninsula. The War Office is most concerned that intelligence about Wellington's plans may reach Napoleon through one of his spies posing as a Royalist. We have many of the emigrés under careful watch, of course, but they are a cagey lot."

Lucien's jaw clenched almost imperceptibly at that last statement, but he left it unchallenged.

"We cannot follow around every Frenchman in London,"

Donley continued. "The clever ones are audacious enough to do their dirty business in public places where they can vanish quickly into the crowds. I understand that Vauxhall, for example, is fast becoming a den of intrigue."

"Yes, sir. It has always been that," Lucien said with a slight smile, his mind wandering to a very different sort of intrigue. Perhaps Vauxhall, with its private walks and secluded nooks, would be an ideal setting for his amorous plans for a certain duke's daughter.

Admiral Donley frowned, and with an effort Lucien disciplined his errant thoughts.

"I have no doubt that the Frenchman will surface as part of the Bourbon coterie. We can do nothing until he shows his hand. The fact remains, sir, that we must catch the traitors out on more grounds than my having seen them one night in Wiltshire."

"You are correct, of course," Donley growled. "It is the matter of the clerk that rankles. I do not like the notion of waiting until he commits treason again before we seize him. I suppose when we identify him, we could transfer him to a harmless operation in another office. He need never know why."

Lucien stroked his chin consideringly. "I think, sir, that if we find this man, we may be able to turn the situation to some use."

Admiral Donley paused, his eyes narrowed and his bushy eyebrows rose in speculation. "Well, Captain Tremaine—or Canfield as I suppose I must call you now—out with it."

"If we do not allow him to believe we are onto him, sir, we might feed him erroneous information that could help Wellington. Moreover, it would lead us to the Frenchman and perhaps uncover his entire network here in England."

The admiral crossed his arms across his considerable girth and weighed the matter in silence. "The idea has merit," he said at last. "But first we must find the little weasel."

Lucien nodded.

"You will come with me to Lord Castlereagh's office this afternoon so we can discuss how to proceed," the admiral ordered.

"Aye, sir."

Admiral Donley nodded a dismissal, but Lucien hesitated. Finally the older man looked up.

"Well?" he barked.

"I was just wondering, sir, how fares the *Intrepid*?"

The admiral's stern features softened for a moment.

"Miss it, do you, Captain? And we you, I do not mind saying. Shipley has her command now. She's off Lisbon helping maintain the threat of our amphibious landings, forcing the French to keep a cordon defense around the Peninsula. Wellington knows he can rely on us for resupply or, if it came to it, evacuation. You would be proud of her."

"Yes, sir."

Lucien's voice held no trace of emotion, but Admiral Donley did not miss his rigidly controlled features.

"You did well, Lucien," he said gruffly. "It is not over, you know. Now you are serving your country in other ways."

"Yes, sir." Lucien bowed stiffly and turned to leave the room.

"Captain."

"Sir?"

Admiral Donley smiled. "You won't forget the bridge ceremony, I trust? I have told Lord Dundas you will be in the Admiralty yacht. It is extremely important. The Regent himself may even be in attendance."

Lucien grimaced. "No, sir. I have not forgotten."

With that, he turned on his heel. And if Admiral Donley's secretary wondered at the resounding slam that followed Lord Canfield's exit from the admiral's outer office, long habit prevented him from voicing such thoughts aloud.

The weather had turned blustery when Lucien set out on foot from the Admiralty, having decided to send his carriage home and walk out his frustrations. At the moment, he did not know whether those arose more from his work at the Admiralty or the matter of Lady Alessandra Ridgely.

Since the Melvilles' ball, she had been at great pains to avoid being alone with him, which seemed to indicate that his strategy had been somewhat successful. After all, he had behaved unforgivably. Any delicately bred young lady would have found her sensibilities gravely offended. But evidently the offensive treatment to which he had subjected Alex had not been sufficient to provoke her to end their engagement, or she would already have done so. The matter puzzled him greatly. Was she thinking it over? If so, she was taking a damnable long time about it. Barely a month remained before he must wed or lose the properties. How could he nudge her into a decision? Regardless of what she thought of his code of honor, and he supposed he had to concede her the point that it was a rather malleable commodity, it would not allow him to be the one to break their engagement. Thus, if she did not cry off soon, he would end up shackled to her for life.

He frowned. Evidently the lady required further persuasion. He quickened his footsteps.

"My dear Alex, I could not believe my own eyes. Why, every feeling must be offended!"

Alex forced her attention to return to Lady Sheffield, who had been speaking some considerable moments now. Alex had missed most of those words, her own thoughts hopelessly trapped in the Melvilles' butler's pantry with one Lucien Tremaine.

Never had she been subjected to such an assault as the one to which her fiancé treated her that night. It had shaken her to the core to realize how closely she had come to ruination behind that locked door. In the intervening week, she had carefully avoided being alone with him, horrified as she was at the prospect of a repeat performance. It had only been in the last day or so that Alex had found the courage to admit to herself that her fears derived more from her own reaction than from any ill use at the marquess's hands.

If truth be told, she had shamefully enjoyed that licentious, lascivious, deliciously salacious interlude. Until the last, of course, when he had dumped her on the divan so unceremoniously. But perhaps he had merely been impatient with her response. She had heard that men had little regard for women's sensibilities in the matter of passion. Odd, though. Lucien had until that last moment seemed quite attuned to her responses. Well, she could certainly not afford to entertain the marquess in that manner again! But how could she get through the remainder of the Season without spending further private time with him? Especially since the idea of it was so enticing!

Alex flushed at her own thoughts and hoped that her face did not give her away to those assembled in the room. Her mother, she saw, was nodding blandly in Lady Sheffield's direction, although Alex knew that the duchess was bored to tears by their guest. Emma was sitting quite properly, hands folded, an expression of respectful interest on her face.

Lady Sheffield was a widow and quite the most intolerable of Alex's acquaintances. She was rich as Croesus, which is why Alex was at pains to solicit her otherwise insufferable company. Lady Sheffield had been a longtime contributor to Mrs. Williams's Home for Foundlings, and now that a new wing was needed, Alex had hopes of furthering her prospects with this benefactor. If only she was not such a dour and righteous woman. What was Lady Sheffield prosing on about now? Something about one of Lord Barnham's lightskirts actually daring to sit in the box with him at Covent Garden.

"It is scandalous," Lady Sheffield was saying, "that so little value is attached to female honor that *prostitutes* are admitted to the same box with the most respectable families."

Emma flushed in embarrassment, and the duchess rolled her eyes to the ceiling, appearing to study an interesting configuration of plaster. Alex was left to respond to Lady Sheffield's statement, but just as she opened her mouth to murmur something vaguely sympathetic, the butler announced the Marquess of Canfield.

He had evidently heard Lady Sheffield's remark, for his face wore an amused grin and his eyes twinkled knowingly at Alex as she rose to greet him. He spared not a glance for anyone in the room save her, and Alex found his warm gaze and frank admiration most disconcerting. His mischievous amber eyes held hers as he brought her hand to his mouth. His lips were warm as they lingered on her skin, and Alex felt her face redden. He squeezed her hand, and Alex saw the unmistakable message of desire in his eyes. She had not seen that expression since the Melvilles' ball. If they had been alone, she knew she would be hard-pressed to keep him at bay. As it was, he was barely observing the proprieties. She swallowed hard.

Lady Sheffield was studying this intriguing display with a frown of disapproval, but just when Alex thought Lucien would cast all caution aside and scandalize them all, he turned and gave Lady Sheffield a courtly bow. She nodded condescendingly, and he then proceeded to greet the duchess and Emma. Before Alex could recover her senses, they were all seated again, and Lady Sheffield was resuming her monologue as if the thread had never been broken.

"Does it not prove a rapid decline in national morals when ladies of rank do not revolt at spectacles of licentiousness?" she asked, adjusting the skirts of her black bombazine dress and treating the company to an outraged elevation of her thin, graying eyebrows.

Alex decided she did not care for this topic of conversation, not with her relentlessly amorous fiancé sitting close by her elbow and the memories of the Melvilles' party still so vivid. She searched her befuddled mind for a way to change the subject, but to her chagrin, her mother decided to pursue the topic.

"Oh, I don't know, Hortense. I do think a man may sit with whomever he chooses in a box for which he has paid," the duchess said, a note of impatience in her voice.

Alex's eyes widened at such an uncharacteristic challenge from her mother. Lady Sheffield "harrumphed" her loud disapproval and wrinkled her brow in irritation.

"That is easy for you to say, Marisa, as your position precludes you from having to endure for a moment any unwelcome company," Lady Sheffield retorted.

"I would not be so certain about that," the duchess muttered softly as Alex started in alarm. Her mother had always been so agreeable and diplomatic. Had she lost her senses? Fortunately

Lady Sheffield did not appear to have heard the comment and was again warming to her subject.

"You demonstrate my point, Marisa. I have always said that ignorance is essential to innocence. Since you have never been forced to endure, as I was, the spectacle of a painted Cyprian comporting herself as a lady in the very next box to yours, you can have no sense of the humiliation of it all." Here Lady Sheffield sat more rigidly in her chair. "But however we may cling to a gratifying illusion, it is folly to deceive ourselves."

Alex did not miss the decidedly militant gleam in her mother's eyes and sought frantically for a way to halt the disastrous course this conversation was taking. Just then, another voice entered the fray.

"I am sure we all share your concern, Lady Sheffield, for the protection of England's virtuous women from exposure to such persons and spectacles as would offend their sensibilities," Lucien said smoothly. "And how shocking if gently bred young ladies were led, through society's apparent acceptance of such loose behavior, to relax their own high standards of morality."

The glance Lucien shot Alex was so elaborately innocent she thought she would die either of embarrassment or the effort to contain her laughter. She held her tongue, helplessly and hopelessly intrigued by this strange discourse.

Lady Sheffield nodded vigorously, the black plumes of her hat tickling the tip of her hawkish nose whenever her head moved up and down.

"I see you take my point, Lord Canfield, and I find I must revise my opinion of you. Not that you have been altogether beyond the pale, of course, but I must say that in the past I have been disappointed at some of your behavior, which has verged prodigiously on the scandalous. . . ."

Lucien bowed his head slightly and fixed her with a mournful look that seemed to gratify the lady. She continued.

"I suppose it is your forthcoming marriage that has reformed you—no, don't bother to deny it—I have heard the rumors."

She beamed at Alex, who was biting her lip in a desperate effort to control her laughter. "I have no doubt your reformation can be laid at the door of Alessandra. You have chosen a young lady whose virtue is beyond reproach, despite her rather unconventional views on some subjects."

Here Lady Sheffield directed a stern gaze at Alex.

"Ma'am, I . . ." Alex began uncomfortably, but Lady Sheffield cut her off.

"All gentlemen must wish for a bride such as Alessandra, whose heart holds both purity and affection. Yet where can a man find such in a city where lust and degradation are the rule of the day?"

"Indeed," Lucien agreed, and directed an innocent look at his betrothed, who had begun coughing into a lacy handkerchief.

"Every woman of character must be offended at the licentiousness represented by these women of ill repute. They cannot but have a detrimental effect on all of us. Why, I understand that these days there are even some females"—she leaned forward in confidential tones—"from the best of families, too, who have even anticipated their marriage vows!"

Lady Sheffield sat back to observe the effect of this shocking statement upon the company. Emma looked as if she were about to faint. But it was Alex's violent coughing fit that soon drew everyone's concerned attention. Lucien was hovering over her in an instant as the duchess, meanwhile, regarded her daughter with an interested gaze.

"There, there, my dear," Lucien said soothingly, patting her on the shoulder. "I am certain that Lady Sheffield did not intend to shock you so completely." He turned to address the older lady. "My fiancée's sensibilities are most delicate, I'm afraid. But then, we gentlemen would ever wish it to be thus for the woman we wed, do you not agree?"

Lady Sheffield nodded approvingly and then rose.

"My dear Alessandra, I do apologize. As one who has been married, I have more knowledge of these matters than you, but

I had ought to consider my words more carefully for your chaste ears. I bid you adieu."

"Wait!" Alex cried, and then as curious eyes turned in her direction, she spoke with more composure: "I had meant to ask you about the orphanage, Lady Sheffield. You know we are in desperate need of a new wing."

The lady waved a hand absentmindedly in Alex's direction.

"Yes, yes. Well, I shall be happy to contribute a small sum, dear. As long as I do not have to set eyes on the place, you understand." Here she looked sharply at Alex. "I still cannot comprehend that you have the temerity to go there. When you are wed, I am sure that Lord Canfield can provide the proper guidance as to more correct behavior in such matters."

This last statement was uttered with a rather pointed glance in the direction of the duchess, but Her Grace merely smiled a thin good-bye, having evidently decided against further prolonging the conversation with Lady Sheffield. Lucien directed a thoughtful look at Alex's flushed face.

Following Lady Sheffield's exit, Emma quickly excused herself to retire to her room. The duchess continued to regard Alex and Lucien with obvious interest. There was an awkward moment of silence, and then Lucien rose to take his leave.

"I called here to inquire if you go to Lady Ellenborough's tonight. It would be my pleasure to escort you ladies," he said, smiling. "I would, of course, claim two of the waltzes from my fiancée as payment."

Alex stiffened. "As to that, sir, I have been considering that it is quite rash to perform the waltz, as we did at the Melvilles'. It is not danced at all at Almack's, you know." Her voice was cool and disapproving.

"Since when have you ever cared a fiddle about what is done at Almack's?" the duchess said, eyeing her daughter with amusement.

Alex bit her lip but did not reply. The duchess turned to Lucien.

"I believe my daughter has taken Lady Sheffield's remarks rather too much to heart, sir. I trust that you shall be able to persuade her otherwise. We shall, of course, be happy to accept your escort."

With that, Lucien bowed and left the room. He felt, rather than saw, the daggers directed at his back by his lovely betrothed.

Chapter 10

"Lord Canfield seems to be enjoying himself."

"Yes, I suppose so," Alex replied indifferently to the lady at her side. Rather much for one who professes such aversion to society, she thought as she watched the corner of Lady Ellenborough's elegantly appointed ballroom, where her betrothed was once again the center of a group of breathless young misses. Lucien, it seemed, had a penchant for the Season's most eligible and insipid young ladies. His behavior was just as perplexing to her now as it had been at the Melvilles' ball.

Alex smiled wryly. Her plan to throw Lucien into the teeth of the Season had not had the expected result; he appeared to be enjoying it to the utmost. Neither had her strategy of donning the protective coloration of the social butterfly given him a disgust of her. If anything, he was more particular in his attentions. Indeed, had she not maneuvered in recent days to keep them always in company, she would have been hard-pressed to hold him at bay. But what game was he playing? Despite his oft-stated contempt for her world, he had thrown himself rather fiercely into the social whirl. And while he was most ardent in her presence, away from her he flirted with everything in sight.

He was holding forth to a bevy of beauties this time, and one particular lady, somewhat older than the others, seemed to be especially exerting herself to afford him a particular view of her décolletage. She was laughing at something Lucien had said and trailing her fan rather boldly along his arm.

"Lady Trenton certainly recovered her figure quickly after presenting the earl with his heir."

This observation from the lady at Alex's elbow was delivered without particular charity, and Alex turned to Miss Constance Motley with a question on her lips.

"Lady Trenton? I do not believe I know her."

Miss Motley's gaze remained fixed on the flirtatious lady.

"She was Lydia Chenilworth before her marriage to the Earl of Trenton," came the bland response, although Alex could see by the pleased expression on Miss Motley's face that she was gratified at being the one to reveal this bit of information. Miss Motley was not precisely a bosom friend, having in the past exhibited a rather obvious envy of Alex's circle of admirers and contempt for the nonchalance with which Alex accepted her bounty.

"I see," Alex replied evenly, and returned her eye to the group around Lucien. This time she thought she detected a bit of strain in Lucien's smile at the brazen attentions of his former fiancée, and though she could not see the expression in those amber eyes, she rather felt that it was not a particularly warm one.

Intrigued, she watched as the raven-haired Lady Trenton found an occasion to brush against Lucien's broad chest, turning to scold another gentleman, who, she seemed to be insisting, had pushed her into Lord Canfield. This worthy responded to her reproach with a mystified expression, and Lucien's smile grew increasingly more brittle.

"Lord Canfield is excessively agreeable to our sex, do you not agree?" Miss Motley continued somewhat maliciously. "I wonder that it does not give you concern about being able to hold his attentions after you are wed. *I* would certainly worry if I were you."

Alex arched an eyebrow at this comment.

"I assure you, Constance, I do not expect that to be a problem . . ."

The other lady returned a skeptical, knowing smile.

" . . . but I can quite understand why *you* would be concerned in my place," Alex finished sweetly.

An outraged gasp was the only response to this statement, but

Alex merely smiled pleasantly and walked away in the direction of Lucien's entourage.

What an enigma he was, she thought as she studied the unruly auburn hair, the hard-planed face, and the strong jaw that had become so familiar to her. At times it seemed as if he were playing at some mysterious game. His performance this morning with Lady Sheffield had been wickedly funny, but there was nothing mean-spirited about it. It was if he were laughing at himself as much as at this society he professed to disdain.

Yes, Lucien could be excessively charming. When he wasn't assaulting her or venting his anger at the *ton* in her direction, she silently amended. Her mother had given her a sketchy account of the scandal involving Lucien's uncle and society's subsequent shabby treatment of Lady Canfield. Alex guessed that Lucien's anger would run deep, even after all these years. Now, as she watched his attempts to edge away from Lady Trenton, who had been the cause of another old wound, she experienced an odd twinge. He was, Alex realized with a start, almost achingly vulnerable. She shook her head and wondered where that notion had come from. This fierce man, with eyes that could impale one with their intensity, vulnerable?

"Lucien." Her quiet greeting was met by a look of relief as her betrothed eagerly reached out to bring her into his circle.

"Alex! May I present Lady Trenton? Lydia, this is my betrothed"—it seemed to Alex he said the word with particular emphasis—"Lady Alessandra Ridgely."

Alex fought the urge to laugh. It was the first time Lucien had publicly introduced her as his fiancée. So this is what it took to have him make such an admission! Well, he would be free of her soon enough. But it was clear that for now, at least, he wished the countess to know where matters stood.

"I am delighted to meet you, Lady Trenton," Alex said with a practiced smile. "Do I take it you are an especially *old* friend of Lucien's?"

The lady's smile grew rigid, and the gleam in her bright eyes was hard and assessing. "Lucien and I were once betrothed ourselves, Lady Alessandra, as perhaps you may know. Alas," she said as she tapped his chest flirtatiously with her fan, "I lacked the ability to defy my father's insistence that I marry dear Lord Trenton."

And the prescience to see that Lucien might come into the title, Alex added silently.

"Pity," was all she said, though her polite smile softened the terseness of her response.

Lucien was beginning to look pained, and Lady Trenton gazed at Alex uncertainly.

"Of course, Lord Trenton and I suit remarkably well," she rushed on. "We understand each other perfectly. We each have our own . . . friends." The countess gave Alex an arch look. "It is odd, is it not, how these things work out? When I knew Lucien, he was fresh from Trafalgar with a chest full of medals. And so horribly wounded! Why, I shudder to think of how his injuries pained him. Tell me, darling, do you still have that dreadful scar on your leg?"

She blushed and fluttered her fan, as if only just realizing the improperness of such a remark. Lucien cleared his throat, but seemed at a loss for words. Alex, however, bestowed a generous smile on the countess.

"You are the soul of kindness to concern yourself with my fiancé's welfare, Lady Trenton. I daresay Lord Trenton considers himself fortunate to have won you away from the wounded, penniless war hero that Lucien was in those days. I can assure you, however, that Lucien's injuries do not pain him overmuch. Indeed, he has put *all* of those unfortunate memories behind him."

With this, Alex beamed affectionately at her betrothed.

"You will excuse us, Lady Trenton. My fiancé has demanded this dance."

Lucien bowed and, taking Alex's arm, bore her away from Lady Trenton, whose cheeks flushed in anger. The lady quickly turned back to the group and, waving her fan unconcernedly, soon made a great show of chatting gaily.

"You were most impressive. I am in your debt," Lucien said as he studied Alex's composed smile.

She accepted the compliment with a nod. "You seemed in need of rescue."

"That is an understatement, I'm afraid."

She caught the apologetic twinkle in his eyes. Her heart gave a small, unsettling lurch, but her words were light. "I cannot believe, sir, that our brave war hero cannot manage to dispatch one obnoxious female." Her face colored as she realized what she had said. "I hope I have not given offense," she added hesitantly. "I realize you once intended to make her your wife."

He regarded her gravely as they walked around the edge of the dance floor. Suddenly he clasped her arm and moved them to a less-crowded spot near a set of open doors leading onto Lady Ellenborough's terrace. The amber eyes were sober as he spoke.

"As to that," he began in a halting tone, "I have long since concluded that my wits were severely wanting at the time." His body shifted uncomfortably, and Alex thought he had never seen him so discomfited. His mouth twisted into a self-mocking smile: "I was too flattered by the lady's attentions to see the emptiness beyond the attractive facade. I'm afraid I was a complete fool."

His eyes clouded with the memory, and quite suddenly Alex was proud of his candor and touched by the effort the admission had cost.

"As to your first statement," he continued, studying her from hooded eyes, "I own I have never dealt well with certain females."

She returned him a curious look. "Now that, sir, is pure faddle," she said teasingly. "I have watched you charm all the young ladies, putting me at the center of no small speculation, I might add, as to whether I am daft in the upper works for betrothing myself to such a fickle gentleman."

He was instantly chastened. "I am sorry. I had not thought about the effect of my efforts upon you." The amber eyes were troubled.

"Efforts? Now that is a curious word for it, but never mind," she said lightly. "I am sure it does not matter to me whether you flirt with all of London. But do not expect me to believe your innocence of the skills required to charm our sex." She gave him an assessing look. "After my own firsthand experience at the Melvilles', sir, I am persuaded that you know precisely what you are doing."

Something flared in those golden eyes, and before she knew what he was about, Lucien had swept her through the doors onto the terrace. His hands burned through the material of her gown as he twirled her to face him.

"By God, you are a strange woman, Alessandra Ridgely," he said, his lips curving in a tantalizing smile. "You dispatch my nemesis with a few, well-chosen words and then calmly tell me that you are onto my tricks. So cool, so self-possessed, this image you present to us lesser mortals. And yet," he continued, his searing gaze taking in her wide eyes and slightly parted lips, "we both know, do we not, that you are a complete fraud."

"A fraud?" she said uneasily. She searched wildly to understand his meaning. Did he suspect her perfidious intentions in this betrothal? Just then he pulled her closer, and she put up her hands in a vain attempt to keep some distance between them. "Sir, I believe you have lost your senses. I do not know what you mean."

"Just this," he whispered, bending to brush her lips lightly with his. "I have it on excellent authority—my own—that the lady is not so cool as she seems."

Softly he moved his lips back and forth against hers, drawing from Alex a breathless gasp as her body moved without a will into his embrace.

"In fact," he murmured against her mouth. "I daresay she is capable of excessive warmth."

This time his lips came down with bruising force. Alex discovered she had no will to move. Indeed she found herself returning his kiss with an enthusiasm that only proved the truth of his impertinent assessment. His hands roved her back, edged around her waist and moved upward to fondle her breasts. Little shock waves rocked her treacherous body.

"Lucien," she murmured, the word intended as a protest but emerging as a sweet whisper.

He lifted his head to gaze languidly into her limpid blue eyes and the errant golden tresses that framed a face flushed with passion. He had to suppress a smile of satisfaction at this evidence of his effect on her. His plan was definitely working. Odd, how he found this lovemaking so pleasurable. It was becoming more difficult to remember that it was but a charade. He frowned. That was not a subject that bore exploring.

"You mean quite correctly to recall me to our surroundings, I am certain," he said, willing his mind to concentrate on the matter at hand. "Very well. I shall let you go for now. But do not think I shall be satisfied to leave it at this for very long."

Her eyes widened at his words, but she quickly rearranged her gown in an effort to make herself presentable.

Just as she moved away from him toward the ballroom doors, he caught her arm. She turned, her lips parted slightly in protest. His eyes blazed with golden fire.

"Alex," he rasped softly, the word almost carried away by the night breeze. "I mean to have you, you know."

Abruptly she turned and fled through the doors.

He frowned. He had intended to be provocative, to alarm her just a bit. The fact of the matter was that he had also succeeded in frightening himself, he realized with a bemused gaze at her departing figure. For he had meant those words, every one.

"I believe I shall wear the Polish instead of this coat, although I suppose it is really more for evening. But with the prince in attendance, I daresay a more formal statement is expected."

This comment precipitated a flurry of action on the part of the duke's valet and butler as the desired coat was procured while Alex and Emma looked on patiently in the foyer.

"I believe you may safely forget the Polish and wear the warmer greatcoat, brother dear," Alex said with a twinkle in her eye. "In this weather, you can be sure that the Regent will be nowhere in evidence."

Clarence favored his sister with a disdainful look as he shrugged into a close-fitting, silk-lined coat fitted with Russian lambskin collar, lapels, and cuffs. It was a handsome garment that would have stood him in elegant stead at the opera, but it was not precisely the sturdy coat one would wish for an outdoor ceremony in the blistering cold and damp of this suddenly inclement May day. Alex and Emma both wore serviceable pelisses of merino wool, and Alex had added a fur-trimmed mantle to hers.

"Nonsense, Alex. The Regent said he would be there, and he will. He is not one to let a few brisk breezes prevent him from laying the foundation stone for a bridge that will so well serve all of London!"

"Or at least that part of it with the time, funds, and inclination to wander around Vauxhall Gardens and indulge in arrack punch," his sister amended wickedly.

"You are all out, Alex, as usual. All members of the public may share in the pleasure of the gardens."

"For two shillings apiece," she returned. "That does not begin to include the cost of the watermen, of course."

Clarence gave her a triumphant look. "My point precisely! Now that there is to be a bridge, it will not be necessary to travel by water or go so far around to Westminster Bridge. Many more people will have access to the gardens."

Emma spoke up. "Pardon me, Your Grace, but I have always understood that the crowd at Vauxhall was a bit rag-mannered. One hears stories of thieves, even spies, and"—here she gave a little shudder—"men who prey on unsuspecting ladies with the misfortune to become separated from their parties."

Clarence took her hand and patted it reassuringly, as Alex rolled her eyes to the ceiling.

"There, there, Emma—and it is 'Clarence,' remember. It is true that despicable persons have been known to frequent the gardens—the walks and grottoes do provide an ideal setting for their nefarious activities. But," he added quickly as Emma's brown eyes grew round, "the gardens are safe enough if one keeps to the well-lit paths. The entertainment is delightful.

There are talented singers and impressive fireworks. You shall see when we attend the opening."

She looked at him dubiously, and he bestowed upon her a paternal smile.

"I would never allow you to become separated from our group, Emma. I shall consider your safety my personal responsibility. I promise you will thoroughly enjoy the evening."

Emma returned him a warm smile, and Alex cleared her throat.

"Well, if we hope to see anything of this afternoon's ceremony, we had best be on our way. Although why anyone would wish to venture out in this is a mystery."

Recalled to their mission, Clarence and Emma joined her in descending the steps to the waiting town coach, a comfortable vehicle emblazoned with the ducal crest and pulled—unnecessarily, Alex thought, since they were only going to Millbank—by six perfectly matched bays. Inside their comfortable conveyance, it was almost possible to forget that it was one of the nastiest days of the year.

The wind whipped around them as they arrived at the cofferdam, which had been fitted up with stages of seats in the manner of an amphitheater. Alex was not surprised to see that the enclosure was nowhere near to being full. They maneuvered near the center platform, which was composed of a plane of double timbers placed on the piles for the northern abutment of the bridge. The Scotch granite foundation stone was in the center.

The Union flag and the Regent's standard flew at either end of the platform, but there was no sign of the prince himself. There was a party of dignitaries, including a shivering contingent borne upriver from Westminster Bridge in an Admiralty yacht.

Alex's eyes crinkled in amusement as she watched the men in the Admiralty party, their faces ruddy from the wind and elements, shakily disembark from the swell-tossed boat to the salute of twenty-one guns. The Regent, apparently, had indeed found it inconvenient to attend, for he was not among the dignitaries. Lord Dundas was evidently to be his representative. The Admiralty representative, who alone of the dignitaries easily negotiated the bobbing yacht, was the Marquess of Canfield.

Lucien did not look thrilled to be in attendance, Alex observed. She was not so far from him that she could not see the clenched jaw, unsmiling mouth, and hard eyes that confirmed her suspicion that he was here involuntarily.

As she studied that set profile she felt the familiar, disconcerting warmth radiating through her body. He had called her a strange woman, and so perhaps she was. From the first moment she had encountered him at the ceremony in Guildhall, his presence had provoked in her strange sensations. When he was in a room, she was conscious of his every move. When he touched her, her insides reacted in a most unsettling fashion. He had been touching her, it seemed, since the time they had first met. Her mind had never been able to banish that encounter in the inn when she had fairly tumbled into his arms without any shame or hesitation. And now, it seemed, tumbling into his arms had become a habit.

I mean to have you, you know. The words had set loose a peculiar thrill that threatened to reduce her to jelly. That was what was truly strange and very unsettling. Since the Marquess of Canfield had come into her life, she had become shamelessly wanton, so far from her usually poised demeanor that she wondered sometimes whether she was in danger of losing her senses.

Lucien moved back a few steps as the ceremony got under way, and with an effort Alex forced herself to concentrate on the activities on the platform. Lord Dundas had positioned himself next to a cloth-covered table on which stood a large silver dish containing British coins inscribed for the ceremony. There was also a wooden mallet, a bottle of port, and a silver trowel. Mr. Rennie, the engineer, poured some mortar into the cavity of the foundation stone and handed the trowel and case to Lord Dundas, who placed them in the cavity and spread the mortar over them. Lucien, Alex observed, was barely able to hide his boredom. His eyes, wandering idly over the audience, found hers. Suddenly they twinkled wryly, that elusive dimple dancing near his mouth. A warm current passed between them, a silent shared judgment about the absurdity of the occasion.

No, he would not enjoy this sort of thing, Alex mused as Lucien returned his attention to the platform. He belongs at the helm of a ship, the battle raging all around him, leading his men and his vessel to triumph. He undoubtedly missed it dreadfully. He was a man of action, certainly not a man to stand on ceremony or to long endure it. Impatient? Yes. Impertinent? Most definitely. Devastatingly attractive? She gave a small sigh. That had never been in doubt.

Lord Dundas struck three blows upon the stone and began to speak. "In the name and by the command of his Royal Highness, George, Prince Regent of the United Kingdom of Great Britain and Ireland . . ."

How was she to manage until June, when she could break their engagement? The month remaining would be one in which, if the past two weeks were any indication, he intended to be most particular in his advances. She could see no way to hasten the process of finding a companion. As it was, she had to be most discreet. She did not want Clarence or anyone else to suspect that this betrothal was a charade. Otherwise, Cousin Agatha would be on her doorstep in a thrice. But even with the assistance of the excellent employment agency she had contacted, it was taking time.

Lord Dundas, it seemed, had finished speaking and turned to pour the wine upon the stone. The ceremony was drawing to a close.

Botheration! She knew she was not being honest with herself. It was more than the specter of Cousin Agatha that had led her to engage in this disastrous charade and prevented her from ending it now. It was more than Clarence's infuriating belief that he could control the conditions in which she would live out her spinster's life. After all, she had always been able to beat Clarence at his game.

No, it was Lucien himself; perhaps it had been all along. There was something about him that infuriated and yet tanta-

lized her from the very first. Yes, she had allowed herself to be
goaded into this rash betrothal, but somehow a part of her that
she could not control or account for wished above all things to
be with him. His amorous assaults on her person had only
served to produce within her breast a passion that she had
barely been able to govern. For the first time, she had encountered a man who did not leave her indifferent and with whom
mere friendship was the furthest thing from her mind.

Their conversations were stimulating—even when they were
quarreling—and she had begun to appreciate that he had a fine
wit of his own. His manners were not perhaps honed to the degree to which those gentlemen of her set aspired. But neither
did he ply her with false compliments or put on airs. He would
never suffer fools. He was always himself—brusque, bold, and
audacious. And it was always clear to those in his presence that
he would never find it necessary to be anything else.

She supposed she would never truly know what made him
tick. And yet she had sometimes glimpsed beneath that hardened veneer a man who was, if he but allowed himself, capable
of great love.

Alex shook her head incredulously. Now she was letting herself go into dangerous flights of fancy. Lucien Tremaine cared
naught for love, although it was clear he enjoyed the delights of
lovemaking. And in that area, she knew she stood in grave danger.

A great cheer erupted along with loud applause and another
twenty-one-gun salute that signaled the ceremony's end. In a
few moments, the Admiralty party boarded the precariously
bobbing yacht.

Standing on deck, oblivious to the wind and rain that had begun to fall, Lucien removed his beaver hat and raised his face to
the elements. Thick auburn hair blew around his face. His eyes,
grazing the shore one last time, found hers. A slow smile spread
over his features.

Alex felt the warmth of his gaze and the heat that suddenly
coursed through her veins. With a curious sense of detachment,
she realized that June was no longer her immediate concern. It

was tonight, and tomorrow, and the next day in his company. She was fast losing control of her awakening passions under the skilled application of his powers of amorous persuasion. The wind blew up again, and to Alex it seemed to whisper in her ear: *Perhaps, my dear, you are already hopelessly lost.* She drew her pelisse around her more tightly and, with a small shiver, turned toward the carriage.

Chapter 11

"Celeste writes that Vivian is feeling fit as a fiddle, although somewhat exhausted by the voracious appetite of little Georgie. You must be thrilled, Emma, to be a new aunt," the Duchess of Farnsworth said, holding Lady Canfield's note.

Emma smiled politely at her hostess. "Yes, Your Grace. Although I have not yet seen him, I am certain my nephew is a handful. In that I suppose he takes after both of his parents."

The duchess looked uncertain at this rather blunt observation from Miss Manwaring; meanwhile, Clarence idly crossed the room and sat in a chair next to Emma's.

"I suppose you will feel constrained to go to your sister now?" he asked casually.

Emma blushed and fluttered her eyelashes shyly. "Vivian writes that while she has every expectation and hope that I will come to see the babe as soon as I wish, she is certain that a prolonged visit can wait until the Season has ended. It seems she has no great need for my assistance, having every confidence in the nurse she has employed for the child."

She looked away from the duke, focusing on her hands, which were folded in her lap. "It is most considerate of her to decline to interrupt my activities here. I ought to go, I suppose, but I confess that I am enjoying Your Grace's hospitality."

With this, her face colored furiously. Clarence beamed. The duchess marveled at this lengthy little speech from Miss Manwaring, who had otherwise demonstrated few conversational skills.

"At least we shall soon see Celeste, and for that I am most grateful," Her Grace said. "London has been dreadfully boring this spring, and I cannot imagine how I should endure the rest of the Season without her company."

"Why, Mother, however can you say such a thing?" Clarence said in surprise. "Have you forgotten the Regent's fete? It is only a few weeks away! 'Twill be the highlight of the year!"

The duchess frowned. "As to that, my dear, no one knows precisely when it is to take place, including, apparently, the prince. There has been one delay after another. It is bad form, if you ask me, to plan such a celebration at the time of the king's birthday. Each day finds the king either much improved or much worse. Far better for the prince to call it off."

Clarence looked at her in horror.

"Never say so, Mother! All of London is envying those of us who have been invited. I understand that even some people with the best *ton* have not been included."

"Mother is right, Clarence, as you would see if you but examined the matter." The eyes of those in the morning room turned toward Alex, who stood at the threshold adjusting a button on her glove. "The prince's celebration becomes ridiculous if the king's condition is so much better as to suggest that there is no need for the Regency. And if the king is worse, then Prinny's party is simply in bad taste."

Clarence sniffed disdainfully. "As always, Alex, you put the least flattering interpretation on the prince's activities. One would think you were not, after all, the daughter of a duke."

At that, Alex rolled her eyes and turned back to the hallway.

"I have no time to lock horns with you today, Clarence. If you will excuse me, I shall be off. It will take an age to get through town in traffic." She nodded to her maid to follow her.

Clarence was instantly on his feet. "You are not going to that horrible place again? I forbid it!"

Alex paused. Her eyebrows rose haughtily, and a casual observer would not have doubted at that moment that she was her brother's sister.

"If by 'that horrible place' you mean Mrs. Williams's orphanage, you are correct, brother. But if you think I will allow you or anyone else to dictate my comings and goings, you are quite out. I am my own mistress, a fact you seem to have over-looked."

Clarence's face had taken on a purplish hue, and he looked at her in outrage.

"Your determination to persist in scandalous behavior is as unwise as it is misdirected," he pronounced angrily. "What you hope to accomplish is beyond me. You cannot go gadding to Cheapside with no more company than a maid. If you come to harm, you have only yourself to blame."

"You may blame me," interjected a deep baritone voice, "as I intend to escort my betrothed. But I assure you she will not come to harm."

Alex turned in surprise to see Lucien standing in the foyer, a bland expression on his face. "I do not need your escort, my lord," she said. "This is a matter I am perfectly capable of tending to myself."

"Nevertheless you shall have it," he said pleasantly, putting a hand under her elbow and steering her out the door before Clarence had the opportunity to frame a response.

They descended the stairs in silence and entered Lucien's waiting carriage. As she sat back against the squabs, Alex turned to Lucien and frowned.

"I am mightily weary, my lord, of the men in my life who believe they must be the arbiters of my behavior."

"And you include me in that number?" His amber eyes held a mischievous gleam.

"In that, sir, I count you little better than Clarence. You are, after all, forever lecturing me about what you believe are my character flaws. I assure you I have no need of such lessons."

Lucien smiled, and his large hand covered hers. "I do not recall such lectures. Perhaps you might endeavor to refresh my recollection."

Alex looked at him in exasperation. "I recall most vividly some of our more lively conversations, my lord. At a certain inn, I recall, you labeled me a frivolous tease, a person not given over to those serious concerns that seem to occupy your inestimable brain. Then there was our dinner party, when you accused me of not caring for those unfortunate seamen. Can you deny, sir, that you have expressed such opinions?"

His eyes swept her flushed countenance, pausing to linger on the full lips that were pursed in irritation. "I find that I am in daily danger of revising my opinions of you, my dear."

She blushed at the heated look in those molten eyes and quickly turned her attention to the passing city scenes. "But where are we going?" she asked with studied calm. "I do not recall giving your coachman my destination."

"When your brother mentioned Cheapside, I assumed he was not speaking frivolously. There is an orphanage of which you are a patroness, I believe?"

She looked at him in amazement.

"Mrs. Williams's Home for Foundlings. That was indeed my destination. We are going there? But how did you know?"

"Please give me the benefit of assuming that I have ears, my dear. I could not but notice when I arrived for my morning call that you and your brother seemed likely to come to blows over the subject. Your quarrel was not precisely conducted in hushed tones."

As her mouth began to twitch he added, "I do believe that the orphanage was your true purpose, was it not, for entertaining Lady Sheffield? I cannot believe you simply desire her company. I think it is rather her gilt that commends her."

Alex sat back in the seat and laughed. "I see I have under-rated your powers of observation, sir."

"A most serious mistake," he murmured, taking her gloved hand and raising it to his lips.

Alex instantly sat upright and withdrew her hand. "I believe we had ought to have brought my maid," she said primly. "This is, after all, a closed carriage. It is most improper for us to be traveling thus."

His eyes danced in amusement. "So the lady suddenly cares for the proprieties, I see. Well, I am persuaded that it is not improper to allow one's betrothed some liberties."

"But not those that you are constantly taking, sir," she returned in exasperation. At his grin, Alex turned her head to stare with great concentration at the passing streets, studiously ignoring the hearty laugh that now came from her companion.

Lucien's smile faded as he contemplated the woman who sat across from him, a portrait of elegance in her dark green carriage dress and tan gloves. Her tawny hair was swirled into a smooth coil at the nape of her neck, but a few tresses had made their escape to hover delightfully about her face.

When had he accused her of being frivolous? It seemed ages ago. And a tease? Lately he had been the one to play that role. While his endeavors had been aimed at giving her a disgust of the prospective passions of the marriage bed, he was beginning to suspect that his betrothed, for all her protestations as to his conduct, did not find passion at all disgusting. Far from inducing her to cry off, his plan may have awakened her to a side of her nature he was certain she had found somewhat disturbing. But apparently not yet disturbing enough to cry off.

Had he misjudged her in other areas as well? Did she actually care about the seamen and some of the issues that moved him? A shared glance was all they had needed to communicate perfectly their opinion as to the absurdity of the bridge ceremony. Here she was braving censure by taking more than a token interest in the orphanage she supported. He sighed. Despite her position in society, despite her outward appearance as a lady mired in the frivolous pursuits of the *ton*, she fit none of the molds into which he had attempted to place her. It was becoming increasingly difficult to decide what to do about Alessandra Ridgely.

Lucien was silent as the carriage rumbled down Newgate, through some of the worst of the city's slums. They turned onto a side street just wide enough for one carriage to pass. Dilapidated row houses sat one after the other, their broken windows staring back at them like so many empty eyes. In the streets, children and drunkards alike scrounged for food, competing with the rats for a scrap here and there. Water was drawn from cisterns that served as receptacles for refuse and perhaps occasionally a dead cat. Lucien looked over at his companion, who watched the passing scenes in somber silence.

The carriage made its way past beggars who rushed up to the well-appointed vehicle, pounding it with their hands in an effort to catch the attention of the wealthy passengers. Lucien put a protective arm out to steady Alex as the carriage shook. She remained calm, however. Finally, as they made their way past one particularly menacing group, he turned to her in exasperation.

"Do not tell me that you have come here alone!" he said, his thick brows drawn together in consternation.

She glanced over at him in surprise. "Why, no," she said. "I always bring Mary."

He swore under his breath. "A maid? The company of a maid is all the protection you think necessary in this den of danger? I begin to think you are as mad as those poor devils yonder!" He gestured to a group of men gathered around a nearby doorstep. Their faces were contorted in unnatural grins as they watched some lads torture a cat.

Alex gave him a cool look and said, "I regret if you are inconvenienced by my errand."

" 'Tis not inconvenience I feel, but horror," he said with asperity. "A woman alone in this part of town is risking the gravest sort of danger to her person. I insist that you leave off this foolishness."

"Oh? I take it you mean to forbid me from future trips?" Alex's voice was low and controlled. "Pray, sir, what gives you that authority?"

Lucien's look was thunderous, but Alex did not flinch. She merely gazed at him, the question still in her eyes. Finally he spoke.

"I am certain that I cannot claim any authority that you would recognize, madam. If you will not listen to your brother, I cannot hope that you will give credence to any admonition from a man who is merely your betrothed." He leaned toward her and added, "I do not intend to allow this to continue. If nothing else, I shall insist on accompanying you in the future."

Alex's brows shot up in surprise. A small smile played around her lips. "I am gratified, sir, by your concern," she said.

They said no more as the carriage neared its destination,

moving slowly past groups of children playing in gutters with bare feet, their faces and hands besmeared with mud. At the end of the block stood a large house several stories high. It was in need of paint and some cosmetic work, but Lucien noticed that its gutters were clean. The carriage came to a stop in front of this structure, where a small neatly painted sign proclaimed it to be Mrs. Williams's Home for Foundlings. Leaving Lucien's coachman rather nervously holding the horses, the marquess and Alex went inside.

They were greeted by a tiny graying woman whose size belied the energy and vigor that radiated from her eyes.

"Lady Alex!" she said with enthusiasm, and Alex took her hands in greeting.

"Mrs. Williams, may I present Lord Canfield? The marquess has expressed an interest in seeing your establishment," Alex said.

" 'Tis more like *your* establishment, my lady," the woman replied, curtsying to Lucien. "If it weren't for you, all of my children would be out on the streets."

Alex blushed. "That is nonsense, as well you know, Mrs. Williams! You were managing quite well before I came along."

Mrs. Williams's smile faded with the recollection. "We were but one step from the end, Lady Alex, but I see no sense in dwelling on those times. Come! Let me show you the new infirmary."

Her skirts rustled as she led them down a hallway, past several rooms that contained, Lucien saw as he peeked in the doorways, several neat rows of beds. They looked immaculate, and the walls were freshly painted and scrubbed. Mrs. Williams stopped at a small room and indicated that they should follow her inside. It, too, was newly painted and contained several cots. In one corner were several basins, some medical instruments, and a cabinet for medicines and other supplies. A scale sat in another corner.

"We are quite proud of this, Lady Alex. I have just hired a nurse who will come every few days to check upon the children. And Dr. Smithson comes at least once a month, more if need be. Our first project is to vaccinate all the children against the smallpox. Dr. Smithson is much in favor of the cowpox vaccine, although I know many people still object to being injected with matter from sick animals." She looked uncertainly toward Lucien. As he remained silent, she continued. "We have much hope that this will prevent many unnecessary deaths. Goodness knows, these children have precious little other advantages. We can at least protect them from this disease."

"I quite agree, Mrs. Williams," Lucien said, and Alex looked at him in surprise. "From my experience at sea, I can tell you that many men die from diseases that could be prevented if we but had adequate food and medical supplies."

They walked out into the courtyard, which was filled with about thirty youngsters jumping and running and otherwise making such noise that it was nearly impossible to speak. One young boy, whose age Lucien judged to be about eight, broke off from his group when he saw them and rushed to Alex.

"Hullo, ma'am," he said. "I was hoping you would come this week! Mrs. Williams gave me a new wooden sailboat for my birthday. See?"

Alex bent down and gravely examined the tiny craft, which the boy had fished from a side pocket in his trousers. Lucien noticed that the boy's clothes were clean, although mended, and he had a healthy glow, unlike the street urchins they had seen earlier from the carriage.

"It is quite the most impressive boat I have ever seen, Danny. By the way, this is Lord Canfield. He is a former sailor, you know. Served with Admiral Nelson, too."

"Really?" The boy's eyes were wide, and Lucien bent down to join them.

"Aye, mate," he said, his eyes twinkling. "Do you care to hear a yarn or two about my travels?"

Danny nodded, his eyes the size of saucers, and was soon hanging on Lucien's every word. Alex rose to join Mrs. Williams, who was looking on approvingly.

"His lordship looks to be enjoying himself," Mrs. Williams observed.

Alex watched the two heads close together. Lucien had removed his handkerchief and was showing the boy how to construct a sail for his craft.

"Yes," she agreed consideringly, surprised by the affection that suffused her as she watched Lucien cut a small patch from the handkerchief with a penknife he pulled from his own pocket.

She was astonished sometime later to realize that they had passed several hours in the orphanage. The time had flown, and she realized she had thoroughly enjoyed being in Lucien's presence. As Mrs. Williams walked them to their carriage Alex extended her hand to the other woman.

"I have no news for you yet, Mrs. Williams, about the new wing. There is no doubt that we will raise the money, but I fear it will take a little more time."

Mrs. Williams smiled fondly. "I am not worried, my lady," she said, and stepped back to wave good-bye to them.

As the carriage made its way back to Newgate Street, Lucien observed a slight frown on Alex's face. "What is troubling you?" he asked.

She looked up from her reverie. "It is nothing, really, just that I wish the money for the new wing were already committed. The home can only take thirty children now. With the additional space, it could take sixty or more. I hate to think of all the children out on the streets, or in worse places, whom we could help if there was the space. They all remind me of Danny. He was drinking from a filthy cistern when I found him, living from hand to mouth, begging for what food he could find, and stealing the rest. It is a sad life for one so young."

"But surely you are wealthy enough to build the wing on your own?" Lucien asked.

Alex gave a bitter laugh. "Oh, I have all the money I need to keep me in gowns and fripperies. My clothing allowance is enormous. My father saw to that," she said angrily. "What he did not see fit to do was grant me an independence. There is a huge fortune awaiting the man who has the good sense to marry me. Unwed, I have not a farthing. What money I have been able to contribute to the home has come from my clothing allowance."

Lucien's brows rose in amazement. He could only imagine how ill such a humbling arrangement sat with a woman of Alex's independence.

"But surely your brother . . . ?"

"My brother does not believe it his duty to provide for 'every street urchin in London,' as I believe he put it. He has rejected my requests for funds to help the orphanage. You saw yourself that he does not hold the home in esteem." Alex settled back against the squabs in resignation. "And so, my lord, you see that my hopes center around the likes of Lady Sheffield and others of her ilk, who lead one a pretty dance for the privilege of relieving her of what few pieces of gold she sees fit to part with."

They rode in silence after that, both absorbed in their own thoughts. They were so engrossed that both looked up in surprise when the carriage stopped in front of Farnsworth House.

"Thank you for escorting me, sir," Alex said as Lucien handed her out of the carriage.

Lucien said nothing but walked her to the door, where a footman stood waiting. "Alex." His voice was strangely harsh.

"Yes?" She waited.

"I shall have my solicitor make over a note to the home tomorrow."

She frowned in confusion. "A note, sir?"

He turned and stalked off down the steps. "Bank note," he growled over his shoulder as he entered his waiting carriage.

Alex stared in astonishment as it pulled away, thinking once again how little she knew Lucien Tremaine.

Chapter 12

Alex interviewed three gentlewomen recommended by the employment agency but was dissatisfied with all of them. She asked the agency to produce other candidates but knew that she would be constrained to accept someone before many more days passed. She found herself unaccountably depressed, especially after she learned from Mrs. Williams that the sum Lucien had bestowed on the home was enough to build the new wing and more. Alex had expressed her gratification to her fiancé but had stumbled over her words so badly she doubted he understood her.

Then there was the small notice she had spotted in the *Times* just this morning: "Lord Canfield to testify before Navy Board on service conditions of His Majesty's seamen." The testimony was to be given in secret, the notice added, it being wartime, but it was widely believed that the marquess, himself a noted naval hero, intended to press the board for better medical supplies and food and was prepared to mount his own fundraising effort if the board did not provide the wherewithal for such essentials.

The matter of Lucien Tremaine preyed heavily on Alex's mind and conscience, especially with this new evidence that he was really quite human after all. Alex's suspicion that his hardened veneer masked a warm nature capable of great tenderness had become a certainty. She felt his bitterness was understandable in the light of all she now knew about his past. She suspected his bodily wounds did not plague him as much as those of the heart—like Lydia Chenilworth's betrayal and his mother's treatment by the *ton*.

Alex sighed. When she broke their engagement, it would be

one more injustice for him to face. Not that Lucien's feelings would be wounded by her rejection. But what if he felt that she had made him a laughingstock? And what if he learned the whole truth—that she had not intended to go through with the marriage from the very beginning? She shuddered at the thought.

She could see no remedy to the situation, however. There was no question of going through with the wedding, for instance. She and Lucien would never suit. He was so intense, so fierce, so determined in his views, whereas she preferred a calmer, more civilized existence. Alex frowned. How boring that sounded! Almost like something Clarence would say. She sighed again. There was nothing boring about those moments spent with Lucien. When she looked into his eyes, what she saw there gave her chills of delight. When he swept her into his arms, she realized it was something she had been waiting for all along. It was mortifying in the extreme to realize that he had such a hold over her.

Meanwhile, the object of her musings was disgusted with himself. He was having no luck finding a suitable substitute bride, despite his tedious efforts to make the acquaintance of every eligible young miss in town. Oh, they were attractive enough, but without sufficient gumption or character to enable him to envision a lifetime enduring their batting eyelashes and simpering smiles. He reminded himself that he was seeking just such a biddable young lady as those he had encountered, but the recalling of that goal did nothing for his spirits or resolve.

His strategy toward Alex had been wrongheaded and dishonorable from the start, he thought glumly. Moreover, he had enjoyed their passionate interludes all too much for one whose chief mission was to find another to wed. These days his thoughts were fixed increasingly on a tall young lady with golden hair and mesmerizing blue eyes. He could not take his eyes from her or prevent his mind from conjuring her image. He was in a fair way to becoming obsessed with Alessandra Ridgely, he realized. That thought left him mired in indecision and gloom.

Thus, both Lucien and Alex discovered themselves stuck in a strange sort of paralysis, relieved only by the distracting whirlwind of social activities on which they embarked together most evenings. There were routs, balls, masquerades, and operas enough to ensure that they would be too weary to think about their next course of action. They attacked this round of relentless activity with a feverish determination that served the welcome function of distracting and distancing them from each other. Consequently the private interludes came no longer, and the atmosphere of tension between them grew almost intolerable as evening after evening left them with frayed nerves, aching feet, and unslaked desire.

One such occasion was the new ballet at King's Theatre, *Les Amours de Mars et de Venus*, which had seemed rich with prospects for diversion. But as the ballet played out on stage Alex grew increasingly uncomfortable. It was as much the subject of the ballet—the frank and delighted courtship of two passionate lovers—that discomfited her as it was the sensual detail with which it was danced.

As the ballet developed, Mars and Venus were seized with a passion for each other so intense that all Olympus was caught at once with the same powerful influence. The dancers were wonderfully expressive, alternating between flight and pursuit, determined resistance and ardent surrender, conquering and being conquered.

Alex shifted uneasily in her chair as the well-muscled Mars clasped Venus to his breast in an intimate embrace, stroking her back and arms with elaborate tenderness. As the sensual movements were exaggerated for the stage Alex seemed to feel them in her very bones. All she could think of was Lucien and his kisses. Her skin began to tingle, and she could not prevent herself from stealing a glance at her betrothed. To her utter mortification, he was staring at her with a strange, unsettling look.

Resolutely she directed her attention to the stage, but when Mars lifted Venus high in the air in a jubilant consummation of their dance, she could not help but remember the feel of Lucien's arms around her as he carried her up the stairs at the inn so many weeks ago. The scene before the fire again played out in her mind, and her insides were queasy with desire.

She dared not look at Lucien again, but she was uncomfortably aware of his hands, accidentally brushing hers with disturbing frequency. Her distraction was such that she failed to join in when the delighted audience gave the troupe several curtain calls. She could only clasp her hands tightly in her lap in uneasy silence.

Her silence continued as they waited for the carriage. Emma and Clarence, who had accompanied them, were likewise silent as they stood nearby.

"Did you enjoy the ballet?" Lucien asked casually as he handed Alex into the carriage later, cursing himself for the thoughts it had inspired in him. He had not been able to keep his hands from reaching for her, despite his best intentions.

"The dancers were quite talented," Alex replied noncommittally, moving to make room for the others and hoping her voice sounded unexceptional.

"Well, I for one thought the whole thing shocking," Clarence said in censorious tones. "Such goings-on before an audience priding itself on its superior morals is beyond anything that is acceptable."

Lucien eyed him without speaking, but Alex spoke up defiantly, determined to pull herself out of the doldrums. "It seemed to me, Clarence, that the audience rather enjoyed it," she said.

He looked at her disdainfully. "Oh, I have no doubt some of the cruder spectators in the pits enjoyed the spectacle. As for me, I find myself quite obliged to apologize to Miss Manwaring for subjecting her to such an ill-bred display."

Emma said nothing, her doe eyes fixed unblinkingly on Clarence as he continued his tirade.

"Being forced to watch half-naked dancers comporting themselves on stage in the heat of uncontrollable passion is not fitting for a young lady's eyes," he said with asperity, looking at Emma for the expected confirmation.

That young lady cleared her throat. She looked up at him

shyly and then spoke in a hesitant voice. "To tell the truth, sir, I rather enjoyed it."

Lucien and Alex glanced at her with astonishment as the duke registered this remark in stunned silence. Emma looked down at her dainty slippers and fiddled with the folds of her gown. No one spoke for a long moment. Finally Clarence found his tongue.

"I collect that you are but voicing admiration for the dancers' technical skills," he said, smiling confidently at this reassuring thought.

Emma returned his gaze with a steady one of her own. "To be frank, sir, it was rather the dancers' unfettered expression of emotion that impressed me. Although one would never sanction such a display in public among well-bred members of society, its evocation on stage in such an elegant medium as the ballet does not, it seems to me, cause harm."

Clarence stared at her as if she had two heads, and Emma responded with a smile that might have held a trace of wistfulness.

"Although I am persuaded that your instincts as to what is proper are unfailingly correct, Your Grace, I confess that I find it difficult to be offended by what is, after all, the mere articulation of love. And that, sir," she added quietly, "is not a dishonorable emotion."

Bravo, Emma, Alex thought as a shocked Clarence pondered this statement. Emma sat calmly with her hands folded in her lap. Alex turned to Lucien in her amusement, but the look in his eyes made her wish that she had not. The amber heat warmed her body from head to toe.

The ride to Farnsworth House was accomplished thereafter in complete silence. Lucien escorted Alex to the door and bowed a terse good night. Alex quickly fled up the stairs to her room, leaving Emma and Clarence alone in the foyer.

"Good night, sir," Emma said, offering the duke her hand.

He took it wanly and hesitantly pressed it to his lips.

"Good night, Emma," he replied in a subdued voice as she withdrew her hand, turned, and walked slowly up the stairs.

Then the Duke of Farnsworth retired to his study and buried his troubled thoughts in a decanter of brandy.

Alex, meanwhile, watched from her window as the marquess's carriage rolled away down the street. She had no difficulty imagining Lucien inside with his feet propped on the opposite seat, his arms crossed on his chest, and a troubled expression on his face. His posture precisely mirrored her feelings.

The very next morning at breakfast Emma cleared her throat and announced her intentions to the family. "I believe, Your Grace," she said, addressing the duchess, "that I will return to Dorset after all."

Clarence's teacup crashed onto his saucer, and Alex sat back in her chair to observe the developments with interest.

"We had hoped to have you with us through the end of the Season," the duchess said graciously, "but of course we quite understand that you must wish to visit your sister."

Emma nodded her gratitude. "Yes, Your Grace. Vivian writes that she has every expectation that George will join her in a few weeks. I should go to her before then, as I think my presence will be unnecessary after her husband arrives."

"A bit superfluous, I imagine," the duchess said with a smile. "Well, we have certainly enjoyed your visit, Emma. I shall have a carriage at your disposal whenever you wish to leave." Her Grace pushed back her chair and began to rise.

"Wait!" Clarence cried, his voice breaking in a high squeak. "That is," he said more quietly, "I thought you planned to remain until after the Season, as your sister had more than sufficient assistance with the babe."

The duchess looked at her son consideringly, but Emma merely smiled politely and dabbed her lips with a napkin.

"You are correct, of course, sir. But as I said, I have learned that George comes to her soon. I would not feel it appropriate to intrude on their reunion. There are some occasions, I feel, when two people in love should be alone."

She placed the napkin on the tablecloth and rose.

So that's the way of it, Alex thought, unable to suppress a wry grin as Clarence, his own breakfast forgotten, rose from his chair as well.

"But what about the Regent's fete?" His voice rose shrilly in a petulant cry. "You surely cannot mean to leave before that?"

Emma turned in surprise. "Oh, I do think I must be gone before then," she replied earnestly.

Clarence's eyes widened in dismay. "But what of the Vauxhall opening? It is only a week away." He turned to the sideboard and took a steadying breath. Then he spoke with labored formality into a tiered candelabra that rested on the massive piece of furniture. "I believe you had expressed great interest in seeing the gardens, Miss Manwaring. Perhaps you might at least stay until then?" He could not quite keep the hopeful note from his voice.

Emma's brows drew together as she considered the idea.

"It might be possible," she said slowly. "If it is only for another week. But I really must leave after that. I would hate to disappoint my sister." There was a reproachful note in her voice.

"Oh, no, of course not!" Clarence quickly agreed, his face breaking into a smile as he turned toward her. "I am certain your dedication to your sister is most admirable."

And I am certain Vivian would be most surprised to learn of such devotion, Alex thought dryly as she studied the calm, departing figure of Emma Manwaring. It seemed she had underestimated Vivian's mousy little sister.

The first week in June brought the long-awaited opening of Vauxhall Gardens, and the party from Farnsworth House was among hundreds in attendance. Her Grace was escorted by Lord Verbank, an old friend with whom she shared a particular love of cards. An avuncular gentleman whose good-natured joviality was somewhat marred by an embarrassing tendency toward off-color jests, his lordship was a widower who enjoyed a rather notorious reputation as a roué. Her Grace, however, had long suspected that he carefully cultivated his lecherous reputation as a way of combating the loneliness which, she was certain, he felt increasingly in his later years.

Whatever Lord Verbank's true motives, he was in rare form this night, enlivening their supper box with such jokes and provocative comments that various other members of the party—excepting the duchess, who seemed to tolerate his lordship's patter quite well—were soon quite uncomfortable. Lord Verbank's relentless jests about a variety of amorous topics left the younger people uneasy, as such matters were much too close to thoughts uppermost in their minds.

And so it was that after sampling the thin slices of ham, minuscule chickens, biscuits, strong punch, and other delights that Vauxhall had to offer, the others began excusing themselves in order to avail themselves of the various pleasures of the garden.

"I am certain I do not have to admonish you to remain together for propriety's sake," the duchess said, her eyebrows arched in barely concealed amusement.

Clarence pulled himself up to his full height and looked down his angular nose with as much dignity as he could muster. "Certainly not, Mother," he said, the reproof at her implication suffusing his words with wounded sensibility.

None of the other members of the party felt obligated to respond, however, and soon the foursome was ambling about in uneasy silence. Not the most compatible of groups under the best of circumstances, they had difficulty finding a mutually agreeable topic of conversation.

"Mrs. Garrick had a sweet voice, I thought," Emma ventured timidly.

"Just so!" Clarence agreed with alacrity. "A graceful woman as well."

Alex frowned. "Actually I thought her tones too thin," she said, "although I suppose her execution was acceptable."

"Too delicate," Lucien pronounced dourly.

They lapsed into a silence that was unbroken until Alex spoke up. "I suppose the fireworks will be spectacular," she said indifferently.

"Oh, yes!" Emma said with feeling. "They shall be the high-light of my visit to London."

Clarence shot her a mournful look at this last statement; nei-ther Lucien nor Alex spoke.

They continued in silence, their gloom undiminished by the laughing couples and boisterous bucks who moved around them as they entered the wide, elm-lined Grand Walk.

"I understand there are some new transparencies added this season," Lucien said stoically after they had walked some yards on the graveled walkway.

"I have always enjoyed the hermit," Alex put in, and Clar-ence shot her a shocked look.

"How came you to see the hermit?" he demanded. "It is lo-cated in quite the most remote part of the garden. Why, there is but wilderness and downs in that area!"

Alex returned an indignant gaze. "That is none of your con-cern, Clarence," she retorted. "For that matter, how come *you* to be so well informed about the hermit?"

Clarence glared at her as Emma appeared uncertain and Lucien studied the two Ridgelys in amusement.

"Come, come, children," he said briskly. "It must be clear to all of us that compatibility—if not combatability—has eluded this group. Perhaps it would be best if we went our separate ways. Farnsworth, perhaps you can show Emma some of the more accessible transparencies."

Clarence opened his mouth to object to the impropriety of such an arrangement, but after one look at Emma's hopeful face, he shut it again.

"I would dearly love to see them, Your Grace," she said shyly, "especially since this is to be my last week in London."

The duke felt the slight pressure from her delicate arm on his and cleared his throat. "Well, I suppose if we keep to the main walkways . . ."

"Excellent," said Lucien impatiently, tucking Alex's arm under his and propelling her down a side path toward one of the other main walkways.

Clarence stared after them uncertainly. The feminine fingers that rested on his arm fluttered slightly.

"Well, sir?" Emma said. "May we proceed?"

The Duke of Farnsworth looked at the small figure at his side. Her doe eyes were wide and imploring, and he suddenly was quite aware that her rose-colored gown exposed rather much of the swell of her pink, creamy skin. He cleared his throat and ran a finger along the inside of his starched neck-cloth.

"Indeed, Miss Manwaring," he said with somber resolve, "I suppose we ought."

Chapter 13

"I wonder that you tolerate living in the same house with those two," Lucien said as he guided Alex under an archway of the South Walk.

Alex looked at him in amusement. "Do you not think Emma and Clarence perfectly suited to each other, my lord? Their sensibilities are much the same. Although," she said consideringly, "Emma has surprised me of late. I believe there is much about that young lady that does not meet the eye."

This statement drew only a grunt from her companion, who was not interested in the affairs of the Duke of Farnsworth and Miss Emma Manwaring, being very much preoccupied with the matter of Alessandra Ridgely. He had once thought Vauxhall's secluded paths ideal for amorous exercises with his betrothed in the furtherance of his ill-conceived scheme. Now, though he craved above all things to engage in such pursuits with her, he knew that he could no longer take her in his arms and be guaranteed of controlling his response. He thought matters therefore would best be served if they kept to the crowded walkways. Nevertheless Lucien continued to lead Alex down a side path to one of the further promenades, reflecting dourly that he seemed powerless to avoid tempting the fates.

"Is your leg troubling you?" she asked suddenly.

Lucien glanced at her, surprised that she had noticed his almost imperceptible limp.

" 'Tis nothing serious," he said. "During the evening damp, it often flares up. I barely notice it."

As they continued their walk it seemed to Alex that the lights filtering through the evening mists gave the gardens a magical glow. After some moments of silence, she spoke again.

"It must have been difficult aboard your ship, since I imagine it was always rather damp."

"What? Oh, the leg." He waved his hand dismissively. " 'Twas nothing, as I have said."

"I see," she said, adding after a pause, "I believe you must be a stoic, sir."

Lucien stopped abruptly to stare at her. "What nonsense are you tormenting me with now, Alex?" he demanded testily. "You make too much of what is merely an old injury."

"Sustained quite heroically, I'm told, during the battle that took Lord Nelson's life." She studied his face. Had he really accused her of tormenting him? What a strange choice of words.

It was impossible to tell in the shadows, of course, but it seemed to Alex that Lucien's face had taken on a darker hue, perhaps a flush of embarrassment. But no, now he was glowering at her, more like the Lucien with whom she was familiar.

"Don't tell me you are going to read me a tribute to my valor and gallantry," he said sardonically. "I assure you I have had quite enough of those empty platitudes."

"I would not dream of it, sir. I was merely curious about your time at sea and what it was like serving with Lord Nelson," she replied easily, placing her arm on his and taking a step so that he was forced to follow suit and resume their promenade.

He was silent for so long that she wondered if he intended to answer her. Finally he spoke. "Nelson was a brilliant strategist and an excellent leader, a man I would have followed to my death," Lucien said quietly, "but in other ways he was a fool."

Alex cocked her head. "How so?"

"For one thing, he hated the French."

Alex looked at him in confusion. "But surely it is permitted to hate one's enemy in war?"

"Nelson hated French people in general. He loathed anything French and could not stand to be in the same room with anyone of French nationality."

Lucien was looking straight ahead, but although Alex could

not see his face, she heard the pain in his voice. An image of Lady Canfield suddenly rose to her mind.

"I see," she said. After a moment, she added hesitantly, "Did Lord Nelson have the occasion to meet your mother, my lord?"

He looked down at her with a rueful look. "Is reading minds one of your talents?" he asked grimly.

Alex made no reply.

"As a matter of fact," he said finally, "I introduced him to her following the ceremony in which I was commissioned lieutenant. She was the only member of my family present, my father being ill at the time and my brother tending to some urgent business in his absence. The minute my mother spoke to Nelson, I saw he wanted to give her the cut direct. Would have, if I had not stared daggers at him. As it is, he merely bowed condescendingly and moved on without a word."

"That must have been very painful for you," Alex said. She was suddenly filled with rage at the admiral.

He shrugged. "At the time, but one outgrows such things. I was proud to serve with him. As I said, I would have followed him to the death. That doesn't negate the fact that about some things he was a fool. In the matter of women, for instance, he was an utter idiot."

Alex gave a soft, melodic laugh. "I assume you refer to Lady Hamilton. But if she made him happy, what difference does it make that she was not his wife?"

Lucien's thick eyebrows rose in surprise. "I imagine Lady Nelson did not see it in quite that light," he said in amusement.

Alex shook her head dismissively. "Lady Nelson was too much the martyr for my tastes, playing the noble wife while her husband was making her a laughingstock by his public adoration of his mistress," she said. "If I had been Lady Nelson, I would have shown his lordship the door and gone on about the business of my own life."

Lucien frowned. "Nonsense," he said sternly. "Nelson was wrong to use her so, of course, but she quite properly acted the supportive wife. She never said a word against him. She made no attempt to interfere with his life or change him in any way."

"And that is your definition of a proper wife, sir?" Alex's voice was filled with quiet laughter. "Pray, is that what you would expect of me?"

Lucien stopped abruptly and stared at her for a long moment, his face unreadable in the shadows. They were quite alone on the darkened gravel walkway, a fact that Alex suddenly found disquieting. He pulled her abruptly into one of the alcoves that skirted the path's edge.

"My expectation, Alessandra Ridgely, is that you would never give a man a moment's peace," he said fiercely, his eyes bright with passion. Before she could speak, his mouth descended to hers.

There was something she wanted to say, something she must tell him, she thought helplessly as his lips burned into hers. She would tell him she could never be a biddable woman like Lady Nelson, that they would not suit, that she had accepted his proposal under false pretenses. It was time for honesty at long last. But as she searched for the words her heart betrayed her; she found herself caught in an agony of indecision that was growing ever more acute as he pressed his kisses upon her. She tried to imagine a lifetime of such kisses. It would not be enough. Her confession died in his embrace.

Gradually Alex became aware of voices somewhere behind them, through the bushes on the side of the alcove, perhaps on one of the side paths. She tried to shut them out, but they were becoming more insistent and louder, apparently raised in anger.

"I am telling you that it is impossible," a desperate voice insisted.

"And I am telling you, M'sieur Mandley, it is not," a heavily accented voice returned menacingly.

"Wellington's troop strength at Badajoz is a closely held secret," the other insisted with a rising note of hysteria in his voice. "My God, man, he has the place under siege! Do you think a lowly clerk can simply walk into the War Office and lay his hands on those kinds of figures?"

"Quiet!" whispered the Frenchman. "Are you a fool?"

"I am beginning to think the answer to that is yes," the other voice retorted angrily. "Whenever I give you something, you want more. From the beginning, all I wanted was to supplement my abysmal earnings for a time. But you do not stop, it seems. Is there no end to your demands?"

Alex looked up at Lucien, who still held her tightly, though he was listening intently. He put his finger lightly on her lips. They waited, perfectly still.

The French voice had taken on a silky tone. "Of course there is an end," it said smoothly. "Just as soon as you give us what we need. Massena was a fool, but our hopes for the Peninsula now ride on Soult and Marmont. So far Wellington has out-maneuvered them. But he cannot continue forever. So you see, it is *essentiel* that we get some numbers from you, *mon ami.*" There was a brief pause. "I promise you that you will be well rewarded."

There was a prolonged silence, during which Alex felt that the sound of her thundering heart would surely give them away. But after a moment, she heard rustling bushes and fading foot-steps.

"Lucien!" she whispered.

"Hush!" he said into her ear. "They may still be nearby."

They remained locked in each other's arms for several more heartbeats until Lucien carefully set her away from him.

"I am going to see if I can track them," he said. "Time is of the essence. Wait here and do not move."

"But, Lucien," she protested, even as he plunged into the bushes. He either ignored her or did not hear her. Most likely, she thought in irritation, it was the former.

After a while, she could no longer hear the sounds of his foot-steps. Suddenly she was cold. She wrapped her arms around her and waited, alone in the silence and the dark.

"This fountain is quite impressive," Emma murmured as she and Clarence passed the imposing structure. Several couples were conversing in the shadows around it; others threw coins into the water and were laughing gaily.

The duke was silent, and they walked on to a slightly narrowed path beyond a group of elms. He was very conscious of Emma's hand as it rested lightly on his arm.

After some minutes, he suddenly stopped and turned to her with such abruptness that his high starcher was wrenched rather awkwardly off to one side. Emma, who had been struggling to keep pace with the duke's long-legged stride, crashed into him.

"Oh!" she said, eyes wide. "I do beg your pardon, sir."

"My fault entirely," he said with studied politeness, although there was an urgency in his voice, and his beady eyes held an agonized look.

They stood there awkwardly for one long moment. Emma's soft brown eyes widened as they remained fixed on the duke's angular face. Finally he cleared his throat in some embarrassment.

"See here, Miss Manwaring," he began.

"I thought we were at 'Emma,' sir," she said quietly, lowering her eyes.

"Yes, well. Emma, then," he said, a gruff note in his voice giving it a rather pompous tone. "What I wished to say was that I can see no reason for you to leave town so precipitously."

"Precipitously, Your Grace?" she replied softly. "I believe I have imposed upon your hospitality for nearly six weeks." She fixed him with a steady gaze.

"Well, it is not long enough," he said, and then colored. "What I mean to say, of course, is that you are welcome to stay for as long as you like."

Emma studied her hands as Clarence awaited her response to this magnanimous gesture. "As I have no real reason to remain, sir, I cannot envision imposing upon you further."

"No reason? Whatever do you mean?" he said, flustered. "An invitation is reason enough, surely."

Emma smiled at him, and Clarence found he could not take his eyes off her face.

"My sister has extended an invitation for me to visit, sir. By your logic, then, that is reason enough to accept."

Clarence shook his head in confusion and clenched his hands. His arms dangled awkwardly at his sides. "That is not what I meant, Miss Manwaring . . . Emma." He frowned at her. "I do believe you are deliberately misapprehending me."

She looked at him innocently. "What is it, Your Grace, that I am failing to understand?" she asked patiently.

Clarence's eyes wandered helplessly over her creamy shoulders and down to the soft roundness of her breasts. He swallowed hard and opened his mouth to speak.

Just then, a pair of wandering bloods jostled him, and Clarence struggled to keep from toppling into Emma. He had just prided himself upon his excellent sense of balance when suddenly he found Emma propelled into his arms.

"How careless these gentlemen are!" she said breathlessly. "I do beg your pardon!"

Outraged that anyone would so ill-use her, Clarence looked around to call the rude chap to account. But whoever had knocked into Emma had disappeared. Indeed, they were quite alone now.

His arms had extended instinctively about her when she had been propelled into him, and there, he found, they remained. Her soft womanly body remained nestled along the length of his gaunt frame. His new parrot-yellow waistcoat was being sadly crushed, but the duke found he did not mind. He looked down his aquiline nose into a pair of limpid brown eyes that riveted him with the message they held.

"Clarence." Her voice was a soft, breathless whisper.

He swallowed hard. "Emma," he said in a raw croak, his heart pounding mercilessly against his chest.

Slowly, without thinking, he brought his mouth down upon hers. It was a tentative kiss, but only for a moment. Her lips were warm and enticing; somehow they parted invitingly, or perhaps it only seemed so at the moment. However it happened, Clarence soon found himself locked in a passionate embrace with a woman who quite surprised him with the enthusiasm and fervor of her response.

He could not have said precisely how some moments later he found himself in the leafy shadows off the main path, caressing Emma's bosom and even going so far as to remove one tantalizing breast from the bodice of her rose-colored gown. When he moved to place his mouth upon the ruby tip, he heard her gasp, but not, he was certain, with displeasure. He paused, waiting for her objection, but found instead that somehow the object of his attentions had been thrust against his lips. Somewhat bemused, but thoroughly captivated by the developing events, he returned to the engrossing exercise.

There followed some long moments of this mostly silent activity, during which Emma's clothing was rather substantially rearranged. Suddenly he heard her cry out in dismay. As she buried her face in his shoulder he looked up to see several bucks and two promenading couples walk by. He groaned in chagrin, but no one seemed to take any notice of their intimate situation. When they had passed, he spoke softly into her ear.

"It is all right now, my dear, they have gone."

She lifted her head and gave him a tremulous look. "Oh, I am undone!" she said, and there was an edge of hysteria in her voice. After a moment, a brave look came over her face.

"I hope you do not feel, Your Grace, that you have compromised me. There is not the least need for you to think such a thing. I am certain that no one noticed my state of . . . undress, and if they did, it is to be hoped that good manners will prevent them from mentioning my disarray to anyone of note."

Clarence's eyes grew wide in horror. "Mention it? Why, I would call out anyone who would do such a thing." He gave her a reassuring squeeze, noticing in delight that she had apparently forgotten to adjust her gown.

A look of irritation flitted briefly across her face and then was replaced by one of infinite sorrow. "I have every faith in the gentlemen, of course. It is the ladies, you know, who gossip so. I doubt that you could call any of them out."

Clarence paused in the act of trailing the tip of his finger along the edge of her bodice. "The ladies?" he asked, his attention arrested.

"Oh, yes. They will quite ruin my reputation, I'm afraid. But do not worry." She smiled bravely. "I am sure they will not blame you for my dishonoring."

"Dishonoring?" He pronounced the word in horror. "Emma, you must know I had no intention of such!"

She said nothing, and he shook his head, baffled. "I do not know how I came to be so carried away," he said slowly. "I have never assaulted a lady before." Looking into her soft doe eyes, he was suddenly overcome with intense guilt. He cleared his throat. "I cannot undo my actions, of course, but perhaps I can make it up to you." He coughed nervously. "Miss Manwaring, will you do me the honor of becoming my wife?"

Emma's eyes widened in surprise. "Your Grace!" she said. "But surely there is no reason for you to make such a drastic offer. I will come about—somehow."

He clasped her hands in his. "I phrased my offer badly, I fear. It is not solely to make amends that I ask for your hand, Emma." His voice cracked, and he coughed again. "Indeed," he continued after a moment, "the events of this night have served to open my eyes to our compatibility. I have always viewed you as a woman of excellent taste, comportment, and conversation. Though I had not thought to marry as yet, I now realize how enjoyable it will be to share with you the . . . delights of marriage." He blushed and then rushed on: "You will be an admirable Duchess of Farnsworth."

"Oh, Clarence!" Emma cried softly. "I am overcome!" She pressed her body closer to his. "I suppose if you truly desire me as your wife . . ."

He groaned as her breasts were crushed against his chest.

"Most definitely, Emma," he replied breathlessly, and brought his mouth down hard upon hers.

Alex waited in the darkened alcove for what seemed an eternity. There was no sound, only the occasional rustling in the bushes from what must have been small animals. She wondered if Lucien had caught up with the men whose voices they had heard. If so, she hoped he had not done anything so rash as to try to capture them. Despite his size and strength, he was outnumbered. She did not like to think of what might happen. In the meantime, she had only her unsettling thoughts for company.

When had she come to enjoy the company of this man whose capacity for love had been so bruised and blunted over the years? When had her own heart become enslaved? She knew his reasons for offering her marriage had nothing to do with love. But lately she had begun to wonder if perhaps he felt something for her, however slight.

It really did not matter, did it? She was not the type of woman who had ever considered trapping a man into marriage, and she would not do so now, despite the fact that she had come to . . . care for him. She would give him his freedom. Her eyes welled unexpectedly with tears.

Before she could dwell on that depressing thought, she heard a sound nearby. Quickly she stepped out of the alcove with a joyful smile on her face.

But the man who stood before her was not Lucien. Indeed, he looked to be a very poor specimen of manhood, suffering the ill effects of too much drink and carousing. Alex looked around quickly. At least he seemed to be alone.

"What have we here, my pretty?" he said, leering at her in undisguised glee, not believing his good fortune in discovering a woman alone in such a darkened, desolate area of the gardens.

Alex eyed him assessingly. She was of a height with him, but he was rather burly and overweight; apparently spirits were not the only thing in which he overindulged.

"I am waiting for my fiancé and am in no need of assistance from you, sir. He is just through those bushes there." She gestured, hoping the man would be persuaded to leave.

He eyed her suspiciously and moved his face closer to hers. She nearly reeled from the odor of spirits on his breath.

"Fiancé, eh? Doubt that, missy. More'n likely some swell abandoned you here after taking his pleasure." He rubbed his hands together and swayed drunkenly. "Some might not like to take another man's leavings. Never been so particular, though, not me. Not one to look a gift horse in the mouth, so to speak."

He laughed at his own joke, and Alex favored him with a

haughty elevation of her brows. "I will thank you to take your lewd comments elsewhere, sir. My fiancé will not like to find your insulting presence here when he returns," she said, adding quickly, "as he will at any moment."

His eyes narrowed in anger. "Insulting, eh? Listen, Miss High-and-Mighty," he said, reaching his burly arms toward her shoulders, "ain't anything at all in those bushes going to stop Jack Hardesty from teaching some manners to the likes of you!"

He crushed her abruptly in his drunken embrace, his arms sliding down her back and bringing her body to his. Alex stiffened, repulsed beyond thought at his touch. His wet lips swamped her mouth, and his hands moved to her waist. With effort she tried to quell her panic. She forced herself to relax, her arms stealing up around his sides as if to return his embrace. His head shot up, and there was an unsavory gleam in his bloodshot eyes.

"That's right, missy. Might as well not fight it. About time you came to your senses!" He held her away from him a bit, allowing his eyes to survey her figure admiringly. "Not so much meat on your bones, but we'll deal well enough together."

"Thank you, sir," Alex said sweetly through gritted teeth. Then, without warning, her foot suddenly shot up and kicked him directly in the area of his most private parts. His face froze, and he dropped to the ground, writhing in pain.

"I was about to offer my assistance, but I see it is quite unnecessary," said a voice at her side.

Alex looked up to see Lucien, his face grim but his amber eyes gleaming as he observed the plight of the man on the ground. Alex sighed in relief.

"Nay, but I am most happy to greet you, sir. Indeed, I might have wished for your appearance a little earlier." Briskly she waved away his hand as he sought to steady her. "I am perfectly fine. Pray, what did you discover?"

He looked over at Alex's assailant and was satisfied he would likely remain incapacitated for some time.

"I caught sufficient glimpse of our quarry to recognize our two friends from the inn."

Alex drew in her breath sharply. "You did not try to stop them?"

"No. They cannot be arrested just yet. But we now have a name—Mandley—and information enough to allow us to lay a trap." His face was hard. "They will be brought to justice, I assure you."

Even in the shadows, she could see the fierce anger radiating from his molten eyes. His brows had drawn together sternly, and his unruly hair framed his face like a fiery halo. Suddenly a name came unbidden to her mind. *Lucifer*. She shuddered.

"Come," she said tentatively. "I think we had best be getting back."

He nodded curtly and then took a last look at Alex's writhing victim. His brow suddenly lightened. "Is there no end to your accomplishments, my dear?" He smiled wryly. "I suppose I should be grateful that you did not see fit to use that technique on me. No doubt I have given you ample reason during some of our more . . . intimate encounters."

Alex looked at him uncertainly, surprised at his broaching of the subject. Did he regret those passionate interludes?

As their eyes met, his smile disappeared and was replaced by a fierce, grim line. Amber eyes held blue for a long, breathless moment as sparks seemed to jump the gap between them. The moment stretched into an eternity, and Alex knew she could not move from this spot if her life were at stake. How could she ever set this man free? She stood silently, returning his gaze, helpless in her longing. He remained motionless, rigid with self-control.

Suddenly the sky lit up behind them. Grecian arches wreathed with flame glided over the firmament as trails of blue, red, and gold swept through the darkness.

"The fireworks are beginning," Lucien rasped in a rough whisper that seemed to come with great difficulty. Alex, wrestling with her rebellious soul, heard him as if from far away. In the distance, she heard the report of the first blasts. Slowly she willed her brain to return to the present.

"Indeed," she heard herself reply in a calm voice as she placed her hand on his arm. "I expect we should be returning."

Wordlessly he walked them in the direction of the heavenly lights.

Chapter 14

"Ah, *ma chère*," Lady Canfield said as she sank back into the velvet cushions. "The country is most relaxing, and Vivian's little one is a delight, but I can see that I have missed much this Season." She sighed deeply, and the Duchess of Farnsworth regarded her in amusement.

"My dear Celeste, I am tempted to mind my manners and reassure you on that score. However"—the duchess leaned back with a satisfied smile—"in truth, you have missed a most interesting time."

"*Je m'y attendais.* It is as I suspected," Lady Canfield replied mournfully as the duchess pulled a face in mock sympathy. Lady Canfield's eyes narrowed in amusement. "Nevertheless, Marisa, I have every *confiance* that I shall have it all from you. But first, pray what is this I hear about you and Lord Verbank? Surely you are not serious about that old *roué*?"

The duchess burst into laughter and said, "The poor man! His reputation has cost him much in the eyes of those very ladies whose company he so dearly seeks. He is utterly harmless, Celeste, although perhaps a bit lonely. I enjoy his company, nothing more. We both have a taste for cards, you know, and I suppose we tolerate each other for the same reasons."

Lady Canfield's smile faded. "You are lonely then? I was afraid of that, my friend. I suppose nothing has been the same since William's death."

"And thank God for that," the duchess replied calmly as she began to pour tea.

She registered Lady Canfield's confusion. "Come, come, Celeste. Well you know that my husband was an insufferable, pompous bore who could not rest until he ordered the lives of everyone around him. Whatever affection I once had for him was destroyed by his interfering and insensitive ways." She handed a teacup to her friend. "It is partly my fault for allowing him to run roughshod over me. But I was young and inexperienced when we wed, and I dared not voice my objections."

She took a sip, staring up at the portrait of the former duke prominently displayed over the parlor mantelpiece. His features were grim and unsmiling, his nose aquiline like his son's.

"Then it was too late," Her Grace continued. "The more I kept quiet, the more I became the woman he wished me to be. The proper duchess." She sighed. "Not an original notion in my head, I'm afraid."

The duchess turned her eyes away from the portrait and smiled ruefully. "William's death was a release, dear Celeste. I mourned him, of course, but I hope it does not shock you overmuch to hear that in many ways, it was a boon. I have become a somewhat different woman, you see."

Lady Canfield leaned forward and patted her friend's hand sympathetically. "A very *intéressante* and brave woman, Marisa. I have no doubt that, should you wish it, you will find a more worthy husband." She settled her tiny frame back into cushions of the claret velvet sofa. "But Lord Verbank . . . ?"

The duchess burst into laughter. "He is a bit much, is he not? I think what I most enjoy about him is how much he shocks Clarence. I fear my son is fast becoming a pattern card of his father. At Vauxhall two nights ago, Lord Verbank made some tasteless joke about the amorous abilities of a Cyprian who managed to juggle three protectors at once. Not at all the thing with which to regale Clarence, much less two unmarried ladies, although I think Alex was rather intrigued. I thought Clarence would never contain himself. As it was, he excused himself for a stroll with Emma, Alex, and Lucien. You can be sure that I upbraided his lordship, but it did not turn out so badly after all. You have heard that there are more wedding bells in the offing?"

Lady Canfield frowned. "I suppose *félicitations* are in order.

But . . . Emma Manwaring?" The marchioness hesitated. "She is a relation, but even so, I do not scruple to say that she is every bit as stuffy as Clarence."

The duchess smiled enigmatically. "I believe we may have misjudged her. There is much to Emma Manwaring that does not meet the eye. At all events, she shows every evidence of being able to wrap Clarence around her little finger, which I can only applaud. Her marriage will be different from mine. I rather think *she* will call the tune."

Lady Canfield's gray eyes gleamed appreciatively before her thoughts took another direction. "But you have told me nothing, Marisa, about what most interests me. How progresses the matter of Alex and my son? I confess I am surprised to see that your daughter has not told Lucien to take himself off to the devil. He can make himself most *désagréable*, although I suppose he is trying to be amenable. He knows it would not do to lose one's fiancée a few weeks before one must marry." Her eyes clouded momentarily. "Sometimes I fear his bitterness has left him beyond tender feelings."

She shrugged and gave the duchess a slight smile.

"*Il n'est sauce que d'appétit.* Appetite is the best sauce, *n'est-ce pas*? I suppose it is not a love match, although I did have hopes. I imagine your daughter does not give him an easy time of it. She does not strike me as the most biddable of young ladies."

The duchess laughed. "No, indeed. She was the only one who could hold her own against William, and I confess I do not know where she came by her determination. She has not confided in me, and at times I have wondered about her commitment to this engagement." She stared curiously at her friend. "But pray, what do you mean about Lucien's necessity to wed in such a short time? Has he some urgency of which we are unaware?"

Lady Canfield was silent for a moment. Then she sighed and replied, "I gather my son did not see fit to inform his fiancée about his father's will. I should not be the one to do so, of course, but it seems only fair that some member of your family not be left in *ignorance*." She took a deep breath. "Lucien was given eighteen months after assuming the title to marry or lose the unentailed estates. He is obliged to wed by July."

The duchess absorbed this information in silence.

"It is perhaps well that Alex has no inkling of this," she said at last. "She would likely do something rash just to be obstinate. There is something about the two of them that seems to engender fireworks."

Lady Canfield's brows arched in delight. "Ah. Fireworks." She repeated the word slowly with a widening smile. "*Alors, peut-être* my hopes are not misplaced."

"Mandley, eh?" The admiral barked the name in satisfaction. "A middling clerk in the War Office. We have been watching him. Spends a lot of time on Lisle Street lately, I believe." He consulted a file. "Yes. Lost a hundred pounds there last week. Wouldn't think he could afford that on his salary."

The others in the room nodded consideringly.

"It fits," said Lord Hasbrook.

Admiral Donley pounded his fist down on the file. "Ought to arrest the traitor forthwith," he said angrily.

"But we might lose the opportunity to help Wellington," Lucien put in smoothly.

Lord Hasbrook, who was the chief deputy at the War Office, nodded. "Just so," he agreed. "With Wellington besieging Badajoz, it is the perfect opportunity to trick the frogs into believing his resources are greater than they surmise."

"Never shared your taste for intrigue," Admiral Donley grumbled, his glare encompassing both Lucien and Hasbrook. "Ought to seize him out of hand. That French bastard, too. Not my decision, of course," he added morosely.

Hasbrook smiled patiently in the manner of one accustomed to dealing with the admiral. "Timing is critical here. I am certain that as a naval man, you will agree, Admiral," he said. "If we can rout Marmont, a great victory will be ours. We must seize every opportunity that comes our way." He looked over at

Lucien. "And while Lord Canfield has identified the traitors, we cannot arrest them without evidence."

Lord Edgeworthy, a balding and bespectacled gentleman given to such quietness as to render him utterly without presence, spoke up for the first time from his position in a shadowy corner of the admiral's office. "We shall help Wellington *and* have our evidence, gentlemen," he said quietly.

Lucien smiled to himself. He would never reconcile this man's unassuming image with the fact that he was one of the great intelligence officers of the time.

The others looked at Edgeworthy expectantly, waiting for the plan that they knew he had been spinning during the past few minutes while they had forgotten he was in the room.

"We will see to it that Mandley finds an opportunity to obtain certain information about Wellington's troop figures and operations. Perhaps Lord Hasbrook's clerk might become ill for a time—it would be only natural for him to turn to someone in the department for a temporary substitute." Lord Edgeworthy removed his spectacles and idly began to clean them. "We will further allow Mandley to pass the information on to this Frenchman. In two weeks, after the false figures have filtered to Marmont, we will set up another such operation and arrest Mandley in the act. He and the Frenchman will hang, gentlemen, in short order."

Even Admiral Donley could not suppress a thrill of excitement. He rubbed his hands together in anticipation. The others drew their chairs closer to hear more about the plan.

An hour later, only Lucien remained with the admiral.

"You have done well in ferreting out the traitors, Captain," Donley said gruffly. "Seems you have found your land legs after all."

Lucien gave the other man a polite smile. "Thank you, sir."

"Captain—dash it, I must remember to call you Canfield." The admiral studied a corner of his desk before continuing. "Heard you were getting leg-shackled. My congratulations."

Lucien bowed. "Thank you, sir," he said once again.

"Always thought the sea was the best mistress," Donley

mused. "So many young men these days think otherwise. First Huntsley, and now you." He smiled ruefully, and Lucien noticed that his face had become flushed. "Not many confirmed bachelors like me around anymore. I suppose there is something to be said for the wedded state. No doubt you will find out what that is."

"No doubt, sir." Lucien's face was unreadable.

The admiral nodded a dismissal. "Your friend Huntsley may have a few ideas about that to pass on, now that he's got his heir. I have sent Gifford to replace him on the *Vanguard*. Huntsley is due here within the week, though I doubt very much he'll do more than report here before hying to Dorset to see the babe." He rose and clapped Lucien on the shoulder with a gnarled hand. "Best of luck, Captain. I know you will do your best."

Lucien tried not to show his surprise at the admiral's sudden warmth. "Thank you, sir," he said, and bowed his leave.

Alex watched as Mary put the finishing touches on a new hair creation that was a bit of a departure from her usual smooth coils. Tonight her tawny hair had been half combed back into curls at the top of the head. The front had been combed forward and arranged in loose ringlets around the face and forehead.

She sighed. The effect was not too girlish, but it was rather coquettish, especially in light of the new and perplexing stage in her relationship with Lucien. Since the night at Vauxhall, he had adopted a demeanor toward her of cordial friendship. They went out at night in a spirit of easy companionship, talking amiably of the weather, the war, the opera, Clarence and Emma—eschewing any topics that could excite passions.

In the afternoons there were trips to the museum, the Tower, Astley's, a balloon ascension, and several other diversions undertaken in perfect harmony and friendship. Lucien was really quite excellent company, Alex reflected. Unfortunately she now knew full well that it was not simply his friendship that she sought.

She frowned, waving Mary away when the maid would have readjusted an errant curl. "Leave it, Mary," she said, rising from her chair. "I am certain his lordship will not notice whether this particular curl resides on the left or the right side of my forehead."

She gathered up her cashmere shawl and let it fall over her evening dress, a charming peach with square décolletage. It was last year's style, but she doubted anyone would notice, least of all Lucien. She sighed. She might as well be wearing sacking.

Lucien was completely unaware of her as a woman these days, it seemed. His smile when he greeted her was easy and forthcoming, much as he might offer his mother or a maiden aunt. There was none of the brooding intensity that had marked his past relations with her or the mesmerizing passion that had left her spellbound at Vauxhall. Indeed, he seemed relentlessly, insufferably cheerful.

Alex was bewildered and depressed by this new development, especially as her feelings had taken the opposite turn since that night. She found herself excessively aware of his presence and his devastating maleness. She could barely prevent her eyes from roaming hungrily over his figure, and her body longed for the closeness of his. Her pulse raced every time he greeted her with an excruciatingly proper kiss upon her hand. She found she had to will her eyes, her body, her hands to behave properly. This chaste stage in their relations was pure torture.

And yet it was probably for the best, she thought as she descended the stairs and forced her face not to break out in an expression of pure delight at the sight of Lucien, resplendent in evening attire at the bottom of the stairs. At least this new friendship would make it easier to break their engagement. There would be no fireworks, only friendly acceptance and perhaps relief on his part.

The Regent's fete was next week. She had to end their betrothal then. There was no reason to delay; she had finally found a woman who would make a most acceptable companion. Her plan had been successful, it seemed, but at what price? The price of her soul, perhaps. *Lucifer*. The word rose unbidden to her mind as she placed her foot on the last step and looked into

those amber eyes. Her social skills served her well, she thought
bitterly as she forced the bleakness from her eyes and gave him
a smile of greeting. She supposed she would never know why
he had suddenly lost interest in her. Or why, at this late date, she
had suddenly realized that she loved him with all of her heart.

She raised her cool blue eyes to his, betraying no evidence of
the devastation she felt. She would never let him see that.

"Good evening, Lucien," she said calmly.

Lucien handed Alex into the carriage, forcing himself to
make chitchat about the opera they were about to see. He would
go slowly, ever so slowly, for the first time in his rash, impetu-
ous life. He dared not give Alex a clue as to his real feelings. He
almost laughed out loud. When had it hit him, this knowledge
that he could not live without her? Vauxhall, perhaps. But part
of him seemed to have known it all along.

She had settled herself next to his mother and was making an
idle remark, something about shopkeepers running out of crepe
as a result of a spurious rumor that the king had died. His eyes
surreptitiously raked her lithe figure. What had she done to her
hair? He wanted to run his fingers through those delightful
curls. How it grated to sit here making silly conversation when
what he most wanted to do was to take her in his arms! But no.
He had done too much of that when he was under the illusion
that what he really needed was some insipid bride who would
leave him alone for the rest of his days. What a fool he had
been. Now he could not stand the thought of being alone, without Alex.

The carriage rolled on, and Lucien made a mental note to
have his coachman see to the door on his side, as it did not close
tightly. A slight wind whistled in through the crack, and Lucien
fought the instinct to put an arm around Alex to protect her
from its insignificant breeze. He must restrain these urges to
touch her. He had treated her badly, taking any available occasion practically to assault her in his misguided effort to induce
her to cry off. It was nothing short of miraculous that she had
not, and he only hoped he had not given her a permanent disgust

of him. He was putting all his efforts now into keeping them on good terms.

Trying to win a woman's friendship and trust was a novel experience for him, but somehow it seemed the best approach. He wanted more than friendship, certainly, but something told him he had not yet earned the right to ask more. When he told her he loved her, he wanted her to return at least some degree of affection. He sighed. He would have only himself to blame if she laughed in his face.

At the opera, they settled into the duke's box, where Farnsworth already was making love-struck faces at Emma. Lucien fought to suppress a pang of envy. He found it unbelievable that he, too, would be sitting here in an agony of longing for a woman. He laughed ruefully to himself. He had never been so awkward with a woman before. Then again, he had never wanted a woman this much.

Lucien saw Alex smile as she offered the opera glasses to his mother. She was not just any woman. So cool, so beautiful, so intelligent. She was worth everything he had, even his pride.

He shook his head. He never thought during those long years at sea that he would find anyone so independent, caring, without airs or guile. A woman he could trust. Their wedding day would be the happiest of his life.

"Look, Lucien. There is Claude Deveaux." Lucien blinked as his mother tapped his arm with the opera glasses. "There. Over in the royal box behind the Duc d'Angoulême."

Lucien glanced at the box, but he could not discern the man's features. He took the opera glasses and raised them to his face. There, sitting with the Bourbon party, was a man with a face that was becoming increasingly familiar.

"You know him?" he queried his mother in surprise.

"*Mais oui.* He was a friend of your uncle Guy. I am surprised to see him with the Bourbons. His politics must have altered a great deal since my brother knew him."

"I imagine so," Lucien replied with a touch of sarcasm. He saw that Alex's attention had been caught by their conversation. Wordlessly he handed her the glasses. When she returned them to him after surveying the royal box, her eyes were wide. He gave her a barely perceptible shake of the head just as the curtain began to rise. Calmly she turned her attention to the stage.

Later, when they walked the corridor during intermission, she put a hand on his arm and pulled him into an alcove. "What are you going to do about the Frenchman?" she whispered.

He stared into her face, drinking in the creamy ivory complexion and those limpid blue eyes. "It is already being done," he said, hoping his own eyes were not burning feverishly with desire.

"A trap?"

"Yes." There was no one in the hallway. He could easily pull her into his arms and rain kisses upon those enticing lips.

"I suppose there is nothing more you can say now." She looked at him inquiringly.

Oh, but there is a great deal I wish to say to you. Lucien shook his head. He must go slowly.

"No. Not now," he said aloud.

She gave him a light tap on his arm. "Then we had best return to our seats, my lord. I would not wish to miss the rest of Catalani's performance. She is in rare form tonight, do you not agree?"

"I do." He arched his thick brows. "Although I must confess that at times she seems a bit . . ." He hesitated.

"Overwrought?" Her eyes were twinkling.

"Precisely." How he longed to turn those dancing blue lights to fire.

She shot him a mischievous look. "Perhaps she had a lover's quarrel before coming on stage. I understand such occurrences make her performances excessively tempestuous."

He forced an answering twinkle to his eyes. *Keep it light.*

"I am certain a duke's daughter is not supposed to speculate on such things." He smiled awkwardly.

"Lovers, you mean? Or quarrels?" Her voice was light, but he thought he detected a strange tone as she continued. "Alas, sir, I fear that you are correct. Those of us in the rarefied altitudes of the *ton* know nothing of such goings-on."

Was it his imagination, or did her voice hold a slight tremor? He said nothing, watching as her eyes glowed with unnatural brightness.

"Tempestuous affairs are the prerequisites of the *lower orders*, are they not, sir?" she rushed on, a brittle smile on her face. "I am sure *I* would know nothing of them. Nothing of lovers' quarrels or passion or anything of the sort! Why should I? For I am certain there is nothing at all passionate about *my* nature."

She stopped abruptly and put her hands up in front of her face. "Oh!" The word was a horrified cry of intense embarrassment.

"Alex." He reached out a hand and rested it uncertainly on her shoulder. The fabric of her gown was like gossamer, and he longed to caress the skin underneath, to hold her close and comfort her. Another moment and, despite his resolutions, he would.

Abruptly she shook him off and removed her hands from her face. A single tear had made its way halfway down her cheek. With a mind of its own, his thumb moved to touch the dewy drop tenderly.

"No." She gave him a wobbly smile before her face assembled itself into a mask of control. "I do apologize, sir, for inflicting my temper on you. I believe I am getting the megrims. Perhaps I can prevail upon you to take me home?"

He bowed his assent, unwilling to trust his tongue.

They rode to Farnsworth House in silence. When he handed her down from the carriage, she lifted her head, and their eyes met in a moment of shared agony. Alex was surprised by the pain she saw in his face. She must have embarrassed him beyond everything with her incoherent talk of lovers and passion, she thought, her mortification complete. She had so wanted to keep the tone of the evening light. If only she could have her words back. She squared her shoulders, forcing herself to regard him with measured calm.

"Thank you, Lucien, for being my friend." She watched him gravely.

He bowed. *She had accepted his friendship then. Or had she merely set the boundaries for all time?*

"It is my pleasure," he replied in a deep baritone that was not entirely steady as he escorted her to the door.

He turned toward his carriage, a forlorn look on his face.

Chapter 15

"The trap is set for tonight." Lord Edgeworthy brushed a speck of lint from the lapel of his ill-fitting coat. "The Regent's fete is the perfect opportunity. Doubtless they think no one will notice their nefarious little transaction in such a setting."

"You are certain all went as planned? Marmont now has the false figures?" Lord Hasbrook asked.

"Quite. Reports from Marmont's camp confirm it. The French are disheartened by what they believe to be Wellington's vastly superior numbers. Indeed, Wellington's latest dispatches show that he has been able to capitalize on their dampened spirits."

Hasbrook nodded, but otherwise there was an uneasy silence in the room. No one doubted that somehow one of Lord Edgeworthy's spies had managed to infiltrate the French camp and that Wellington would outmaneuver Marmont. But each man was somberly contemplating the evening ahead.

"What is the plan for tonight?" Lucien spoke for everyone.

The rumpled man in the corner cleared his throat. "Mandley has been told he is to accompany Lord Hasbrook to Carlton House tonight to obtain the prince's signature on some papers. The papers themselves are meaningless. But due to an oversight on Lord Hasbrook's part"—here he gave just the hint of a smile—"the safe in his lordship's inner office, which contains some highly secret details of Wellington's plans for Cuidad Rodrigo, has been left open for"—he checked his timepiece—"about an hour now."

Lord Edgeworthy rubbed his spectacles as he continued.

"Lord Hasbrook had to rush out, you see, and in his hurry no doubt forgot to secure the safe. At all events, we expect that Mandley will have these papers with him to peddle to the Frenchman when he accompanies Hasbrook tonight. When he hands them to Deveaux, we will arrest them both."

A man who had until now remained silent cleared his throat from his position on a claret leather divan, and all eyes were instantly directed to him. "The Bourbons must not be publicly embarrassed. If it should become known that they unwittingly fostered a Bonapartist spy who was arrested at the Regent's fete, of all places, I should not like to have to answer to the prince for the ensuing hubbub." He spoke in clipped tones. "I assume you have thought of that."

Lord Edgeworthy nodded. "Yes, Lord Castlereagh. The man Deveaux has been very clever. The Bourbons believe him to be a loyal friend, never realizing that his true dedication is to the Corsican. We expect Deveaux will be eager to meet Mandley privately, out of view of the Bourbons, of course. That is when we shall act. I believe I can safely promise that none of the Regent's royal guests will suffer public humiliation, sir."

Lord Castlereagh considered this for a moment. "I assume you will manage to watch these two without their suspicions being aroused? Else the whole plan will go awry."

Lord Edgeworthy hesitated. "No plan is perfect, sir. Our men shall be as unobtrusive as possible—they will pose as waiters and the like. In addition, Lord Canfield has promised to stand available. He has had some dealings with the two in the past."

Admiral Donley spoke up for the first time. "But will they not recognize him? That could very well scuttle the plan."

"I do not believe so, sir," Lucien responded. "They last saw me many months ago at a dingy inn in Wiltshire. I assure you my appearance was vastly different at the time." As so many things were then, he added silently.

No one spoke as each digested the arrangements. A clock sounded the hour. Finally Lord Castlereagh rose.

"Proceed then," he said, "but if aught goes amiss, Edgeworthy, I shall remember only that I arduously counseled you against such a plan."

He left the room. Lord Edgeworthy subjected his spectacles to one final inspection and put them on.

"Good day, gentlemen," he said, and shuffled out the door.

Tonight. Alex repeated the word to herself as she stood motionless before her cheval glass, willing herself to calmness. Her gown was last Season's, to be sure, but it had nevertheless risen to the occasion, the silver lamé on blue gauze shimmering in the candlelight like so many stars. Her mother's sapphire-and-diamond necklace added the last elegant touch. A small cluster of diamonds and sapphires nestled in her hair, which was swept into a high-crowned coil from which a few lustrous curls cascaded.

"Drat and botheration."

Alex's maid looked askance at her mistress. "Why, you look like an angel, my lady. Is aught amiss?"

An angel is precisely what she was not, Alex thought, but she turned to her maid with a smile. "Nothing at all, Mary," she said smoothly. "I am merely envisioning the long night ahead."

"But what a night!" her maid said dreamily. "All the ladies dressed up in their finery. The prince and all the princesses and the queen . . ."

"I do not believe the queen or any of the princesses will be in attendance," Alex said as she picked up her fan and shawl. "The Regent's fete is not viewed by his esteemed family as being quite the thing just now."

"Never you mind, my lady, 'twill be a grand party just the same." Mary smoothed a wrinkle in Alex's shawl.

Alex hurried down the hall away from the maid's oppressive cheerfulness. *Tonight.* After tonight, her betrothal to Lucien Tremaine would be a thing of the past. She had rehearsed the calm and reasoned words she would say to him. They simply did not suit. As they had quarreled excessively from the beginning, by now it must be quite clear that their discourse was lacking in the qualities of reasonableness necessary to marital harmony; it could therefore only be the fondest wish of both parties to extricate themselves from such an ill-advised arrangement.

Except, of course, that that was so much dibble-dabble. Rot. Rubbish. Pure humbug. Well then, what about the truth? Oh, yes, Alex thought sarcastically as she started down the stairs. She could only imagine Lucien's face as she explained that the betrothal was not only a ploy to avoid the dreariness of Cousin Agatha but that she had also conceived the disastrous idea that it would teach him a lesson. About what she could not precisely recall at the moment. Oh, yes. That he was arrogant and insufferable in condemning her and her set as superficial ninnies. Well, this little farce had only proven his point, had it not?

Nevertheless tonight she would hand him his freedom and set everything right, she vowed as she took a deep breath before greeting him. Her eyes took in his black-laced shoes, black Florentine silk breeches, white marcella waistcoat, and corbeau coat. A dress sword hung at his side, and he carried a cocked crescent hat under his arm. She lifted her eyes to his face and saw the amber eyes light up. A smile spread slowly over his sensuous mouth, and that tantalizing dimple danced in his cheek. She tried to remember when she had first been awed by the magnificence of those features. Was it that very first meeting, at the unveiling? Or at the inn later? A glowing fire flickered in her mind's eye. She took a step toward him, her brain somewhere in Wiltshire, a foolish half smile on her face.

Suddenly her toe caught in the carpet, and she plummeted into him. Lucien's arms immediately went out to steady her.

"I trust you do not plan to treat the prince to such a warm greeting." For a brief moment, Alex thought she saw a flame kindled in those amber eyes. He had not looked at her like that in days. But just as suddenly the look was gone, and he was setting her on her feet and adjusting her shawl like a congenial brother.

Her own brother was frowning at them in his own uncongenial fashion. "Must you always subject one to such embarrassments, Alex? I do hope you have no such inelegant moves to display for the Regent. For that matter, I had quite given up hope that you would present yourself downstairs at all. Such preening that women do." He patted Emma's arm, which was tucked inside his own. "Thank goodness all women are not slaves to vanity."

Alex normally would not have dignified such a remark with a response. But her equanimity was so shaken from that small encounter with Lucien's firm body that she took refuge in the familiarity of her contempt for Clarence's prosing.

"If anyone in this house is guilty of preening, it is not I," she said crossly. "Why, I have never seen so many fobs and decorations in my life, Clarence. One would think you a head of state from the pretentious manner in which you are decked out. Why do you not simply open a jeweler's shop and be done with it?"

The only sound following this statement was Lucien's muffled cough. Clarence's complexion had begun to turn a dangerous shade of purple as Alex spoke, quite ignoring Lucien's gentle warning pressure on her arm. The duke moved toward his sister, apparently with the intention of boxing her ears, the dignity of the occasion quite forgotten in his anger. Lucien stepped quickly in front of Alex and found himself staring into the duke's beady black eyes. Clarence blinked at the ferocity of the amber gaze that held his.

Suddenly a light footstep sounded in the hall.

"Children! I could hear your quarreling from the drawing room," the duchess said, her eyes flashing. "Please set aside your differences for the nonce, if you please. Lord Verbank is here, and it is past time to leave. As it is, it will take half the night to maneuver through the streets."

Emma's delicate hand reached out for Clarence. "Come, sir. If Alex is overset tonight, I am certain it is not *your* doing." She gave him a shy smile with her doe eyes, ignoring the indignant look from her future sister-in-law. "I am counting on you to show me all the special treasures of Carlton House."

His vanity thus appealed to, Clarence allowed himself to be mollified for the moment, and soon the party was being bustled into two carriages for the ride to Carlton House. Lord Verbank and the duchess took one carriage. Since Lucien had ordered his to return for Lady Canfield, who had been delayed by a problem with her gown, the duke reluctantly extended the hospitality of his crested conveyance to the marquess. The two couples sat opposite each other for the drive; as the streets were filled with other carriages and hundreds of onlookers hoping to catch a glimpse of the *ton* and its finery, this journey occupied some time, much of it marked by an uneasy silence among the parties.

"I daresay we shall not eat until the morning," Alex said at one point. "And then there will be so many dishes, we will never wish to eat again."

"Shall we meet the prince?" Emma asked shyly.

"Of course," Clarence replied quickly. "His Highness has always taken a particular interest in our affairs."

"I rather think it the other way around, Clarence," Alex began, but broke off as Lucien shot her a warning look.

Fortunately her brother had launched into a painstaking description for Emma of the kindnesses and attention the Regent had paid him since Clarence had come into the title.

"Why do you silence me, sir?" Alex whispered to Lucien. "I shall say what I wish to my own brother. You need not fear that I will lose any battle of words with him."

"I do not doubt the strength of the weapons at your disposal, my dear. Please remember that I have been on the receiving end more than once. What I do fear is that you will have me and the duke at fisticuffs before the night is through." Lucien studied her closely. "Are you certain you are yourself tonight?"

Alex swallowed hard. *No, I very much fear I will never be myself again.* "Quite," she replied briskly.

Those cool blue eyes did not flinch before his gaze. Lucien smiled approvingly.

"Excellent. I was beginning to wonder if you were overcome by the magnificence of the evening."

Alex looked at him disdainfully. "Certainly not. My opinion of this ridiculous fete has not changed." The blue eyes twinkled mischievously as she added, "Although the spectacle is not to be missed."

"No, indeed," Lucien agreed with an answering gleam in his eye as the carriage at last rolled to a stop.

The band of guards was playing in the courtyard, and the guests were received by the members of the prince's household, dressed in their grandest livery. The prince himself entered the staterooms shortly after nine. He was wearing his field marshal's uniform, which was heavily and ornately embroidered. He wore the garter star and a magnificent aigrette. The Bourbons arrived shortly thereafter.

The Farnsworth party was presented to the French royal party by no less a person than the Regent himself. Clarence beamed, and Emma sank into a deep curtsy. Alex followed suit. The prince himself raised her from her curtsy.

"Ah, Lady Alex. And Canfield. We have not had the occasion to offer our felicitations upon your betrothal. May I say, my dear Alex, that you have snagged one of the most valued officers in our navy. It was a loss to the nation when he left the sea, but it is a pleasure to have him with us in town."

Alex smiled politely as the prince spoke, but her emotions were in a turmoil. By singling them out for congratulations, the prince had inadvertently assured that the ending of their engagement would be made the topic of public speculation and gossip all over London.

"Thank you, sir," she said through gritted teeth.

She only half heard Lucien's response, and saw with some relief that the prince was now speaking to someone else. Her eyes were wandering idly over the Bourbon party when suddenly they came upon a cold pair of eyes staring back. She nearly gasped. It was the Frenchman, the man Lucien's mother had called Deveaux. Had he recognized her? Perhaps not if she had been alone, but here she was standing with Lucien, precisely as she had been at the inn. Lucien had alluded to a trap. Would this chance encounter sabotage it?

Alex looked uneasily at Lucien, but he gave no evidence that anything was amiss. The Frenchman, too, was studying Lucien. When the man's eyes returned to hers, her heart sank at the cold speculation there. But she willed herself to evince no recognition, only a blank politeness when he bowed a greeting.

Moments later, the Farnsworth party joined the rest of the guests in meandering through the great hall, the library, golden drawing room, and a small bowroom where some Dutch pictures were hung. As they often stopped to greet acquaintances, there was no time to speak privately. An hour passed in this frustrating fashion.

"Lucien," Alex whispered fiercely as Lucien picked out a delicacy from a tray held by a man in the prince's dark blue livery, "I *must* speak to you."

"In a moment, Alex." He bit into the pastry and smiled his approval. "I must command a few more of these from this man."

Alex turned away, exasperated, and it was some moments before Lucien stood in front of her, gesturing to the garden.

She followed him out onto a long covered walk decorated with flowers and mirrors. He guided her to one of the exits from the walk into the garden itself, and soon she found herself sitting on a stone bench some distance from a group of large lanterns.

"What did you wish to speak to me about?"

"The Frenchman. The one from the inn. The one your mother called Deveaux."

She saw that she finally had his attention.

"What about him?" The nonchalant note in his voice belied the arrested expression in his eyes.

"He was with the Bourbon party."

"Yes." It was a statement of fact, delivered without apparent concern.

Alex shook her head in frustration. "Don't you understand, Lucien? I believe he recognized me."

Lucien's countenance darkened, but his tone was light. "Nothing for it now."

She looked at him in surprise. "But will he not be suspicious?"

"Of what? I can think of no reason why he should suspect

you of anything simply because he now knows you are a lady, not a serving wench. As far as he knows, English ladies often take great delight in donning servants' garb to meet their paramours in out-of-the-way inns."

"You must be daft, sir, to think you can persuade me to swallow such a clanker." Despite her fears, her tone was teasing. Then she sobered. "Let us not mince words, Lucien. I am perfectly aware that you posed as a seaman for that Captain Harnsby in order to ferret out just such characters as the Frenchman and his Mr. Mandley. No doubt Monsieur Deveaux came over on Captain Harnsby's boat, for I suspect our seafaring captain of dipping into some nefarious business."

Lucien frowned, an expression that Alex immediately took as confirmation of her suspicions.

"When Deveaux saw you later at the inn, you needed to throw them off the scent, so you seized upon me as your decoy. Just a common drunken seaman wooing the local tavern wench." She smiled mischievously. "You have considerable acting skills, Lucien."

Lucien, meanwhile, was watching her with interest, his arms crossed in front of his chest. "I might say the same for you, my dear. You never did explain why you were masquerading as a serving girl."

" 'Twas not a masquerade. As usual, you put the most unfavorable interpretation upon my actions," Alex retorted indignantly. "My carriage lost a wheel, and I walked through a downpour to the inn. The landlord found me a dry frock when he saw the deplorable state of my clothes."

"And a most becoming frock it was, as I recall," Lucien said with a teasing smile.

Alex frowned. "Be serious, sir. Now your Monsieur Deveaux sees us at Carlton House, with you introduced as the Marquess of Canfield and I as the sister of a duke. He must wonder at our game. You cannot make me believe that this does not put your plan in jeopardy, Lucien." Her eyes widened in concern. "And you as well."

He shrugged. "I think we must hope that my Monsieur

Deveaux cannot take action immediately. By the time he for-
mulates a plan to save his skin, it will be too late."

"Too late? You mean the trap is set for tonight?"

Lucien moved closer and took her hand. "Hush, my curious
one. There is no need to speak of this further. Let us simply say
that the matter is well in hand. Which brings me to another matter I have been meaning to put to you."

Alex was taken aback by his casual change of topic.

Lucien hesitated. Their friendly standoff of the past two
weeks had been more than enough for him. He did not think he
could endure it any longer. He had to make her see that they
must wed immediately. Once married, he could surely win her
love with other powers of persuasion that were not presently at
his disposal. He cleared his throat.

"It concerns our betrothal."

Alex nearly jumped from her seat in dismay. Must they speak
of this now? She had envisioned a later hour for her confession,
perhaps after they had danced their fill and had enjoyed the evening. But no, here it was. She would have to tell him now.

"What about it, Lucien?" she said weakly.

"I wish us to marry next week."

He watched the alarm leap to her eyes and felt his hopes fall.
He should have guessed this would not go as he had hoped. Not
with Alessandra Ridgely. He trailed his hand lightly along her
arm as he spoke again, his voice gently cajoling.

"Would it be such a burden for you to accommodate me?"

Alex felt a treacherous sense of joy beginning to rise in her.
Did he really wish to marry her so much then? Perhaps he
would wave aside her confession and sweep her off to the altar.
She was shocked by the realization that she wanted him with
every fiber of her being. Suddenly she allowed herself to hope.
She took a deep breath.

"That is a matter I, too, have been wishing to speak to you
about," she said hesitantly. He moved closer, and she felt a tiny
thrill ripple through her body. She fought to remember her carefully prepared speech. "There is no need for haste," she began.
"In fact, I ought to tell you now that—"

"There is every need for haste," he interrupted in a harsh rasp, his eyes burning into hers.

Alex felt the tiny thrill surge into a wild wave of joy. He *did* want her. He would not care that she had trapped him into this silly, unworthy engagement.

"I should have told you before," he said, and now his voice was oddly tentative, "but my thoughts about this have not been in any coherent order for some time."

Alex smiled. He intended to make a declaration! She would not even mind hearing all those fulsome compliments, not from him. Indeed, she was certain she would hang on his every word.

"You have driven me quite to distraction." His eyes were warm, but suddenly he waved his hand dismissively. "However, that is another story altogether."

Alex was confused. She would have thought that the matter of his amorous distraction was quite germane. "My lord?"

Lucien did not notice her puzzled expression. He was pacing the ground in front of her, speaking with great determination. "I must marry in a fortnight or lose the unentailed properties for my heirs."

Alex looked at him blankly.

"It was a condition of my father's will," he explained.

Alex's brow furrowed as she sought to make some sense of his words, and he smiled at her confusion.

"So you see, there is some urgency about our wedding date. Oh, I suppose I should have told you at the outset of my reason for marrying," he said as he began to pace again, "but it was easier somehow to allow you to believe that tale about my having compromised you at the inn and feeling compelled to live up to my own code of honor."

Alex sat perfectly still. Her heart was pounding, and there was a rush of noise in her ears that she rather suspected came from the toppling of her foolish hopes.

"You offered for me because of a condition in your father's will?" Her voice was low and controlled.

Lucien's hands were clasped behind him, and his face was a study in concentration. "That was it initially. You were the only candidate at hand, although at the time it did not seem a very happy choice. I thought you would make my life miserable, you know."

He smiled ruefully, not noticing Alex's stricken look. "You should have seen the pains I was at to find another bride, someone more biddable. I thought that was the kind of wife I needed."

"And when no one jumped at the opportunity to be your marchioness, you decided to confess all and marry me forthwith," Alex said slowly. "It would not do, after all, to lose all those properties."

"No—yes." Lucien stopped pacing. He ran a hand through his thick auburn mane and looked at her. For the first time, he sensed that something was wrong.

Alex was beginning to laugh, but the sound held no mirth, and her eyes were shimmering with unshed tears. Lucien looked at her uncertainly.

"What you say is true, of course, but the point is that I *do* wish to marry you as soon as possible and not for that reason. I have much more to say."

"I am certain that you do, my lord, but I shall not be around to hear it." She gave a shaky laugh. "If you will excuse me, I feel a pressing need to remove myself from present company."

Alex rose and walked to the main path, although her legs were trembling so she felt as if she would collapse at any moment.

Here she had felt guilty for misleading him, and all along he had played her for a fool! She would take great delight in handing him his congé, although not just now, most definitely not now, when she could not seem to stop shaking. Later, perhaps, if she could somehow get through this evening. Later, if she could recover from the aching hurt that crippled her heart.

She walked unsteadily back to the main house, oblivious to the sound of her name on his lips. Was that her own hysterical giggle? Her predicament was laughable, was it not? Foolish to hope that he cared just a little. Foolish to nourish that one small hope.

Chapter 16

By the time Alex reached the Grecian hall, she was beginning to envision the pleasure of telling Lucien that she had never intended to marry him, never cared one whit for him or his bloodless proposal, and was happy to fling his prospects for saving his precious estates to the bottom of the sea.

She seized a glass of champagne from a tray offered by an expressionless servant in blue livery. How she would love to toss the bubbling liquid in Lucien's face! Instead, she took a deep gulp and, finding that most satisfying, quickly downed the remainder.

"Oh, there you are, my dear. *Pardon!* I tore my gown at the last moment, you see, and had to wait for my maid to repair it. *Mon Dieu! Mauvais quart d'heure.* I hope you and Lucien were not so very inconvenienced."

Alex looked down at the petite Lady Canfield, whose gray eyes danced with her usual high spirits. Inexplicably Alex wanted to fall into the marchioness's arms and weep her heart out like a small child. Given the difference in their respective heights, that would probably topple them both into the ornate crimson draperies, Alex reflected wryly. Perhaps she could simply retire behind those solid-looking curtains until this dreadful night ended.

Alex realized that Lady Canfield was looking at her curiously. She attempted a lighthearted laugh, only to have it emerge as a tremulous cackle.

"Nonsense," Alex trilled hastily. "We were not inconvenienced in the least. Indeed, Lucien and I have been enjoying the best of evenings." She broke off, not knowing what else to say.

"That is not precisely how I would have put it," said a deep voice behind her, "but welcome, Mother. You look *ravissante*, as usual." Lucien bowed over his mother's hand as Alex's face flushed a deep red. Lady Canfield, looking from Alex to Lucien, smiled uncertainly.

Alex did not think she could yet meet Lucien's gaze with composure. She stood motionless, her eyes fixed at a point beyond his shoulder. Part of her did not want to spend a single moment in this man's company. But a small voice inside wondered how she could possibly justify her anger, since her intentions on going into the betrothal had been no better than his. Alex tried to block out that irritating voice.

"Please excuse me, ma'am," she said, curtsying. "I believe I shall tour the house."

Lady Canfield smiled pleasantly, her expression giving no evidence of the concern she felt as she observed her son and his fiancée. *"Mais oui,"* she replied lightly. "You must be eager to see this home *extraordinaire*. No doubt there is some lively dancing in the ballroom. Run along, *mes enfants.*"

Alex hesitated as Lucien offered his arm. She saw that Lady Canfield's eyes were suddenly filled with lively speculation and something else—sympathy?

"Il n'y a que le premier pas qui coûte. It is only the first step that is difficult," the marchioness said gently, patting Alex's arm.

"Mother," Lucien said sternly, a warning note in his voice.

Alex smiled weakly. She felt the pressure of Lucien's arm and did not object when he began to lead her away.

"Now *I* must insist that we speak privately," Lucien whispered in her ear, and Alex nearly jumped as his moist breath hit her skin. She could not suppress a shiver and was instantly furious at betraying any sign of his effect on her.

"I do not think I can endure a conversation with you at the moment," she replied with chilly control as they entered the ballroom.

"Then we shall dance until you feel yourself up to the task," he replied, and, without preliminaries, swept her into his arms.

The orchestra was playing a cotillion, but Alex found she could not keep her mind on the dance or move her feet properly. There were not many dancers, the room being excessively stuffy. Alex's clumsiness notwithstanding, she and Lucien made an elegant couple as they moved about the floor over a chalked arabesque figure, in the center of which were the initials *G. III. R.*

Alex felt her head growing light, but whether it was from the heat or the champagne or simply Lucien's presence she could not have said. Finally, in the midst of their third dance, she stopped still, her head spinning.

"No more, sir, I pray!" She weaved slightly and fluttered her fan weakly.

"Are you ill?" He regarded her carefully.

"No—yes—that is, I simply need to stop," Alex replied, feeling more foolish by the moment.

Lucien quickly put his hand at her elbow and steered her out of the ballroom, through another set of rooms, and into the conservatory, which was set for the enormous dinner that would not be served until well after midnight. Alex could not help but stare as they moved through the chamber, its vaulted ceiling lending it a cathedral-like air. Small colored lamps were set in little cornices and Gothic niches, and hexagon lanterns hung from the points of the arches. The ceiling was filled with glass, and the many stained-glass windows bore the arms of the sovereigns of England.

Alex had never failed to be impressed by the florid Gothic chamber, but tonight the conservatory rose to new heights of lavishness. A grand table that extended the length of two hundred feet held in its center a canal of water flowing from a silver fountain at the head of the table. Fish swam through the bubbles; flowers and moss lined the banks. Crimson-covered tables behind the prince's seat held a profusion of silver and gilt plate, fountains, epergnes, and other ornaments. Others held gold vases, salvers, and an exquisite Spanish urn.

"My goodness!" she exclaimed.

"Quite," Lucien agreed. But he did not allow her to linger

and soon had maneuvered them both into a small adjacent room. It looked to be an antechamber of some sort, as there was a large door that presumably led into a larger inner room. Heavy crimson draperies trimmed in gold braid lined the windows and walls, putting Alex in mind of an ornately hung bedchamber. The laughter that rose to her lips at that thought was immediately stifled by the fierce expression burning in Lucien's molten eyes. What was he thinking?

Lucien stared at the beautiful woman before him. What a fool he had been. In the garden earlier, he had only intended to clear the air, to get the matter of his father's will off his chest. But he had handled it clumsily, allowing her to believe that was his only motivation for pressing his suit now. The only way to make her believe otherwise was to declare his love—a daunting prospect. For so long he had not allowed himself to trust a woman. Perhaps she would reject him out of hand. Then again, perhaps he could persuade her to give her feelings a chance to grow.

"I think it is time to be completely truthful," he said, and took a deep breath.

"I could not agree more," Alex interjected before he could continue. She strode purposefully to the center of the small room before whirling to address him.

"Our engagement is at an end, Lucien," she said, and was instantly dismayed at the slight squeak in her voice. She took a calming breath and continued: "If you must know, I never intended for us to wed from the outset. It was all a ploy, you see."

There was a moment of silence.

"I am afraid I don't see." Lucien's thick brows were knit together, and his forbidding tone sent a tiny tingle of fear down her spine.

Alex turned away to address the curtains, thankful that her voice now seemed steadier. "I was weary of Clarence's harping on my need for a companion—he was going to force our dreadful cousin Agatha on me—and so I thought that if it appeared that I was betrothed, I could find my own companion. Which I have—a very nice female, incidentally, perfectly suited to my temperament."

She rushed on, heedless of the ominous silence and increasingly aware of how lame her words sounded. "It was not very sporting of me, I suppose, but you were so insufferably arrogant that I thought to teach you a lesson. You made it clear that you held me in no great esteem, and your opinion of my family and friends was no better, so when you offered for me, I decided it would serve you right if I accepted. And so I did."

Alex turned to face him and nearly jumped when she found him not two feet from her. His eyes were gleaming dangerously under those thick brows, and his mouth was drawn into a grim line. Auburn lights glinted in his unruly hair. *Lucifer*. She steeled her nerves.

"It is really for the best," she said with determined calm. "It is not as though we really care for each other. You made your feelings perfectly clear earlier tonight. It must be obvious that we do not suit."

Fire leaped to his eyes, and Alex could almost feel the heat on her skin. But no, that was from his hands. When had they come up to grasp her shoulders, his fingers sliding easily under the thin fabric to send the most disturbing sensations through her?

"Not suit." He repeated the words slowly in a low voice, his hands kneading her shoulders, gripping them like a lifeline in rough seas. His eyes were lit by the hard glint of hot anger and cold loss as they bored into hers.

Alex found she could not speak. She stood riveted to the spot as he continued his rough caress of her shoulders. Was he going to choke her? She could almost imagine the feel of those rough hands around her neck. Suddenly one hand checked its relentless pressure to allow his fingers to trail softly along the top of her bodice, where her breasts rose and fell with her pounding heart.

"Not suit." The words were barely a whisper now as he bent his head to hers. Alex's eyes widened at the ferocity of his expression and felt herself drawn inexorably into those burning amber eyes.

"Lucifer." Had she said the word out loud?

It seemed not to matter as his mouth covered hers, forcing her lips into submission as he pulled her violently to him. Her breasts, crushed against his broad chest, arched from the pressure as he continued his assault, but she did not resist, and her swollen mouth opened readily to receive his probing tongue. The warmth of that intimate contact raced down to the pit of her stomach, and there it was again, that strange sensation that engulfed her when she was in his embrace. She shivered as she felt the hardness of his body. Her skin stung from the roughness of his chin as he swept kisses down her neck and along her shoulders, moving lower to kiss the soft roundness of her breasts. Every nerve ending seemed to be alive. Every sense burned for him.

"Lucien." Now she had the name right. Lucien, Lucien Tremaine. No one else. Never anyone else.

He raised his head and looked at her from eyes drugged with passion and anger. "It is too bad I intend to wring your lovely neck," he said fiercely, his deep baritone rumbling in her ear. "Otherwise I would enjoy showing you the ways we suit very well."

"And I would enjoy watching such a display," came a heavily accented voice, "but unfortunately I have other, more pressing needs."

Claude Deveaux stood in the doorway to the larger chamber. At his side was the clerk Mandley, looking distinctly uncomfortable.

"Voilà, Mandley, our *amoureux* couple from the inn. The seaman and his tavern maid, looking remarkably like the Marquess of Canfield and Lady Alessandra Ridgely. How appearances can deceive."

The Frenchman pulled a pistol from his waistcoat and pointed it at them as Mandley eyed him nervously. Casually Lucien moved to stand in front of Alex.

"I could not agree with you more, Deveaux," he said softly.

The Frenchman moved a step forward, but Mandley put out his arm to halt him.

"There is no need for this, Deveaux. And I really must be getting back to Hasbrook."

The Frenchman's eyes narrowed. "You have no heart for the game, Mandley, and I am beginning to find it *très exaspérant. Peut-être* our association is nearing the end of its usefulness."

Mandley's eyes moved nervously, but he remained silent. Lucien, however, watched the pair in mock amusement.

"What is the matter, Deveaux? Never say your partner in treachery has disappointed. From the looks of that thick packet you are carrying, I would say he has come through for you very well."

Deveaux fixed Lucien with an ugly look. "So you know. *Je m'y attendais.* It is as I suspected. Well, I have arranged a surprise for you, *monsieur le marquis.* I am not about to let you spoil my plans."

Alex recoiled at the menace in his voice, but Lucien merely shrugged his shoulders in Gallic fashion.

"I quite see why it might be inconvenient for you if we informed the Bourbons that there was a Bonapartist rat in their midst."

Deveaux leveled the pistol at Lucien, and Alex knew a moment of sheer terror. Please, she thought, let help come through that door.

"As you say, Englishman, it would be most *inopportun.* And now let us see what can be done about you and your lady."

At that moment, a rumpled, bespectacled man stepped out from behind a large crimson curtain. "I think not, Mr. Deveaux," said Lord Edgeworthy.

The Frenchman turned toward Edgeworthy, his pistol at the ready, but before he could fire, he was brought to the floor by Lucien's running tackle. Instantly two waiters in the prince's dark blue livery materialized in the doorway from the large chamber, and two others appeared from behind the curtains in the smaller room. They clamped their burly arms on Mandley, who had been quietly edging away. After a brief scuffle, Lucien

wrested the gun from Deveaux and drew the Frenchman
roughly to his feet.

"I shall relieve you of this burden," Lucien said as he removed the incriminating packet from Deveaux's waistcoat. "I
think you shall trouble us no more."

Alex sighed in relief. But Deveaux, it seemed, was not finished. He gave Lucien an odd smile.

"As to that, *m'sieur*, I would not be so *certain*."

Alex could not suppress a tiny chill as the Frenchman was led
away, but her eyes were riveted on Lucien, who was brushing
some floor dirt off his coat.

"Are you all right?" She endeavored to make her voice calm,
but a small tremor betrayed her efforts.

He fixed her with a cold, curious look. "Is it indeed a matter
of importance, Alex? I could have sworn you have been at pains
to persuade me that we do not care for each other."

The discreet sound of a throat being cleared prevented Alex
from answering. She had forgotten the presence of Lord
Edgeworthy.

"I will not burden you overlong by my presence, Canfield,"
he said apologetically, "but I shall be happy to relieve you of
the evidence."

Lucien smiled wryly and handed the packet over. "Well done
as usual, Edgeworthy. Did your men also manage to witness the
exchange of documents?"

Lord Edgeworthy nodded. "We overheard Mandley and
Deveaux agreeing to meet in this room—it's called the Royal
Tasting Chamber, incidentally, I suppose because the food is
sampled here before state occasions. It seems that the prince is
most preoccupied with the possibility of suffering potentially
fatal cases of indigestion."

Lucien shifted impatiently. "Edgeworthy, please get on with
it."

His lordship removed his spectacles and began to polish
them.

"Yes, well, our waiters overheard the hasty arrangements for
this meeting—no one notices waiters, you know, yet they are

constantly hovering about. When we discovered that the room actually consisted of two rooms—the inner chamber and this outer one—we were somewhat at a loss. So I stationed men in both chambers, concealed behind the curtains, a wise move considering that Deveaux and Mandley chose the inner room for their clandestine activities. As it happens, my men heard every word in there. With this"—he patted the packet—"we have enough evidence to hang them both."

He put his spectacles back on his nose and smiled broadly. "I am most grateful, Lord Canfield, for your excellent work in the capture of these villains. And now, if you will excuse me, I must report to Lord Castlereagh."

He bowed and walked to the doorway, hesitating for a moment on the threshold. "I hope you will pardon me for venturing an insignificant opinion," he said gravely. "But I think you and the lady suit most admirably."

He turned and vanished through the doorway as Lucien and Alex stared after him. Alex let out a small shriek of dismay.

"Lucien! He was hiding behind the curtains all along. He heard every word we said!" She flushed in mortification. "And I suppose he saw . . . everything."

Lucien smiled grimly. "Edgeworthy is most discreet. Your reputation is safe. Which is more than I can say for your person at the moment. Come. I am going to take you for a carriage ride. I have quite a bit more to say to you on the subject of our little engagement."

He gripped her arm forcefully, and Alex found herself half dragged from the room, propelled through the conservatory, and quickly thrust outside past the prince's waiting servants to wait for the carriage. Lucien said nothing, but his expression was foreboding. Alex bit her lip. Her plan had never seemed so unworthy as it did now. If only they could somehow start anew. But of course, she was now beyond redemption in his eyes.

"Lucien," she began as they waited near the gravel drive.

"Not now, Alex. Perhaps later, when I explain to you the notion of trust. It was a commodity I thought you valued and understood, but I was wrong. Indeed, it appears that I was wrong about you in quite a few respects."

Alex felt her own temper rise. "Perhaps so, Lucien, but do not come all sanctimonious with me about the subject of trust! Do not forget that *you* misled *me* about your intentions in this betrothal. I do not think you are in any position to judge my actions. But of course that has never stopped you in the past. You are so eager to condemn others that you simply cannot see the truth. Even when it is before your face!"

He turned to her, and Alex shrank from the blazing anger in his eyes. But she squared her shoulders and quickly drew herself up to give him the full force of the cold rage in those icy blue eyes. But just as she was about to speak, the crunch of the carriage wheels intruded.

In an instant, Lucien had thrust Alex inside his carriage. They rode in silence for several blocks, the *clip-clop* of the horses' hooves the only sound as both parties wrestled with their own emotions. The night had misted over, and with it had come a damp chill. A wind had whipped up, too, and Alex wondered idly whether it would rain before the night was done. She drew her shawl around her against the breeze that seeped through a crack in the carriage door, but it was thin comfort. She turned to Lucien, rigid on the seat beside her, his hands clenched tightly on his muscled thighs. The harsh planes of his face were barely softened by the misty light of the street lamps. Alex could see the tightening of a small muscle in his jaw, and she could only guess at the expression in those amber eyes. She knew she had to find out. When Deveaux had pointed that pistol at him, she had felt her life's blood drain away. She had to know if somehow they could come about.

"Lucien?" Her voice was a whisper.

He turned. With dismay, she saw that his eyes held only the blank, deadened stare of a man whose senses have been numbed.

"Lucien," she repeated softly.

His eyes blazed briefly with contempt, then an ineffable sadness. He shook his head and turned to stare out the window as the carriage slowed for a crossing.

Alex folded her hands in her lap, trying to comprehend her own profound sense of loss. This was it, then. A temporary engagement, and now it was over. This was what she had wanted. Only her scheme had not worked out quite as she had planned. She had hurt them both. He would recover, no doubt more embittered than ever. But would she?

She felt the tears in her eyes and put her hands up to cover her face. That was when she heard the carriage door open. Was he so disgusted with her that he suddenly preferred to walk home alone on such a threatening night? She sighed, but the sound was lost in the sudden noise of a sickening thump. Alarmed, Alex uncovered her face, only to be grabbed violently by a pair of rough hands. Then came a nauseating smell as a damp cloth was thrust over her face. She struggled briefly, but the hands held her pinioned. She felt herself begin to retch as the cloth was pressed tightly over her mouth and nose. Finally, mercifully, there was darkness.

Chapter 17

A low moan intruded into Alex's numbed brain some hours later. It took her a moment to realize it was the sound of her own voice. Why did her head ache so? Then she remembered the damp cloth, the unpleasant odor, the rough hands. She seemed to be lying on a dank wooden floor that was vaguely unsteady, but her fogged mind could not quite comprehend the strange sensation.

In the dark, her eyes could just make out the shapes of barrels and crates. She appeared to be in some sort of storage area. There was an insistent odor of fish that made her stomach turn. When she tried to move, she found that her hands were bound. She cried out in frustration.

"Quiet."

The soft, fierce command came from the shadows to her right.

Lucien! Her relief turned to dismay as she saw that he was likewise bound. "Where are we?" she asked in confusion.

"Well past the mouth of the river, I should imagine. Heading to open sea."

"You mean to say we are on a *boat*?" Now she understood that strange unsteady movement of the floor. Indeed, the rocking seemed to be getting stronger even as Alex took another look at her dank surroundings. The night's events were becoming clearer.

"We have been abducted," she said, half to herself. "But by whom?"

"Our French friend," Lucien replied. "I suppose when Deveaux recognized us at Carlton House, he decided to dispose of any threat we might pose to his operation. He had already given the orders for this little journey by the time he was arrested."

Alex remembered the rough hands that accosted her. "Deveaux's men waylaid our carriage?"

Lucien smiled grimly. "The task was rather simpler than that. They were driving our conveyance, as perhaps I would have noticed if I had not been so preoccupied while we were waiting. We fell right into their hands."

Now that her eyes had adjusted to the dark, Alex could make out Lucien's features. He was propped against a wooden barrel, his face a study in concentration as he worked his hands behind him. His feet were bound, and there appeared to be a darkened area near his eye. Alex saw a jagged line of dried blood.

"You are hurt!" Her heart skipped a beat.

Lucien shook his head. "Nothing significant. Fortunately Deveaux's men are handier with their fives than with the half hitch."

Alex blinked, uncomprehending, until she saw Lucien's arms move more vigorously. Suddenly he pulled them free, the thick piece of rope that had bound them now dangling uselessly from his wrist.

Quickly he untied his ankles and crawled over to her. Alex saw his grimace of pain. She studied him as he worked her bindings.

"I believe you *are* hurt," she insisted.

"I said it was nothing." He bit off the words angrily, and Alex lapsed into silence. She sensed that he was bothered not only by the wound but likely by his old leg injury as well. Stubborn man to keep his pain to himself. But she did not press him.

"What shall we do now?" Alex asked as Lucien removed the last of her ropes and began to massage her numbed wrists.

"Trickery, I expect." He studied her closely. "Do you think you are up to it? Without female hysterics, I mean?"

Alex sat upright, indignant. "I have never succumbed to hysterics in my life, sir, and do not intend to begin now." Her cool blue eyes were steady.

Lucien could not suppress a smile.

"Somehow I do not doubt it." His eyes flicked over their surroundings. "Now. This looks to be an old tartan, a small craft— three men or even two could manage it in a pinch. I daresay we are not so very outnumbered. The key will be surprise."

Alex registered the intensity of his eyes and the grim line of his mouth. His large hands moved decisively as he outlined his plan, his face a picture of determination. His once elegant silk shirt was pulled taut across his chest as he limbered his cramped arms. After a while, the boat began to bob quite dramatically, and their small prison grew uncomfortably stuffy, but Lucien seemed not to notice. He moved easily about the rough cabin searching for weapons, perfectly at home in his surroundings. When he found an old carpenter's chest and ax tucked into a corner with some rigging, he smiled as if they were great treasures.

Captain Lucien Tremaine was in his element, Alex thought, taking comfort in the realization. He would do his best for them. And if the unthinkable somehow happened, she knew she would never find a better man to follow to the bottom of the sea.

"It will not be long now," Lucien said. "We must have rounded the point and started south toward the Downs. Our captors will wish to be certain of our condition before they are into the crossing."

"The crossing . . . you mean to France?"

Lucien nodded. "If they had wished to put a period to our existence, my dear, they would already have done so. I believe they have decided to question us to see what we know about their operation."

Alex was perplexed. "But *I* can tell them nothing."

"They do not know that. Remember, you were seen with me in Wiltshire." His mouth quirked into a grim, ironic smile.

Alex blanched, and Lucien's eyes were suddenly filled with regret. "I am sorry to have gotten you into this misadventure." His voice was harsh with emotion.

The boat gave a lurch as Alex reached out for his hand. But he frowned suddenly, preoccupied.

"Unless I miss my guess, we are already in deep seas." His frown deepened. "Rather much sea, I would say."

Alex did not have time to examine his statement, for at that moment the door began to creak. Quickly, as he had ordered, she got into position on the floor, draping ropes over her ankles and wrists. She moaned, an insistent cry that grew more shrill.

The door opened.

"Zut!" a rough voice exclaimed. The man advanced into the cabin, so intent on Alex's condition that he failed to see Lucien behind him holding a thick timber he had scavenged from spare rigging. It crashed down on the unsuspecting seaman with a sickening thud. Quickly Lucien had the man's hands and feet bound.

"Now we wait for his mates," Lucien said, resuming his post.

It was amazingly simple, Alex thought. Apparently the crew did not consider that a drugged female and an unconscious Englishman would pose any threat. Another man was similarly disposed of. Lucien seized the man's pistol and started out the door.

"Where are you going?" Alex asked in alarm.

"To determine how many others are on board."

Before she could protest, he vanished, and Alex found herself preoccupied with the violent motion of the craft. Her stomach felt uneasy, and it was becoming harder to move about without falling.

When Lucien returned, his face was drawn. "As I suspected, there was only one other. I'm afraid he fell overboard during our struggle. No one else will bother us," he said grimly. "However, I fear our problems are just beginning."

"What do you mean? Can we not simply return to England?" Alex fought the rising fear in her chest.

He shook his head. "We can try, certainly, but there is the small matter of the weather. Our crew would not have seen it last night, but by dawn's light, it is clear that we are heading straight toward a squall. What's worse, there are treacherous shoals off South Foreland, where, if I do not miss my guess, we

should be about now. I do not relish trying to steer this rackety
between reefs and a storm."

Alex fought off her panic. She would not let him down.

"You have but to tell me what to do." There was quiet resolve
in her voice.

Lucien shook his head. "I will not have you washed overboard," he rasped gruffly. "You will remain belowdeck."

Alex rose to her full height, the effect of this grand effort
somewhat marred by the fact that she was immediately forced
to grab Lucien's broad shoulders to avoid falling.

"I will not, sir," she said, facing him squarely, "and you will
not insult me by treating me like some hen-hearted miss. If we
perish, so be it. At least we will *both* have done our best."

A violent movement of the boat unsteadied her as she finished this speech. Lucien instantly pulled her closer. Despite the
chill and damp, Alex felt a wave of warmth flow into her body
from his. His eyes burned molten gold, and her heart thrilled at
the message there. She moved toward him, her own eyes reflecting his fire.

"Lucien."

"Shhh. There is no time, Alex." He lifted a finger to silence
her and then gently traced it over her mouth.

They stood there, lost in the silent depths of the other's eyes,
their hearts filled with words that would have to go unspoken.
Lucien's eyes clouded with regret. The boat gave another shudder, and he gripped her tightly before releasing her.

"Here!" He grabbed a coil of rope and tied it around her
waist. They moved to the deck, where he secured the rope
through some fairleads and quickly began to grapple with the
sails. But the ship was careening precariously. The sails only
worsened their plight as they caught the wind and sent the craft
lurching seaward.

"It is worse than I thought!" he shouted to her. "We can only
hope to ride it out!"

Wind whipped around them, and heavy seas pummeled the
little craft over the next half hour. Speech became impossible.
Alex found she could not move in her drenched gown, so she

hitched her skirt under the rope at her waist. She stood behind Lucien, trying to help him as best she could, but the sea repeatedly broke over them, undoing their futile efforts. Her dainty slippers gave her no hold on the slippery deck, and she was repeatedly thrown to her knees. More than once she would have been dragged overboard but for the lifeline Lucien had provided. She saw that he had no such trouble; his legs were spread slightly as he made his way with practiced ease, his body a study in fluidity and grace.

The wind was piercingly cold against her chilled skin, and the wet lamé and gauze of her dress clung mercilessly to her thin body. It seemed that every moment would be their last. The boat heeled over again, out of their control as Lucien suddenly gave a warning cry.

"Reefs hard to starboard!"

A crashing jolt knocked Alex to the deck. She saw Lucien groping his way to the cabin and wondered how anyone could walk at such an angle. He returned with the ax and began to chop at the mainmast rigging.

"What are you doing?" Her shout was nearly lost in the tumult.

He pointed at the deck. "Throw anything you can overboard!"

Alex heard the rocks battering the hull as she tried to drag herself to her feet. One devastating thought came to her mind. *We shall perish here in this icy sea, and I have not told Lucien that I love him.* Heart-stricken, she tried to work her way over to him.

"Lucien!" she shouted, grasping the rail and holding on to her rope line for dear life.

He was struggling with the mainmast and did not hear her. Alex began to inch along the railing toward him, but just as she reached his side the waves crashed with thunderous fury. She clutched at him for one desperate, heart-stopping moment as the watery tentacles curled around her. Lucien's arms closed strong about her as he braced them both against the hull. The wave retreated empty-handed.

He planted a fierce kiss in her wet, tangled hair and then, without speaking, turned to renew his struggle with the mast. The hull heaved against the reefs with a sickening crunch, and the wind swirled ferociously around her as Alex fought to muster the vestiges of her strength. With a desperate effort, she reached out to help Lucien push against the mast. There was an ominous creaking, a thunderous crack, and then the glorious sight of the mast tumbling overboard.

Giddy with triumph, Alex caught his arm.

"We did it! Lucien, I—" But her words were lost as another wave shattered over the boat, slamming them into the deck. Alex felt a blow to her head, and suddenly her world began to grow dim.

"No!" she protested, even as the edge of her awareness faded. But the word emerged as a muffled groan. Then darkness descended.

Someone was rubbing her legs, her arms, her torso, sending life into her numbed limbs. Despite an ache in her head, there was a wonderful, comforting warmth that spread to the tip of her toes, banishing the chill of her damp clothes. She felt that her skin was no longer wet, and basked in something warm and welcome. The sun.

Alex opened her eyes and blinked against its brilliant rays. She was lying on deck, and Lucien was hovering over her, carefully kneading her limbs with his hands.

"Shall I live?" she asked groggily.

Even in her disoriented state, she could see joy leap to his eyes. They were bloodshot, and his face was lined with fatigue. There was a night's growth of beard on his chin.

"You appear to have no serious injuries." But his eyes were grave.

Alex tried to sit up. On the second effort, she was successful. She scanned the horizon. The sun stood high in the sky, turning the now placid sea into sparkles of light.

"But we are still in difficulty?" She saw the answer in his

somber face. She smiled hopefully. "The storm is gone, at least."

Lucien nodded grimly. "We sustained quite a blow on the reefs. I could not attempt to repair it until the storm blew itself out. We are still taking on water, although it is only a trickle now. With luck, we may stay afloat for some time. But our rudder was lost, and of course we have no mast." He smiled wryly. "We are drifting at the mercy of the sea, my dear. She is kind for the moment, but I must tell you that she is a rather fickle mistress."

Alex stretched, happy to see that her limbs still functioned.

"There is nothing we can do for the nonce?" He shook his head, and she gave him a direct gaze. "Then perhaps, my lord, we may take care of some unfinished business."

At his puzzled frown, Alex reached out her fingers and stroked the deep furrow between those thick brows. He sat unmoving as she moved her finger to the ugly, purplish bruise on his head and then touched it lightly with her lips. Her brave, dear love.

"Oh, Lucien! Can you ever forgive me?" Alex's voice broke as she threw herself into his arms. "I never meant to behave so abominably. I didn't really care about Cousin Agatha or the companion, you see, not at the end anyway. As for teaching you a lesson, all I really wanted was to love you with all my heart."

With a muttered oath, Lucien caught her to him, his strong arms fiercely encircling her. Gently his hands began to stroke her hair as he whispered against her ear.

"Do not cry, Alex, my love," he said. "I am as much to blame for this bloody mess as you." He held her away from him for a moment, and she could see that his face was suffused with chagrin. "As you have pointed out on more than one occasion, my insufferable arrogance leads me astray."

"No more than mine." She smiled through her tears and touched his face gently, mesmerized by the warmth emanating from those golden eyes. He caught her fingers and brought them to his lips.

"I really bungled it last night with all that talk of preserving my estates, did I not?"

She shook her head in denial, but the corners of her mouth tugged upward into a betraying smile. He pulled her closer.

"You are the only woman I could ever want, Alex," he said in a hoarse voice. "I would be lost without you. It is life itself to hear you say that you love me. When you ended our engagement last night, I was devastated. And angry at your scheming." He gave her an embarrassed smile. "It was, however, no worse than mine."

Alex winced, but Lucien put his finger lightly on her mouth to still her words of apology.

"Hush, dearest," he murmured. "Perhaps we both have something to learn about trust. I failed to trust in the strong, courageous, independent, and quite beautiful woman of my dreams. I wore my hurt and my disillusionment as my armor against any tender feelings that might filter through. I can only beg your forgiveness and say that I, too, love you with all my heart."

Alex looked at him wonderingly. "Oh, Lucien!" Her cry was lost as he pulled her to his chest and brought his mouth down upon hers.

The sun was at its zenith, beaming its full strength on them as their lips joined in exultation. Alex gloried in the feel of his lean body against hers and the sea scent of him so close to her skin. His hands roamed over her body, and Alex felt as if they belonged there, caressing her, playing her senses like a joyous symphony. She clutched him tighter, allowing her own hands to wander as he trailed kisses along her neck and shoulders. She knew the fire that had begun so long ago in Wiltshire would be denied no more. As his mouth moved to her breasts she entwined her fingers in his hair and called out his name.

Suddenly he was still. Alex looked up in stunned dismay.

His amber eyes were soulful and apologetic. "I have forgotten myself, my love," he rasped with difficulty. "I must remind myself that we are not married. If we continue like this, I will forget that fact entirely."

Alex's blue eyes twinkled, but the dancing lights did not obscure the barely restrained flames of desire.

"But can you not see, Lucien? I *want* you to forget it entirely!" She gestured around them. "I do not intend to be deprived of you simply because we are drifting helplessly at sea. All the more reason to pursue the matter, since there is no one to notice or to care but us."

He stared at her. Finally his eyes gleamed in comprehension.

"I do not believe what I am hearing from this proper duke's daughter," he said, his sensuous mouth widening to a grin.

"I have never been proper with you around," Alex retorted. "I am afraid you have an inflated notion of my sense of propriety."

"That may be, but a gentleman would save you from yourself." He regarded her gravely.

Alex sniffed. "I do not doubt it, sir. I am thankful there are no such creatures on board today."

Lucien's laughter shattered the calm sea air like triumphant music, rising to join the cries of the gulls hovering overhead. He drew her to him and rested his chin on the top of her head.

"You are serious, are you not?" His voice was quiet.

Alex nodded. "I know very well, sir, the state of things here. Who knows if we shall ever see our wedding day?" Her voice did not falter, and her steady gaze did not waver as Lucien held her away from him for a moment and took her face between his hands.

"You are a remarkable woman, Alessandra Ridgely." He kissed the tip of her nose. "I do believe you have won this particular battle—or perhaps I should say engagement."

His lips descended gently, moving back and forth over her swollen mouth with a softness that made her whimper with yearning. Eagerly she returned his kiss with a fire that ignited them both. Lucien swept her into a bruising embrace, his caressing hands moving to command her response. Alex savored the feel of him until her impatience took hold.

"Please, Lucien." Her words were barely audible, but he heard them and groaned with desire.

He lay her back gently on the deck as the sun blessed them with its warmth. Alex's heart was full of joy. Whatever else happened, Lucien would be hers. The fire from their love would burn forever. She closed her eyes and sighed in breathless anticipation.

"Ho, there! Ho!"

The sound came from a distance, but Alex and Lucien heard it clearly. They sat bolt upright and squinted hard at the horizon.

"Ho, there!' The voice sounded again, and through the sun's glare, Lucien saw the schooner that was swiftly bearing down on them. They watched in amazement as it closed the distance, making recognizable the figure looking at them through his raised glass.

"If I were not so glad of rescue, I would gag him to the rigging for his timing," Lucien muttered.

Alex's eyes widened as she, too, recognized the figure.

"George?" Her voice squeaked in amazement.

"Bound for the Admiralty, no doubt, before racing down to Dorset to join his wife and heir."

The craft was nearly upon them. If Sir George Huntsley was startled to recognize them, his voice did not betray his surprise.

"A bit of trouble, Lucien? Don't seem as though they are giving you much in the way of worthy craft these days." His voice carried clearly across the few feet of placid sea that separated the two vessels.

"As you say, George," Lucien responded calmly. "Perhaps you might care to assist. This tub does not endear itself with time."

Sir George's eyes narrowed speculatively as he studied them.

"Seems to me you were doing quite well on your own a moment ago." He did not flinch at Lucien's warning gaze, but added with aplomb, "I own I was surprised when Vivian wrote me of your betrothal. Never thought my letters would play Cupid. Trust you are well, Alex?"

"Your letter had nothing—" Lucien began in irritation.

"Why, yes, George, how kind of you to ask," Alex interrupted, giggling helplessly. At his puzzled look, she explained lamely, "Lucien was just about to explain about gagging someone to the rigging."

Sir George frowned. "Nasty sort of punishment. Not a bit funny. Tie a man to the rigging with a piece of iron in his mouth. Can't think why you want to know about that."

"Because that might well be your fate, Huntsley, if you do not allow me to bring my fiancée on board this instant," came Lucien's menacing growl, but Alex could hear the laughter in his voice.

A rope ladder was quickly thrown over the schooner's side.

"Your virtue is safe, love," Lucien whispered as he helped her up the rope. There was the smallest note of regret in his voice.

"For now, you mean," Alex retorted with a provocative arch of her brows.

"Precisely what are you plotting, Alex?" Lucien demanded. "Now that we are rescued, I give you fair warning that I intend you to have a proper wedding, as befits a proper duke's daughter."

"And I have said, sir, that I cannot be proper with you around," she replied. "I intend you to secure a special license the moment we reach land. We will be wed before nightfall."

"Doubt your brother will like that, Alex," Sir George interjected. "A bit high in the instep about the proprieties."

"I do not give a fig about the proprieties, George," Alex said, her blue eyes flashing.

Sir George absorbed this information, then broke into a grin.

"It seems, Lucien, that you are in for an exceedingly short engagement," he said.

Lucien's heated amber gaze never left Alex. "I do believe that you are correct, my friend," he said with an exaggerated sigh.

Alex's pulse raced, but her countenance remained unruffled. "For once, my lord," she replied serenely, "I find we are in perfect accord."